HIDDEN HEAT

LEAH BRAEMEL

Somerlane
Publishing

HIDDEN HEAT

Cover Art by Flirtation Designs

Second Edition June 2017

Somerlane Publishing

Digital ISBN: 978-0-9959429-2-9

Paperback ISBN-13: 978-0-9959429-3-6

Paperback ISBN-10: 0995942935

ABOUT THIS BOOK

Wedding rings, babies, commitment? No thank you. Working for a company that's wall-to-wall, testosterone-fueled alpha males, Sandy Hallquist is in her element. By day, she's the picture of calm, cool efficiency. Off hours, her inner adrenaline junkie is off the chain.

His whole professional life has been all about being invisible, but nothing about Troy McPherson is real, not even his name. It's the only way he can manage Hauberk's international offices while hiding his other career: assassin. But in one moment of weakness, Troy's carefully constructed mask begins to crack. Cracks that reveal his yearning for things he can never have. Family. Stability. Love.

Too bad they're the last things on Sandy's must-have list. By the time she realizes the heat between them will last a lifetime, his next mission could make him disappear from her life. Permanently.

ABOUT THIS BOOK

WHAT REVIEWERS ARE SAYING ABOUT HIDDEN HEAT

...almost too hot to touch ~ *RT Book Reviews*

...a very complex and suspenseful story ~*Guilty Pleasures Book Reviews*

...a powerful and fun story full of all the emotion, sensuality and suspense ~ *Romance Junkies*

... The sexuality, sensuality, passion and suspense blend together perfectly ~ *The Romance Studio*

∼

Nominated as Best Romantic Suspense of 2012 by the reviewers at The Romance Studio for their annual Cupid and Psyche Awards (CAPA)

ONE

THE RED DOT of the laser site centered on the target's forehead milliseconds before a hole appeared in its place. Not until the body dropped to the ground did Troy McPherson lower the pistol.

"Subject neutralized." With the call sent out, the agents positioned around the perimeter closed in. Leaving them to bundle the corpse, he walked onto the porch and surveyed the ranch bungalows along the street. No lights went on, no heads poked outside. Perfect. They'd be long gone by the time the residents of this middle-class neighborhood awoke, never realizing they'd harboured a killer in their midst.

As one of the agents pulled the black van into the bungalow's garage, Troy tucked the gun into a bag, stepped off the porch and onto the sidewalk. He kept his step casual, just an insomniac out for a pre-dawn stroll. Up ahead, another insomniac stopped to let his German shepherd leave his mark on a light post. Once the dog finished his business, Troy stopped by the grey-haired man.

Cooper Davis, the head of the ultra-secret Brigade, pulled on the leash when the dog sniffed Troy's pant leg. The shepherd whined then settled at Cooper's feet, his nostrils flaring as he sampled the air. "You haven't lost your touch. Harris didn't even get a chance to react. Are you sure you won't come work for us?"

"Not a chance." Troy waited as the garage door reopened and the van pulled onto the still-quiet street. Once they were again alone, he handed over the weapon. "Here's your POS gun."

The bag Troy held out disappeared into Cooper's coat pocket, no doubt to be disposed of in the Chesapeake or some nearby swamp. "I doubt Harris would like his gun being called a piece of shit. It was his favorite piece."

That the man had been killed by his own weapon lent a certain irony to the hit that pleased Troy. "Then you're better off without him. No self-respecting marksman would use a laser sight. They're for lazy assholes who couldn't hit the broadside of a barn."

"I'm not shedding any tears getting rid of him, but he had his uses."

"Until he went rogue." Troy couldn't resist the dig.

"There is that."

Both men stilled when an Audi started a half block away. Once the sedan pulled away at a leisurely pace in the opposite direction, Troy relaxed. "I'll tell Chad that it's safe for him and Lauren to return."

"How are they getting on? Do you think they'll get back together?" The question was asked oh-so-casually but there was an alertness to Cooper's expression, an expectancy, that had Troy wondering at the interest behind it.

He'd lay big bucks Cooper was more interested in convincing Lauren to return, or more likely, using her as bait to lure Chad away from Hauberk. "What do I look like? A fuckin' dating service?" He reached down and scratched the shepherd behind the ears. "You'll let me know when Garcia's on the move, *and* let me in on the op to take him down?"

"That was our agreement." A light flicked on in the kitchen window of the house two doors down. "You'd better get going. You'll be hearing from me."

After giving the shepherd one final pat, Troy continued along and turned down a side street. Five minutes later, he merged his SUV in to Beltway traffic and headed back to headquarters. The empty stretches of highway filled in around him as the first of the early morning commuters began their daily trek. The radio serenading him with a Shostakovich adagio in the background, he analyzed the takedown. It had been a textbook op, all the players performing their parts with precision. Not that the head of the Brigade would have accepted anything less. That Garcia, the head of the drug cartel who had ordered the hostage-taking in Colombia, had escaped had frustrated them all. If he didn't soon hear about a raid on Garcia from that damned rat bastard Davis, he'd pay him a visit in person.

He parked beside a Jaguar XK in the Hauberk parking lot and walked to the company's main entrance. Once he'd passed through the security doors, he headed to the weapons room.

He'd just opened his locker when Sam Watson, owner of both Hauberk and the Jag, filled the doorway from the indoor range, his own pistol in his hand. "Good work liaising with the feds about Harris."

"Thanks. You can call Chad and tell him it's safe to come back now."

Sam opened his locker and grabbed his cleaning kit, then straddled the bench and broke down his Glock. "Are you gonna tell me what went down?"

"Nothing to tell. I handed over the transponder Lauren's people had given her and the Homeland Security grunts used it to lure Harris into their nets." For a brief—very brief—moment, he considered telling Sam the whole deal. About the existence of the Brigade, and Sam's good buddy Cooper Davis's involvement in it. Everything. Except he understood the need for secrecy. Especially if he wanted to be part of the group nailing the head of the terrorist group who had kidnapped his agents in Colombia. He owed Scott that much.

"Were you in on the takedown?"

Uncomfortable with the question, Troy turned to his locker,

choosing between his four favorite pistols. He lifted the Heckler and Koch P2000 as well as his favorite Sig Sauer, trying to decide between them. "Only on the fringes. You know they don't let civilians into their investigations."

Sam accepted the lie at face value, or gave the appearance of accepting it. "So you plannin' on sticking around once Chad's back in D.C.?"

"For a while. Got a couple things I need to do before I head back to London."

Screw it, he'd shoot both. He grabbed some ammo and headed to the range. If anything did go wrong with today's mission, at least this way he'd have a reason for a positive GSR test. Not that anything had gone wrong, so there'd be no need for him to be swabbed for gunshot residue. For the next half hour, he fired his gun until he was satisfied with the near-perfect formation of holes in the silhouette's head and heart. He flipped off his protective earmuffs and hit the switch to bring the target to him. His hearing no longer muffled, his senses screamed there was someone behind him. Right behind.

"Nice shootin', Tex," a bright female voice said from behind him.

He whirled, his weapon raised, his finger milliseconds from pulling the trigger when he recognized the speaker. His heart pounding, he lowered his weapon. "Jesus, Sandy. You shouldn't sneak up on me like that."

"I've been standing here watching you for a few minutes now." She pulled off her own earmuffs with one hand, dislodging strands of blonde hair from its French braid. As incongruous as they should have been, the bright orange headset she'd donned on entering the firing range complemented her dark blue sweater. The combination of blonde hair and blue eyes gave her an almost doll-like look from far away. Up close she had a smattering of freckles across the bridge of her nose as if some fairy had sprinkled her with cinnamon. He'd often wondered if she tasted like cinnamon too. "You should have been aware I was here. I could have had a knife and slit your throat and you wouldn't have been able to stop me."

Although she thought she was teasing, she was right. But only about how he should have been aware she'd been behind him; he'd argue the part about him not being able to stop her.

Exhaling, he shoved his gun in his shoulder holster. "Don't do it again. You wouldn't want to stick me with a load of paperwork if I'd killed you, would you?"

"Not to mention cleaning up all that blood and trying to hide my body would be a real bitch of a job." Her light tone lowered his blood pressure. Thank God she had a sense of humor and wasn't the type of woman to run screaming in fear.

"I leave the cleanup for others." He wondered if she knew he wasn't joking.

"Good plan. But aren't you supposed to warn your suspect before shooting?"

He exhaled as he released the cartridge and replaced it with a fresh one. "That's only in the movies. Same way the bad guy always takes the time to reveal his plan, giving the good guy time to figure a way out. In real life, you shoot first. Is there a reason why you're standing here, plotting my demise?"

"Scott's psychiatric report just arrived." She held up the brown, legal-sized envelope. "I figured you'd want to see it right away."

It didn't surprise him that she'd brought it straight to him instead of leaving it in his office. He lifted his hand to take the folder then dropped it. Did he really want to confirm his suspicion that Scott had fooled everyone else about being better, even the shrink? "I think I'll hit the showers and get changed first. Why don't you put it on my desk for now?"

Sandy brushed her bangs out of her eyes. After a breath or two, she nodded once. "You betcha."

"Thanks." He watched her walk away, her long legs swinging giving her ass a nice hitch. After this morning's hit, his body craved release. Pity she was Sam's assistant and therefore relegated to the hands-off list.

Once she reached the inner door of the airlock, she turned around. "Hey, Troy? Scott's going to be all right, isn't he?"

Good question.

~

THREE HOURS LATER, the sealed manila envelope still sat unopened on top of Troy's inbox. Unable to stand it any longer, Sandy stood in the doorway to Troy's office while violins and some other stringed instrument softly played over the speaker system. Maybe he found it relaxing; it would put her to sleep listening to it all day.

"Be right with you, Sandy. Take a seat." He motioned to his guest chairs with a casual wave of his hand, not taking his eyes from his laptop's screen.

She perched on the chair, using the time to surreptitiously watch him from beneath lowered lashes. Not that he'd ever notice her watching him. Even now she doubted he was aware of her, he was so involved in whatever document he was composing. But whenever he was in the office, she'd always noticed him. When he was there. For Troy McPherson, the D.C. office was more of a pit stop, one of a half-dozen international Hauberk offices he hopscotched between.

Runnels created by his fingers through his thick dark curls betrayed his frustration with whatever problem his agents posed. Her fingers itched to smooth the wayward curls that had sprung up at his crown. If he saw them he'd head straight to the barber for another awful buzz cut like he'd had in the spring.

Instead of the black tracksuit he'd worn in the shooting range, he'd changed into an expensive designer suit, though he'd carelessly discarded his jacket on the chair beside her. A hint of chest hair peeked from the V in his shirt where he'd loosened his tie and undone the top two buttons. He'd rolled up his sleeves, his muscular forearms hinting at the power barely contained by the shirt. Drawn to the fingers stabbing impatiently at the keyboard, her body heated as her imagination provided images of them removing her clothes, touching her private places.

His scowl deepening, he hit the enter key before shoving his keyboard tray under his desk. "So what's up?"

My libido, she wanted to answer. Damn, it hadn't been that long since she'd had a lover, though he'd been almost as uninventive as her ex-fiancé Glen had been, but something about Troy told her he'd never let her be bored. Instead she tapped the envelope. "You haven't read this yet."

"Been busy. I'll get to it."

"Sam wants an update." She pushed the envelope across the desk. Okay, so Sam hadn't asked about it, but he would soon enough.

Troy wielded his letter opener like a surgical instrument and slid the report onto the desk. To her surprise, he glanced up at her and waited before looking at it. *Shoot*. He expected her to leave.

"You know Sam will give it to me to file so I'll see it later anyway."

"It's not that."

So he *was* afraid to open it. "I thought he was getting better. He seems happier."

Troy angled the envelope until the report slid out. He skimmed the contents, flipped back to the front page and read it again, slower this time, then held it out to her. "Here. See for yourself."

His fingers brushed hers as she took the report. Strong, callused, with a hint of roughness that would feel good on her skin, touching her everywhere. Pity he'd never given her any indication he was attracted to her. If he did, she would be all over him like snow on a Minnesota field in January.

She flicked through the psychiatrist's recommendation that Scott was well enough to be placed back on active duty. "He'll be glad to get back into the field. He's been grumbling for months about being on restricted duty."

"Yeah. I guess." Troy tugged his shirt collar.

"You don't think he's ready, do you?"

"I didn't say that." Tug. Tug.

"You don't have to."

He huffed in exasperation. "What are you talking about?"

She settled back into the chair, tucking one foot beneath her. "Whenever you don't agree with something, you tug at your collar."

"I do?" He pulled his hand away from his neck and stared at it as if it didn't belong to him. "Any other tells I should know about?"

"If you're impatient or annoyed with something, you fiddle with your watch band. If you're worried, then you rub the pad of your index finger over your thumb nail."

"Remind me never to play poker with you. You'd bankrupt me in short order. Or better yet, I should bring you to my next poker night and introduce you to a couple of my friends with big wallets I'd love to take from them."

That he would never invite her, that none of the agents, male or female, ever thought to invite her to any of their parties or events stung. Private club didn't begin to describe the clique mentality of the Hauberk operatives. Either you were an agent or you were invisible. "Name the time and place and I'll be there."

Shooting him a bright smile that she didn't feel inside, she hurried back to her desk.

WHILE HE ENJOYED the sight of Sandy walking away from him—what man wouldn't enjoy ogling her curves?—he wondered at the smile she'd plastered onto her face. Oh, it might have fooled anyone else, but there was something missing in it. Did she think he wasn't doing enough for his agent?

He flipped through the report to ensure the shrink hadn't missed some sign Scott was still having trouble. True, his nightmares had lessened, as had his requirement for meds. So what was it that was bugging him about placing his friend back on active duty?

Unable to see a satisfactory answer, he tossed the file back on his desk and shoved his chair back, intent on asking Sandy if she'd noticed anything about Scott. Standing up would be a waste of motion—Sandy was busy with a client, or potential client. While he couldn't hear exactly what the woman in her late thirties was saying, Sandy's glance toward Sam's closed door told him that the woman was demanding to see Hauberk's owner.

If she was a potential client, Chad's agents had their work cut out protecting that walking safety deposit box. With the almost-floor-length fox coat she wore, the visitor presented a fantastic target to the PETA crowd. Snatch-and-grab artists would have a field day with the expensive designer purse tucked beneath her elbow. Or maybe they'd pull a gun on her and demand some of the diamonds glittering on her wrist, ears or the finger she wagged in Sandy's face.

Despite Sandy's smile, the tension in her shoulders betrayed that the woman had hit some sore spot. Yet she rose and poured the woman a cup of coffee and chatted to her, smoothing whatever remaining feathers—or fox fur—might still be ruffled.

With a little training, she would have been a good asset in the field. Not as an agent. No, she would have been a perfect mole. She could slide into any environment and adapt, make herself useful while extracting information people wouldn't tell others.

The door to Sam's office opened and Sam sauntered out, greeting the woman with his trademark smile. While everyone else might buy the mellow persona Sam exuded, Troy knew it was a façade. Only Rosie had found the way to dispel the demons he'd fought to hide.

Sandy's shoulders relaxed as Sam's southern drawl thickened, charming the client, leaving Sandy free to return to her desk. The sweater she wore covered her cleavage but it couldn't hide the curves he found so erotically enticing.

He forced his attention off the outer office and back to the folder on his desk. He'd finally managed to lose himself in his operatives' reports when his secure phone jangled.

"Garcia's planning on meeting his people in Val Varde next month," Cooper Davis's voice barked down the line. How Davis had managed to get hold of the private secure line, Troy had no idea, but he could only guess the Brigade had resources from all the alphabet agencies. "If you want in on it, tell me now."

So why hadn't Davis revealed that nugget earlier? "I want in."

"Just so we're clear, I'm only inviting you. Phillips gets nowhere near the op. In fact, I don't want you breathing a word about it to him."

If he'd been the one held captive, the one forced to watch his partner tortured to death, he'd demand to go. He'd see the bastard's death as justice served. Did Scott deserve any less? Yet if he insisted Scott be included in the op, Davis would hang up and neither of them would be in on taking Garcia down.

"All right. Just me," he agreed. Scott would be pissed, but knowing Garcia was dead should placate some of his ire. "Consider it a quid pro quo for keeping silent about Harris going rogue."

"I can give you no more than two hours' warning so be ready to leave whenever I call. Oh and, McPherson? If you're not at the airport, the plane will take off without you." Cooper cut the connection before Troy could respond.

Troy laid the receiver in its cradle and fingered the psychiatrist's report. Would knowing Garcia was no longer a threat, that Scott's partner Devon King had been avenged, help Scott heal? Or would it drag him back into the morass of pain and doubt? Either way, he wanted to be in on the op.

"I'll get him for you, buddy," Troy whispered.

His inbox notifier dinged. Almost absently he checked his inbox and found a note from John Lake, Hauberk's IT manager, requesting a meeting with all department heads in an hour. Wonderful. Just how he wanted to spend the rest of the day. Trapped in a fucking meeting talking computer crap.

TWO

.

SANDY CLOSED her apartment door behind her and leaned against it with a sigh. Her purse fell with a thump at her feet. She set her laptop case down with a little more care. It wasn't hers, after all. "Hey, Jazz? You home?"

Jazz didn't answer but an orange tabby padded out of her roommate's bedroom to wind around her ankles. Its purr strengthened when she bent to scratch behind its ears. "Hey there, Xander. Did you miss me?"

As if in answer, the cat jumped up on her desk, meowing at the bag of treats Jazz had left there. "You miss them more than me, huh? Those things will make you fat, you know?"

Xander blinked and nudged the bag until it toppled onto the floor.

"Yeah, you don't care, do you? Must be nice not to have to worry about your weight."

She kicked her heels into the closet, taking a certain satisfaction in the thump they made. With a sigh, she bent to pick them up and place them together. They'd cost her over four hundred dollars, far too much for her budget, but they'd looked so good in the store and even better on, she hadn't been able to resist. Her mother would be horrified to learn she'd spent that much on a pair of shoes. But then her mother didn't have to meet and greet millionaires and some of the country's movers and shakers on a day-to-day basis. Women—and occasionally men— who would judge her by what she wore on her feet. Her now-aching feet.

She headed into her bedroom, stripped off her clothes, and pulled on her favorite pair of fuzzy plaid pajama pants and matching top. So it wasn't the most glamorous outfit she owned, but it was comfortable. Besides, it wasn't as if anyone would see her.

She'd just settled onto the couch and turned on the television when someone thumped at the door. After unfurling herself with a groan, she peeked through the spy hole.

On the other side of the door, a stunning redhead juggled a pizza box, her purse and her keys.

Recognizing her roommate, Sandy unlocked the door and opened it. "Hey, Jazz."

"Thanks. Couldn't hold all this and work the keys."

Sandy opened the door wider to let her roommate in. The scent of cheese and pepperoni quickly filled the apartment. "What are you doing back so soon? I thought you had a date tonight."

"I did. My date turned out to be a snoozefest so I ditched him." She dumped the pizza on the tiny table by the front window before heading into her bedroom.

"Any luck on the job hunt?" Sandy grabbed a plate from the cupboard, flipped open the box and slid two slices onto the plate.

"No." Jazz's voice was muffled as if she were pulling a top over her head. "I thought I had a nibble but it turned out they were looking for someone who knew video editing software."

"Rats. I was really hoping you'd find something."

"So was I. I'm so frickin' tired of working at that call center. Do you have any idea of how nuts people can get?" Jazz padded back, wearing a slinky black silk chemise and a pair of pink boyshorts. She piled three slices onto her plate and then curled up on the couch beside Sandy.

When they'd finished their pizza, Jazz grabbed the remote and muted the sound. "I'm bored sitting here. Let's go down to Rusty's and see who's hanging around."

"I don't know. I just got comfortable. Going out means I'd have to get dressed again—" The phone rang. A quick check of the caller ID had her groaning as she answered. "Hi, Mom."

"Oh, Sandy honey, I'm so glad you're home for once. I wanted to make sure you're coming home for your sister's anniversary party next weekend."

"Uh, gee, Mom, I don't know if I'll be able to make it. Things have been pretty busy lately." Fat chance she was going to fly all the way back to Minnesota to spend forty-eight hours listening to how wonderful her boring brother-in-law was. He was a former prison guard who had been fired and become a salesman. Of cardboard, for criminy's sake. When he wasn't talking about his experiences in the jail, he waxed poetic on corrugation. Talk about yawnsville.

"You work too hard. You should find yourself a nice man and settle down. Are you seeing anyone, dear? You could bring him along. We'd love to meet him."

Usually her mother waited until later in the conversation to get to the "who are you dating" questions.

"Mom, considering your history of interfering, I'm not talking about my dating life." She rolled her eyes at Jazz while wondering how many more times she'd have this conversation before her mother got a clue that she had no intention of getting married. Ever.

"If you come back for Jennifer's party, you can meet Ernie's cousin, Donald. He's a very nice young man who lives a little ways outside of St. Charles. You could move back here and we could see each other every day. Wouldn't that be nice?"

Nice? "Um, I like living in D.C., Mom." *I like having a life that doesn't revolve around dishes and babies and diapers.*

Her mother ignored her. "Donald sells used farm equipment so he's got a steady job. Not like that awful boy you brought home last time."

She'd brought home Tank specifically to shock her mother. His tattoos and piercings had accomplished that the minute he'd walked in the door. That he'd had a respectable job as a paramedic hadn't mattered one whit to her mother. "He sounds a lot like Glen and I'm not going through that again."

"Oh honey, Glen wasn't so bad, I still don't know what your problem with him was or why you broke off your engagement."

Sandy gritted her teeth to stop herself from launching into a rant at her mother.

"Donald is a perfectly lovely young man. You should see how he worries about his mother. Gives her a part of his paycheck every week like clockwork." Her mother lowered her voice. "Now, Donald's a little bit shorter than you are, I think. So it's best if you don't wear heels when you meet him and it should be fine."

Just shoot me now. "Mom, he doesn't sound like my type."

Her mother sighed. "Dear, you're nearly thirty. You can't afford to be picky. It's time you settled down. Got married and had babies. Like your sister and Cathy and Patti." She named Sandy's brothers' wives. "Seriously, dear, this isn't something you can put off until you're my age."

Sandy thumped her head against the back of the couch. "Mom, I'm only twenty-eight. I've got lots of time." *As in the rest of my life.*

"Sandra Elizabeth, when I was your age, I'd already been married ten years and had Eddie and Dwayne and was about to give birth to Frank. You've only got a few years left if you want to have a family without having to resort to medical intervention. And I want to be young enough to enjoy my grandbabies. I'm not getting any younger either, you know."

God, sometimes she swore her mother had gotten stuck in the fifties. "Mom, you're not even sixty yet. You've got lots of time to enjoy your grandchildren." She hurried to cut her mother off before she could launch into a recitation of this neighbor or that friend and their health problems. "Was there anything else? Because I'm on my way out." *Please don't let there be anything else, please please please.*

"Oh, you've got a date? I suppose I shouldn't keep you then."

Her mother's interest was palpable. "Is it someone you might be serious about?"

"No, Mom, it's not a date. I'm going out with Jazz." Rats. She should have just said yes, it was a guy she'd picked up at a bar. Another one with lots of tattoos and piercings. No, that wouldn't be enough to discourage her mother's grandbaby obsession. "I really need to go. I'll call you later, all right?"

"Oh." From her mother's hopeful tone, she hadn't completely accepted that a date with what's-his-face was out of the question. "So we'll see you home for Jennifer's party?"

"No, Mom, I think you should plan that I'm not going to be there." If she had to get herself arrested to keep herself in D.C., she'd do it. Not giving her mother a chance to launch onto another topic, she said good-bye and hung up the phone. She glanced up to find Jazz shrugging on her coat while Xander attacked the pizza she'd abandoned.

"Go get changed. I'll wait."

She flipped through her various outfits, carefully choosing a top and skirt that matched her mood. Pity it was winter or she'd wear something baring her belly. Her mother would be horrified with her choice of skirt, her father scandalized that she'd had her belly button pierced. Whatever.

Maybe it was time to get her nipples pierced.

THREE

THE HUBBUB of the other patrons blended with the mellow jazz playing in the background. Troy sipped his Guinness as Scott's current partner, Andy Walters, thanked the waitress for the Coke he'd ordered.

Once the waitress left them, Andy lowered his voice so any other Hauberk operatives who frequented the bar couldn't listen in on their conversation. "So are you putting Scott back in the field as a bodyguard?"

"Not yet."

Andy swirled the ice cubes in his glass. The halogen over the table spotlighted the edge of his tattoo peeking out beneath his sleeve but left his face in shadows. "Look, I know I don't get to read those reports from his shrink, but I've worked with him a couple times now and I'd let him cover my back in a high-pressure situation any day. You keep him out of the field much longer and he's gonna walk. He'll find some other way to get back into the action. Even if it means quitting Hauberk and going to work for the competition."

The doc had felt it possible that if Scott were partnered with the right person or given the right assignments he might be fine. Andy might be the right person, but assignments were tricky. Too many times an assignment an agent thought was routine blew up into a major showdown. He trusted Andy's judgment a lot more than he did a shrink who sat in an office all day, never seeing what it was like in the field. But he also trusted the sick feeling in his gut that Scott was still hiding something. Besides, putting him back in the field meant sending him overseas. Somewhere Troy couldn't see for himself how Scott was coping.

Before Troy could answer, the agent's gaze fastened on the bar door, his eyes widening. He blew a low whistle, drowned out by a wolf whistle by some drunk at the bar. "Whoa, momma, if she came into the office dressed like that, every agent near or far would find a reason to come in and you'd never get any work done."

It took Troy the stereotypical double look to verify that *she* was Sandy. Instead of her hair being tucked neatly into the French braid she'd worn earlier, it hung loose, brushing her shoulders in a tousled just-got-fucked look that had every man in the place eyeing her speculatively. If they weren't, they were either gay or blind.

Her winter coat hung open, revealing a silky fire-engine red number that was unbuttoned damned near to her navel, displaying cleavage that a man would pay good money to bury his face—or his cock—in. And her skirt? If he'd seen it in a drawer or hanging in a store, he'd have sworn it was a wide belt, nothing more. Her well-toned legs stretched a mile, ending in a set of sparkly stilettos that matched her blouse. Why the bloody hell hadn't he ever noticed she had such a fantastic set of legs?

His position allowed him a long, unhindered look as she walked by. The view from behind was just as spectacular as from the front. Bloody fucking hell, she strutted the length of the room with the grace and ease of a New York runway model. She followed her companion to the far end of the bar where they hitched themselves up onto barstools. Sandy draped her faux fur jacket over one leg, leaving a long expanse of bare thigh exposed to the drunken masses.

"Huh," Andy grunted. "I swear I know her."

"Of course you do. It's Sandy."

Andy shook his head in disgust. "Not Sandy. Her friend. What do you think I am, an idjit?"

Troy glanced at Sandy's companion. She had her back to him, giving him a sneak peek of a tramp stamp—a set of bat wings?—above her leather skirt. Her flame-colored hair with its half-dozen black streaks didn't match her skin tone, leading him to make a mental bet that the collar wouldn't match the cuffs.

The friend glanced over the bar, her gaze passing over them, lingering for a second, assessing them as if they were salmon in the fish market. She didn't look older than Sandy, but she had a harder look about her. The word "jaded" popped into his mind, though perhaps that described him better.

"Have at her, mate."

Andy grimaced when his phone warbled. He answered the phone without checking the caller ID. Troy didn't need to hear the other side of the conversation to learn that Andy's chance at getting to know Sandy's friend had been ruled out.

"I gotta go. Husband of one of the women from the Safe and Sound program just showed up at her door."

"Watch your back," he warned as Andy slid from the booth, his expression grim.

"I always do."

As Andy went out the door, Scott walked in. *Shit.* Hiding out at the bar hadn't worked. Scott stayed in the doorway, scanning the bar until he saw Troy. He beelined straight for the booth and sat on the bench Andy had vacated.

"I haven't changed my mind, if that's what you're hoping."

Andy's warning replayed. Had he pushed Scott too far by keeping him on restricted duty?

"I didn't think you would. So I've decided it's time for me to look for a new job."

Shit. Walters was right. "Where will you go? Have anywhere in mind?"

"I haven't a clue. But I can't work with people who will continue to think I'm *unbalanced*. That I can't be trusted to keep my shit together."

"That's not what we think." Or maybe it was. Every time he'd come home from work the first few months after Scott had moved in, he'd had to steel himself against the fear he'd open the door to find Scott had hung himself or eaten his gun.

"Yeah, you do. Otherwise you'd have given me a non-bullshit assignment after reading the doc's report."

Troy tugged at his collar, then, remembering Sandy's earlier comment, forced his hand back to the table. "So I'm concerned about you. I'm concerned about all my agents. Shoot me for being cautious and keeping you out of the field until I'm sure she's right."

They both leaned back when the waitress appeared to take Scott's order. Once she'd left, Scott resumed his attack.

"So you're saying if it wasn't me, if it was someone like Russell or Snider or Goffin, you'd keep them out of the field because your gut holds more sway than a psychiatric report?"

"That's what I'm saying."

"Bull. Shit." Scott leaned over the table. "I'm ready to get back to work, Troy. Sitting around in the office doing background checks on the Internet or on my ass in the car teaching a rookie how to stakeout some douchebag cheating on his wife is driving me to a whole new level of batshit crazy. If you won't give me an active assignment, then I walk. I'll find some other company who will put me back out in the field. I'll fucking move back to fucking Alaska if that's what it takes."

Christ. Scott hated Alaska and all it represented. Troy pinched the bridge of his nose. "All right. How about I ask Chad if he can use you? You can plead your case with him."

Scott narrowed his eyes, suspicious. "And you wouldn't try to interfere if he wants to put me out in the field?"

"No." Fuck it all. "You're my friend, and yeah, maybe I've let our friendship influence my decision." He broke off, glad for the interruption when the waitress placed Scott's ale in front of him. "You're the only friend I've got, damn it. I thought I'd lost you in Colombia. But that's not why I'm keeping you out of the field."

"Yeah, it is." Scott raised his mug and then carefully placed it back upon the coaster. "Look, I haven't had a chance to say thanks for letting me bunk with you and putting up with my shit all these months." He shrugged. "Thanks."

"Least I could do, mate," Troy said quietly. "You've been there for me when I needed help."

"But I knew when to walk away and let you stand on your own two feet. I'm okay, Troy. I'm ready for this."

The sound of Sandy's laughter wound its way through the rest of the babble, catching Troy's attention.

Scott glanced over his shoulder at her. "You like her, don't you?"

Troy gave a half-hearted shrug. "Doesn't matter."

"Yeah, it does."

"It doesn't matter because she's not my type."

"Because she's got that whole wholesome Midwest thing going on? Come on, I know you. I'll bet you've got a hard-on for all that soft blonde hair and blue-eyed sweetness." Instead of the sorrow and pain that had filled his expression most of this year, Troy saw interest in Scott's eyes. Maybe he was getting better.

"The keyword there is wholesome. She's too damned innocent for my tastes, and you know it."

Scott laughed, a sound Troy hadn't heard from his friend in far too long. Probably because he finally got to turn the spotlight off him and on to Troy. "You know what they say about the quiet ones. They're usually the kinkiest. I'll bet she'd surprise you."

"I'll bet she's looking for Mr. Right who will hand her a wedding ring and follow it up with a white picket fence and two point five babies instead of getting involved with a fucked-up bastard like me."

Scott ran his fingers through his hair. "To be honest? Settling down doesn't sound so bad."

To be honest, it didn't sound so bad to him either. Feck it all, if his life wasn't fucked up.

～

"YOU'RE NOT from around here, are you, sexy lady?"

Was it her Midwest accent that told him she wasn't a native to D.C.? Or did she have an I'm-a-small-town-hick sign plastered to her back? "I'm from Minnesota."

He must have come straight from work, one that involved heavy labor, because when he lifted his arm to grab the beer he'd ordered, his body odor had Sandy holding her breath. "That's one of the states up north, right?"

Wow, forget trying to be a Jeopardy contestant, this guy would never qualify for *Are You Smarter Than a Fifth Grader*? "Yeah. It's west of Wisconsin."

"Guess we'll have to go back to my place tonight then." His mouth split into what he probably thought was a smile but only thinned his already-too-thin lips. And did the man not know what a toothbrush was for? Or floss? What was that stuck between his teeth? Pepperoni from the smell of it.

Dear God, if this was the type of man this outfit attracted, she'd willingly don a wimple and nun's habit. And she was Lutheran for Pete's sake! All right, so she hadn't been to church since she'd left Minnesota, and her pastor and most of the rest of the congregation would be horrified to know what she'd done since she left, but she still had standards.

"Get lost, Ray." Jazz muscled between her and pepperoni breath. "Hell will freeze over before I let her go home with a loser like you."

To Sandy's surprise, Ray shuffled off without an argument. "You know him?"

"Oh, honey, everyone around knows he hits on anything without a dick between its legs." Jazz glanced at Ray's rapidly retreating figure. "In fact, I think that may not even be part of his criteria."

Sandy took a sip of her virgin daiquiri then turned her attention to the rest of the bar. The two of them discussed, and discarded, half a dozen men who might be boyfriend material. More than once she let her attention return to the booth where Troy sat talking with Scott.

Jazz followed her gaze. "I know him, don't I? The guy on the right? He seems familiar."

"That's Scott Phillips. He's the guy who got kidnapped in Colombia last year."

"Oh yeah, I heard about him. Pity. I don't do damaged guys. I've got enough baggage of my own. What about the other guy? He's cute."

"That's Troy McPherson, the head of the International group. I've told you about him before." About a gazillion times.

"Oh, so that's Mr. Tall, Dark and Mysterious. Shoot, girl, why haven't you made a move on him yet? With shoulders like his, and those smoky eyes, I'd do him in a heartbeat."

Jazz's overt ogling rankled. "As I've told you about a hundred times before, he's one of my bosses."

"So? It didn't stop your boss from dating one of his agents, did it?"

True. And considering the thumps, moans and groans she'd heard coming from Sam's office when she'd locked her desk earlier, he and Rosie were doing very well. Often. And a little too loud for her comfort.

"I don't think I'm his type. At least he's never given me any indication he might be interested in me. I think he may have a girlfriend over in England or something."

"Pity." Jazz swung her stool to assess the rest of the crowd. "What about that blond guy? Do you know him?"

"That's Kris Campbell. Sorry, but yeah, he's a CPO too. No baggage that I know of so he's fair game for you."

"I'm not asking for me, dodo. Why aren't you hitting on him?"

Seeing that they were looking at him, Kris smiled, then ducked his head. "Kris isn't my type. Besides, he's younger than me by a couple years."

"Oh, hon, younger just means he's more eager to learn what pleases you. Besides, they're usually the best fun because they're not looking for a commitment. Not that any guy is." Jazz observed the young agent for a long moment before pointing out another potential prospect. "Oooh, there's a good candidate. Nice suit, expensive shoes. Lawyer maybe?"

"Yeah, he's not bad." The man in question placed an order with the bartender at the far end of the bar. When he noticed them watching him, he took his beer and threaded his way through the crowd toward them.

"Don't forget to check for his wedding ring." Jazz jumped off her barstool.

"Wait, where are you going?"

"I'm going to see if I can get some action with Kris. I don't mind robbing the cradle a bit. For a night, anyway." With a saucy grin, she leaned in and whispered, "Let me know if you aren't going to need a ride home," then wound her way through the crowd.

The potential candidate for the evening stopped beside Sandy. He leaned against the bar, lifting a foot to rest on the brass rail of her stool. "Where'd your friend go?"

"She saw someone she wanted to talk to." Shoot, so he wasn't interested in her but in Jazz. Still, Sandy did a quick check for a wedding ring and found none, though he did wear a rather expensive gold link bracelet. First test passed. What about the rest of him? Height, hard to tell considering she was sitting, but she thought he was taller than her by a couple inches at least. Brown hair, trimmed shorter than she preferred, but no biggie. No body odor, always a check mark on the plus side of her list, though perhaps he'd gone a tad heavy with the aftershave. Suit, blue, single-breasted, no vest. But it had the same type of expensive look as Sam's and Chad's suits. Probably tailor-made.

What else had Jazz told her to check? Shoes. His were black. Shiny. Expensive, though she couldn't tell the brand the way Jazz would have been able.

Damn it, she was judging him by his clothes exactly the way she never wanted to be treated herself. She lifted her gaze and met a set of arctic blue eyes watching her.

"I'm Mitch." He held out his hand, waiting for her to shake it. "And you are?"

"Sa—mantha McPherson." No harm in using her bar name. It was smarter, right? And Troy wouldn't object that she'd borrowed his last name. Not that he'd ever know.

"Nice to meet you, Samantha." Mitch held up a hand to catch the bartender's attention. "Bring the lady another of whatever she's drinking."

"Thanks." She accepted the glass the girl tending bar handed her. After taking a sip, she straightened her spine and smiled at Mitch.

"So tell me about yourself, Samantha. Do you work around here?"

TROY'S FINGERS curled tighter around his glass as Sandy tugged her skirt down her thighs, rewarding that wolf in the blue suit with her beautiful innocent smile. "Hey, Scott. Do you know him? The guy staring down Sandy's cleavage?"

Scott shifted to get a better view of the couple. "Not by name. He started hanging out here a couple weeks ago. Heard him bragging about working for some financial firm or something. Why?"

When Sandy placed a hand on the guy's forearm and accompanied him to a booth at the back, Troy wanted to snarl. "Something about him sets off the alarm bells."

"It's your own fault if she goes home with him, you know," Scott said quietly. "You could have gone up there and talked to her yourself."

Flipping Scott the bird, Troy looked for some sign she was uncomfortable. To his disgust he found none. A half hour passed before Scott finished his drink and excused himself.

As the night wore on, Troy's mood darkened. He had no justifiable reason to plow his fist into the overconfident fucker's nose and wipe his smug smile off his face. It was none of his business the number of times the bastard's gaze dropped to Sandy's cleavage. Or how he'd placed a hand on her hip as if staking his claim.

Hidden in the shadows, he allowed himself to picture Sandy shrugging out of her blouse. He imagined her shimmying out of her skirt, letting the fabric puddle at her feet to stand in front of him wearing only a scanty bra and perhaps, if he were lucky, a lacy thong. First thing he'd do would be to lick the freckles above her breasts and let the spice of her skin excite his taste buds. Then he'd suckle on her plump nipples until they were hard, maybe he'd let her feel his teeth on them. Once she was moaning her pleasure, he'd fill his palms with those full globes of her ass and part her legs, bury his cock deep inside her.

His breath hissed through his teeth when his fingers brushed the hard-on pressing against his fly in his attempt to create more space in his trousers. Talk about a glutton for punishment, letting himself fantasize about her. Now he was in desperate need of a little hand action to ease the ache in his balls. If he didn't get himself under control, he'd either spill in his pants or he'd be forced to seek the men's bathroom and find his relief in a stall.

The asshole stood. Good. He was leaving.

Shit. Sandy was standing too. And taking the asshole's hand. Three steps later Sandy slipped and Troy had seen enough. He slid from the booth, blocking their way before they could pass.

"I'll take her home."

Sandy huffed. "Troy, please."

"You know this jerk, Samantha?" Asshole's jaw tightened.

Now wasn't that interesting? Sandy hadn't given Asshole her real name. Troy sized him up. Manicured hands, not used to hard labor. The start of a pudge around the midriff. Desk jockey, at least lately. Not that it made him any less dangerous. The guy could be carrying a gun. Or a knife. Hell, he could be a former agent who'd been retired a few months too long but still retained the knowledge of how to incapacitate someone with his bare hands. "Yeah, she knows me. And I don't know you. So why don't you take a hike?"

"I don't think so." To his credit, Asshole placed himself between

Sandy and Troy and stuck out his hand. "Mitch Young. And you are?"

Troy dropped his gaze to the outstretched hand and let it hang while he returned to meet Young's gaze. Okay, so maybe he wasn't a complete jerk. "McPherson. Troy McPherson."

Young's demeanor completely changed. He held up both hands and side-stepped Sandy. "Sorry, man, I had no idea she was married. She never said a word."

Married? Why the fuck would the asshole think he was Sandy's husband? Then again, who cared? Troy watched the man scuttle away before turning to Sandy, who glared at him. Rather than give her a chance to get away, he grabbed her wrist and hauled her out of the bar.

"Troy, stop it. You have no right to act like this." Despite Sandy's protests, she didn't struggle against his hold. "Will you slow down, please? I'm in high heels here."

He slowed but didn't stop until they were beside his SUV in the parking lot. "Damn it, woman, you don't have the sense of an overbred cocker spaniel, do you know that?" A spaniel with big blue puppy-dog eyes and soft wavy hair, lush curves and plump lips.

"Are you calling me a dog?" She flattened her hand against his chest and shoved him. At least she tried to shove him but ended up staggering backward herself.

"No." He crowded her against his SUV, trying to ignore the way her breasts brushed his shirt, or the way her lipstick glistened in the moonlight. *Focus, mate.* "Have you ever met this Mitch guy before tonight?"

"No, but who I decide to have a drink with is none of your business. I'll date who I want, when I want."

"Then you can get together with him another day, but I won't stand by and let you go off with a guy you don't know when you're drunk and not fit to make a decision."

"I'm not drunk. I was drinking virgin daiquiris, for Pete's sake."

"Sure as hell looked like it to me from the way you were stumbling your way out of the bar. Shit, did you take your eyes off your drink? Maybe he slipped you a roofie." He checked her eyes to see if she might be drugged only to have his hand slapped.

"Oh for heaven's sake. I'm not drunk and I'm not drugged. Someone must have spilled a drink, my heel slid. That's all. Besides, have you ever tried walking on four-inch heels? Do you know how hard it is, especially if some asshole is forcing you to keep up while he runs outside?"

He mentally took a step back, wondering if he had misjudged the situation. Then he made the mistake of looking at her again. Sparks of blue fire snapped out at him from those big puppy-dog eyes. Her chest rose and fell as she fought her anger. His body urged him to lower his head, to kiss her and capture her mouth with his, to draw some of that passion into his long-dormant soul.

A breeze whipped around the parking lot. She shivered and her nipples beaded beneath the silk of her blouse. As much as he wanted to be the one to warm her, he stepped back.

"You're cold."

"Because you dragged me out here without giving me the time to put my coat on, asshole."

Unable to argue her point, he took the jacket she clutched in one hand and held it open.

Her anger didn't disappear precisely but it was joined by questioning bemusement as she slid her arms into the sleeves. "Thank you. I'm still ticked off with you, you know."

Placing his hands gently on her shoulders, he turned her to face him. "Same goes. You need to be more careful about who you trust. There are some nasty types out there who will gobble a pretty girl like you up for a snack."

He couldn't resist playing with her collar as a way to cover his need to touch her hair. To touch her.

Her expression softened. "I know about the nasty types, Troy. I have to file the reports that agents submit, as well as sit in on the initial meetings with clients, which means I know exactly why they require bodyguards. I also volunteer with the Safe and Sound program. I've seen what those women have experienced before they made it to the shelter."

When she shook her head, her hair brushed the back of his hand in a soft caress.

All his protective instincts bristled that she could be put in danger from one of those abusers. "Tell me no one's been harassing you from there. None of the husbands who think it's easier to blame you than himself."

Her eyes closed briefly and a soft huff of exasperation escaped between her lush lips. "I'm fine. And stop trying to distract me about how you interfered back there. I'm still mad at you."

Smart girl. He caught a strand of hair and rubbed it between his fingers. "He wasn't your type."

"And you are?"

Not hardly. "No. I'm the big bad wolf. That's why you need to trust me that he wasn't right for you."

"What big eyes you have, Grandma?" Her lips compressed though the corners twitched as if she were trying not to smile. Then she tilted her head until her ear touched his thumb and the ground slid from beneath him. Why was it so hard to breathe from such a simple touch?

He gave in to impulse and lowered his head. Her eyes widened briefly, then they closed as he took the kiss he'd dreamed of for so long.

She tasted of strawberries and sugar. And everything good that must be found in heaven. Heaven became even more attainable when she slid her hands beneath his coat, around his waist and flattened them over his back, pulling him closer. He sank deeper into the kiss, her innocence a benediction, a cleansing of all his sins.

The Honda parked beside his SUV beeped and its headlights flashed, breaking the trance he'd fallen into. He couldn't remember a time when he'd ever been so reluctant to break off a kiss, but he forced himself to lift his head. To step back.

As the owner of the Honda cleared his throat and gestured to the door Troy was blocking, he took Sandy's hand and led her to the front of the car. She didn't say a word as she followed, but the look of complete trust she gave him wracked him with both guilt and desire. Her tongue darted out to moisten lips swollen from his kiss. In what seemed to be an unconscious gesture, she touched a hand to smooth the hair he'd managed to further tousle. Is this what she'd look like waking up beside him?

Stop it. She'd run screaming if she knew you killed an unarmed man this morning.

FOUR

SANDY SHIVERED at the breeze swirling around the parking lot. Or maybe she felt the loss of Troy's warmth. What had just happened? She'd been angry enough to spit railroad spikes when he'd sent Mitch packing and hauled her out like a caveman dragging his woman by the hair. Then out of the blue he'd kissed her. And, oh man, did he know how to kiss.

She'd loved how he'd held her head in his palm, with a firm yet gentle touch. She'd loved the heat radiating from his body, making her forget they were outside and her coat open to the wind that now chilled her to the bone. She'd loved the strength she'd felt beneath her palms.

He'd made her feel protected. Feminine. Desired.

Troy cleared his throat. "Let's get you home."

His voice matched the night, hinting of danger lurking in the shadows. A delicious thrill crawled up her back and into her psyche. Maybe this was a man she could trust with her darkest desires, the ones she'd trusted with very few people.

He unlocked the Porsche and held open the passenger door, helping her climb into the seat before slamming the door shut. She sat in the darkness, watching as he rounded the hood and opened his own door. He didn't speak as he eased through traffic with a competency that left her no question he was in complete control. Come to think of it, she couldn't remember ever seeing him lose control. Everything about him seemed planned and guarded. Every word weighed and measured before spoken, his movements efficient.

As the stereo serenaded them with a piano and violin sonata by Bach—or perhaps Mozart, she couldn't tell the difference—she pondered the speculations as to his background, the questions about the trace of Irish accent that appeared at random times. Jazz had speculated that maybe he'd been raised there—

"Shoot."

He glanced sharply at her. "What? Did you forget something at the bar?"

"I forgot to tell my roommate I was leaving." She scrambled through the contents of her purse, searching for her phone. "Damn it, my battery's dead."

"Were you her ride?"

"No, she drove, but she'll worry if she can't find me."

He shifted in his seat and pulled his cell from its holster on his hip. "Here, use mine. Do you know her number?"

"Thanks. I'll just text her, so I don't interrupt her if she's hooked up with someone." She composed a quick note and hit send before handing him back the phone.

Four blocks later, he glanced at her. "Are you hungry?"

Startled, she nodded before she thought.

"Good." He flipped on the turn signal and pulled into another parking lot, this time beside an upscale restaurant. The type with a valet who took a good long look at her legs when he helped her from the car.

"Eyes up, mate," Troy practically growled, a territorial claim that secretly thrilled her. He laced his fingers with hers. "Shall we?"

The door opened to muted voices mingling with the sounds of cutlery on china, all accompanied by a string quartet at the far end. The maître d' greeted Troy by name and led them through the half-filled dining area. Once they were seated, Sandy opened her menu but studied the man across from her instead. Other than the Christmas party the year before, she'd never been around him outside of the office. She hadn't missed the heads turning when they'd walked in. It hadn't been her the restaurant patrons had noticed. He had a presence about him, one of confidence along with a hint of danger. Even though he was dressed in jeans and a cotton shirt where most of the other men wore high-powered business suits, Troy fit in.

He glanced at his menu for a minute before meeting her gaze. "So why did you tell that jerk your name was McPherson?"

"I always use a bar name. Just to be on the safe side."

"It's a good idea, but why McPherson?"

"Because you were..." She stopped herself from admitting it had been him she'd been thinking of, substituting, "the first person I saw when I was trying to come up with a name. I didn't figure you'd mind."

"I don't." A furrow marred his forehead. "You were leaving with him."

Was he asking if she was going home with Mitch? Going to sleep with him? Why was that any of his business? Unless...no, he couldn't be jealous. Could he?

"He was a nice guy who spent most of this evening listening to me babble on about Hauberk. He wasn't a serial killer or anything."

"You're too trusting. For all you know he was plotting to get you out into the parking lot, shove you into his car and abduct you. Promise me you won't take that type of chance again."

She couldn't stop her eyes from rolling at his overprotective tone. "So what should I have done? Told him I didn't trust him and he needed to wait while I fetched my big, bad bodyguard to protect poor little old me? Believe it or not, I can protect myself."

"What would you have done?" He sat back in his chair and grimaced. "Because there's no way you could have run from him in those damned shoes."

"I keep a Taser in my purse. I would have used it, kicked off my heels and run back into the bar, screaming the whole time."

"A Taser? Well, that's something I guess, but I hope to bloody hell you don't take that into D.C. with any of your dates. They'll throw your pretty little behind in jail."

What was it with guys thinking she was an idiot? Of course she knew about D.C.'s laws. "Look, you're not my father or my brother. And you're not my boyfriend, or my husband as you let him think. So what's with the twenty questions? What difference is it to you who I go home with?"

He hesitated for a second. "I'm an expert in security. I've been trained by the best to keep people safe. I've seen too many women get badly hurt because they trusted someone they shouldn't have." He dropped his gaze for a second. "I didn't want to go into the office tomorrow to discover you'd been raped. Or worse."

His answer didn't surprise her, but the disappointment she felt did. He'd been analyzing the situation as part of his job when she'd hoped he'd been jealous. "I appreciate that. I guess. But I'm a big girl. I know how to look after myself."

"You're no girl, Sandy." He leaned forward, his voice husky. "You're a beautiful woman. And dressed the way you are now, it's enough to drive any man crazy with lust."

"Not you," she muttered.

"Yes. Even me."

The arrival of their waiter forced her to wait until they'd finished ordering to ask for an explanation of that bombshell. Once they were alone again, she asked, "So am I to look at this as a date? Or a business meeting, with you advising a potential client about security risks?"

"Which would you prefer?'

She started to answer but was interrupted by the waiter who had returned with the wine Troy had ordered. Frustrated, she tapped her foot until the waiter finished pouring. As soon as the waiter had taken two steps away, she folded her arms across her chest and glared at Troy. The hell on playing coy and all these stupid games. "I don't know what to think. Considering the kiss you gave me earlier, I guess it's possible you see it as a date. But, for all I know, you're using me as a smoke screen as a way to stay in the closet."

Okay, it was a low blow but hell, he was so freaking confusing.

Troy lowered the wineglass, his jaw dropping, his eyes wide. "I beg your pardon? Do you mind explaining how you came to that conclusion?"

"You've never once mentioned being on a date with a woman that anyone can remember. You always find a way to back out of going to any parties that might require a date. Not to mention that Scott's been living with you ever since he got back from Colombia. What else are people to think?" Okay, so it was pretty thin in the telling but the thought had crossed her mind.

"I don't talk about my dates because I don't like bringing my personal life into my job—it's a bad idea on too many fronts. And right back at you, by the way. I don't like going to parties because I can't abide small talk." His lips had firmed, and his words were clipped. The hint of Irish accent that came and went thickened.

"As for Scott, not that it's anyone's business, but he has no family to rely on, and since I didn't like sending him back to his flat in London where he might be tempted to eat the end of his gun, I invited him to stay with me until he got back on his feet." He stared across the restaurant to the entrance to the kitchen and swore beneath his breath, anger radiating from him.

"I'm sorry," she whispered. "I just...you confuse me. You've never given me any sign in the office that you're even aware I'm anything more than a piece of furniture."

His head swiveled back, his gaze as piercing as a hawk's. "Oh, I'm aware of you. You can count on it. But it's safer if I keep my distance."

Safer how? By not making her a target in case one of the baddies his type went after decided to go after someone he cared about? Or was he one of those egotistical assholes who thought every woman he met would swoon at his feet for him to ravish? "Safer? For who?"

"Safer for you." The unblinking gaze didn't relent, making her sympathize with the criminals caught in his sights.

A shadow fell across Troy's face as another diner stopped beside their table, a much younger woman at his side. Troy got to his feet and shook the man's hand. "Senator Brannally, how are you, sir?"

"Fine as always. Please sit." From the way the senator greeted Troy, not just with his trademark smile but also how he clapped his hand on Troy's shoulder once he'd resumed his seat, Sandy realized this was not a casual acquaintance but a dear friend. She knew Sam had friends in high places, but she'd never realized Troy did too. "I just thought I'd drop by and say hello. I was going to have my assistant contact you tomorrow, but since you're here—I understand Senator Hirst has hired your firm to provide extra security for his wife's birthday party at the Hay Adams next week. Will you be there?"

"That's part of the D.C. office's responsibility so no, I have no plans."

"Pity." His gaze wandered to Sandy, lingering, she swore, on her cleavage.

Troy followed the Senator's gaze. "Senator Brannally, may I introduce you to Sandra Hallquist."

Hmm, that was interesting. Not my assistant or my secretary as Sam had once mistakenly referred to her.

"Miss Hallquist." The senator nodded his head before returning his attention to Troy. "Have you decided to stay in D.C. permanently?"

"Semi-permanently. The head of the D.C. office has been out of town so I've been covering for him."

"We should get together one night. I'd like to hear what you're up to. Give you some ideas for the future."

The Senator persisted until Troy agreed to join him for dinner the following week before excusing himself. Sandy waited until he was out of sight before raising an eyebrow.

"I don't know if I'll ever get used to the circles you guys run in. Movie stars, senators..." She brushed her bangs from her eyes. "He's not a client, is he?"

Troy placed his napkin back on his lap. "No. He was in Ireland when my parents died and my mother's brother, who lived in his district, asked him to intervene with the Irish authorities and bring me back to the States. When my uncle died, he became my guardian and paid for my room and board at the Academy where I went to school, and when I decided to go into the Diplomatic Service he put in a good word for me. He's kept an eye on my career ever since."

"That was nice of him." On impulse she reached across the table and laid her hand on his. Something flared in his eyes; with a simple movement he reversed the position of their hands.

"Yes, it was." His thumb stroked the fleshy part of her palm, light strokes up and down, soothing and yet her body quivered at the simple touch. "This is nice too."

His thumb made circles on the inner flesh of her wrist. Who knew that part of her hand could be an erogenous zone? None of her other boyfriends had made that connection before. She pressed her thighs together at the promise in his words. From the heat in his expression, this was most definitely a date.

Not trusting her voice, she nodded. Only when the waiter arrived with their food did Troy release her. The rest of the meal he found whatever excuse he could to touch her. Reaching for the salt, refilling her wineglass, handing her the dessert menu. Each time he touched her, his eyes locked on hers.

"Taste this." He held a spoonful of his crème brulee to her lips. Electricity zinged through her body, bouncing beneath her skin like a summer field filled with fireflies. His gaze locked on her lips, her tongue, as she cleaned the spoon with light licks. He lowered the spoon only to lift it, filled again, with yet another command to taste the creamy dessert. By the time they finished, every inch of her body was ready to spontaneously combust. The wait for the check seemed interminable and she found herself squirming, trying to find relief from the need he'd spawned.

Less than ten minutes after they'd pulled out of the restaurant's parking lot, Troy parked the SUV by her apartment building's front door. The hand he placed on the small of her back as they walked to the building firmed her resolve. It's not that she'd never considered

Troy *that way* before but now he was really here, touching her, and her body simmered with anticipation.

She waited until the elevator doors closed and then turned to face him. Reminding herself he'd already kissed her once, she curled her fingers around the collar of his coat and tugged him closer. With her stilettos, she was almost his height. All she had to do was tilt her face and press her lips against his. His body went rigid for a moment, then his lips parted and his tongue brushed hers.

Warmth quickly spread from his lips through the rest of her body, caressing and curling around her breasts until they were heavy, her nipples hard, weakening her knees. He slid his hands down her side and around to cup her backside. The heady scent of her arousal wafted between them, her panties dampening as he rocked his erection against her mound.

Intoxicated to be in his arms once again, to be under his control, Sandy lost herself in the kiss until the elevator bounced to a stop and the door slid open.

"This is your floor." Though he'd broken the kiss, his hands didn't move from their place on her ass.

"So it is." Reluctantly, she stepped back and captured his hand before it dropped to his side. She led him down the hall, fumbling one-handed in her purse for her keys, afraid that if she let go of him he'd find an excuse to leave. The key turned in the lock and she pushed the door wide. There were no lights on, and Jazz's boots weren't in their usual place on the boot mat. Xander looked up from where he'd curled on the couch then dismissed them as unimportant.

To her disappointment, Troy attempted to extract his hand from hers. "I should go."

"No," she whispered. "You should stay."

She stepped into her apartment and tugged. He resisted a moment, then took one step—only one—across the threshold before he stopped and shook his head. "This isn't a good idea, Sandy."

Perhaps not, but it was exactly what she needed. Besides, if they had any chance at having a relationship, he needed to know from the beginning exactly what she expected.

Not caring that the door was open, she tossed her coat on the couch, disturbing the cat. She undid the remaining buttons on her blouse and shrugged out of it. Struck by the cool air, her nipples furled into hard buds beneath the lace of her bra. "I want you to stay. All night."

His eyes closed and his Adam's apple bobbed as he swallowed hard. "I may want things you aren't prepared to give."

"I won't know until you ask me, will I?" Before he could say no, she let the silk fall to the floor at her feet, then she captured his hand and pressed his warm palm against her breast. "This is what I want. Trust me."

WELL, *this evening had turned out to be a bust,* Jazz thought as she nursed the last of her ginger ale. While Kris had been a promising diversion for the night, his phone had rung and he'd begged off. Now here she was, alone.

The bartender and owner of Rusty's ambled over and hooked a thumb toward the front door. "If you're looking for your friend, she hooked up with one of the Hauberk guys and left a while ago."

Damn it, Sandy had waltzed off without letting her know? Was she coming back or was she finding her own way home? She dug out her phone and hit the speed dial for Sandy's cell. Only to reach voice mail. Damn. Muttering under her breath, she composed a text message and hit send. "I guess all I can do is wait until she replies. You wouldn't happen to have some coffee handy, would you?"

"Sure thing. I always make a fresh pot at this time of night for those people who need to sober up." Rusty poured a cup and placed it in front of Jazz, his eyes sharp in their assessment. "Was she your ride? Do you need me to call you a cab?"

"No, she came with me but now I don't know if I'm supposed to wait for her or assume she's finding her own way home." Jazz sighed and swivelled on her seat, assessing the nearly empty bar. Three couples lounged at the larger corner booth, but other than that the place had cleared out. The remaining guys at the bar eyed her with a voracity that left her queasy.

"If you want my opinion, all the good guys left long ago." Jazz straightened when the men's bathroom door opened and the guy Sandy had been talking to earlier appeared. "Or maybe not." She caught the bartender's eye and gestured to where the guy now sat. "Hey, Rusty? Do you know him?"

"He's come in here fairly often the past couple weeks. Pays his tab, though he's a little stingy with his tips. Seems to seek out the Hauberk guys—haven't figured out if he's looking to hire them, if he wants to join them or if he's a guy version of a badge bunny. Haven't had any complaints about him though, if that's what you're asking."

The object of interest noticed them watching and settled on the stool beside Jazz.

"I saw you earlier, didn't I?"

Before he'd zeroed in on Sandy, she reminded herself. "You were talking with my roommate earlier so maybe you saw me with her."

"That's right. You left before I had a chance to talk to you." He rested an elbow on the bar, his eyes on her face instead of her boobs like most of the guys that night. "Why'd you take off?"

Wait. He'd been coming over to talk to her, not Sandy? Well, hell. This night was looking up.

He leaned in to whisper in her ear. "Tell me you're in need of a bodyguard because I'd love to guard your body."

Okay, for a pickup line it was way cheesy, but it still made her laugh. She stuck out her hand. "Hi, I'm Jazz."

Shoot, she should have used her bar name. There was something comforting in knowing if the guy turned out to be a creep, he wouldn't know her real name and be able to stalk her. But this guy didn't seem like a loser. Besides, if he did start stalking her, she had an in with Hauberk Protection, didn't she?

"Hi, Jazz. Nice to meet you. I'm Mitch. Mitch Young."

. . .

AFTER A BRIEF HESITATION, Troy's mouth claimed hers, resuming the kiss they'd started in the elevator. One arm snuck around her waist, his hand molding her behind, pulling her against him. Yes, this was what she wanted. Craved. Yet she needed more. She wiggled her mound against his erection. A groan rumbled deep in his chest as he took control.

He walked her backward until her spine touched the wall. Her gasp at the coolness of the plaster against her bare skin let him break off the kiss. His mouth trailed kisses along her jaw and down her neck, his breath kindling a fire with each soft exhale. With an incomprehensible murmur that may or may not have been English, he pushed aside the lace of her bra and bent his head over her breast. His tongue swept a long stroke around her nipple. The heat was immediately followed by a cool breeze as he blew on the moist path he'd left.

When she attempted to reach between them and loosen his fly, he caught her wrist and stopped her, his eyes smoldering dark with heat. "No."

The single word had her melting against the wall. This was a man who knew what he wanted, would give her what she needed.

He stepped closer again, his lips recapturing her mouth while one hand undid Sandy's skirt until all she wore were her heels and the skimpiest pair of panties she owned.

His hand dipped beneath the fabric to part her folds. Sandy closed her eyes and concentrated on the sensations he aroused. Her cream coated his fingers as they slid over her clit and curled around the opening, dipping in to tease the tissues until her breath stuttered then skated away.

She held on to his biceps as if she would fall down if she didn't, and from the way her legs trembled, perhaps she would. Beneath her fingers, his muscles were hard, the contours well defined from more than hours in the gym. He knew just what to do to make her body melt around him. That he was still fully clothed and she was nearly naked added a delicious naughtiness to the equation that heightened the entire experience.

He hooked his fingers in the side bands of her panties and drew them down her thighs, his body following their path until he knelt at her feet. With a single tap on her ankle, he signaled for her to lift first one foot then the other.

As soon as she was free of any restrictions, he nudged her legs farther apart and leaned in to bury his nose in the thin strip of curls covering her mound. She threaded her fingers in his hair as he ran his tongue through her folds, his beard rasping the tender skin of her inner thighs. Her low moan filled the room as pleasure assailed her.

"Tell me what you want, sunshine. Do you like this?" His fingers pressed deeper inside her then withdrew, coated with the musky scent of her arousal. "Yeah, look how wet you are. You do like this, don't you?"

"Yes." Oh God, it was better than anything she'd ever fantasized. Even his accent had thickened to that sexy Irish lilt. Pure unadulterated lust leapt in her belly, sent another wave of cream from her pussy.

When he sucked his fingers into his mouth, she couldn't take her eyes off of his lips. *Put them back on me.* His lips curved, as if he knew what she was thinking.

Anyone out in the hall could probably have heard her gasp when he speared two fingers into her sheath but she couldn't stay quiet. Nor did she try. He must have kicked the door shut because a part of Sandy's brain heard it click shut. Then her brain shut off too. The passion he ignited scorched every part of her body as his tongue and fingers branded her in places that had slumbered for years, if they'd ever awoken before. He drove her higher, harder until she was shaking and breathless, unable to stand up unassisted. "Do you like that?"

"Yes." At least that's what she tried to say, but she could barely breathe.

"What else do you like, sunshine?" His voice was rough,

rippling through her body, commanding without being oppressive. Despite his questions, he continued to stroke her both inside and out. He worked with a sense of purpose, finding the right spots the way no one else had.

"I like it hard. I like being stretched so full it hurts a little." She rushed the last admission.

A third finger joined the other two and he rasped his teeth over her clit, nipping and biting. "You're too tight for any more."

"Then put your dick inside me." She tilted her hips, pushing her pelvis into his face. She needed more. More teeth, more tongue, more fingers...more. "Please."

She almost cried when he slid one finger along her crease and circled her anus then thrust past the tight ring of muscles. Both passages filled by his fingers, her brain overloaded by the cascading sensations. She rocked against him, urging him on, until she found the sharp edge she craved. Her body clamped around him when he nipped at her clit, her orgasm exploding like an expanding ball of liquid fire.

No breath left in her lungs, her head spinning, her legs weak, she slid down the wall.

Before her butt hit the floor, Troy lifted her easily, carrying her to her bedroom. After stretching languidly over the quilt her mother had given her for her eighteenth birthday, Sandy reached up to touch his cheek. "Your turn."

A shadow flickered across his face as his gaze roamed down the length of her naked body. To her surprise, he shook his head. "Not tonight, sunshine."

Instead, he pressed a kiss to her forehead and headed to the bathroom. She heard water running, then the light flicked off. Yet he didn't return. Instead she heard the front door open then shut. "Troy?"

There was no answer.

Unable to believe he'd walk away like that, Sandy lifted herself up on her elbows and stared at the empty doorway.

What had just happened?

FIVE

A LONG, sleepless night later, Troy sat at his kitchen table and stared at the pre-dawn sky. What the hell had happened to the control he had over his life? Scott threatening to leave, Sandy asking him to stay. What should he be bracing himself for next?

Scott walked out of his bedroom and headed straight to the kitchen in search of his first hit of caffeine for the morning. "You look like shit."

"Fuck you."

One of Scott's eyebrows arched but he didn't say anything. Instead, he reached for a mug from the cupboard, letting the silence ask the questions Troy knew he had.

Before he could stop himself, he found himself saying, "I think I crossed a line." Shit. "No, I know I crossed a line."

Scott stopped filling his mug. "What did you do?"

"I stuck my nose in where I shouldn't. I ended up taking Sandy to dinner and then back to her place last night and we..." He blew out his breath. "You're right about the quiet ones. She's not what I expected." She was more. So much more.

The eyebrow arched higher. "Just how far did things go?"

"We didn't...shit. I didn't fuck her, all right? But I came damned close."

Both eyebrows arched this time. "Damned close? That tells me a whole lot of nothing." When Troy didn't elaborate further, Scott frowned. "At any point, did she say no?"

"No. It's just—"

"It's that it's Sandy we're talking about here," Scott finished for him. "And you have this crazy idea that she's a virgin who'd be tainted by hanging around you."

He snorted. "Oh, she's no virgin." Not from the way she'd dropped her blouse or her skirt. Christ, that had been so unexpected, and so freakin' hot to see her strip down right there in front of God and country. He'd nearly come in his pants.

"So what's the problem? Ask her out on another date. See what happens from there."

He shook his head. He could imagine what would happen from there. She'd see who he really was, what he really liked. "I don't think that's a good idea."

"I do," Scott said quietly. "I wonder if you're selling Sandy short. I'm willing to bet she's as responsive as hell and knows what she wants in the sack."

She is, he wanted to respond but didn't.

Scott didn't need it to be voiced either. "So what's your problem?"

Damned if he knew. But getting involved with Sandy was a bad idea, of that he was certain.

"If you're worried she'll wrap you around her little finger and have you sitting up and begging instead of the other way around, don't be afraid to ask for help. You know I'm always happy to help a friend out."

Why hadn't Scott turned around, damn it? He couldn't tell if he was sincere or not. "Are you? Still my friend?"

Even though I don't want to send you out on active duty?

Scott faced him, his expression closed so Troy couldn't read him. That Scott felt he needed to guard his reactions, to shut himself off, caused an ache deep in his gut. "Are you going to talk to Chad about transferring me to his group when he gets back?"

"Yeah. I promised, didn't I?" *Fuck it all. Don't go out there yet. Haven't you been through enough?*

"Then yes." Scott nodded once before turning back to his coffee. "We're good. But if I find that you've lied or gone behind my back to make him doubt me? Then all bets are off."

≈

"SO HE'S NOT ASKED you out yet? It's been, what a week now? Hand me the ketchup, will you?"

"Four days." Sandy handed Jazz the squeeze bottle. "And in all that time, he's not said a thing that isn't work related. You'd think the other night never happened."

"Maybe he's been busy covering for that guy who got shot."

The news that Chad had been shot still made her nauseous. At least he was already out of the hospital and due back at work in a couple of days. The news that his ex-wife had returned and had moved in with him had the office grapevine buzzing more than usual.

"Yeah, but I don't think it's that." She leaned in and lowered her voice. "I don't understand. He made me come so hard I could barely walk afterward. Yet here he's pretending it never happened." Everything in her body softened at the memory of his head buried between her thighs and the orgasm he'd driven her to. "What am I supposed to think? Do you think I was a pity fuck or whatever that was?

"I know he was turned on too. His hard-on was pretty hard to ignore. But all he said was 'not tonight, sunshine' and then he walked out." She leaned back, letting out a huff of frustration. "So now I have no idea what to think. Does that mean he wants to get together again? Or that he wasn't interested in *me* in the first place?"

Jazz flipped the top on the ketchup and squeezed the bottle. "I doubt he would have gone down on you if he wasn't interested in you. And for a guy to walk away from a guaranteed night of sex?

That's really weird. But he called you sunshine. That's got to mean something."

"Why does that mean anything? I always figured it was what guys called a woman when they couldn't remember her name."

"I don't know. I've never had a nickname from anyone. If a guy called me something sweet like sunshine, it would make me feel...I don't know special."

Wow. If that's all it took to make Jazz feel special. Sandy shoved her speculations away from Jazz's love life and back to Troy.

Jazz grimaced as she removed the pickle from the hamburger's bun. "So is he in the office today?"

Sandy snagged the discarded dill slice from Jazz's plate. "I know he was there when I got in but by the time I finished going over the morning agenda with Sam, Troy's door was open and his office was empty. So I haven't a clue if he's coming back or not."

"Maybe he had a meeting."

"Maybe. But he didn't have any meetings scheduled on his calendar for this morning." Sandy frowned at the turkey club she'd ordered. She should have ordered the salad instead. At the very least she should have had them hold the mayo. "Do you think carrying me might have turned him off? Maybe he hurt himself because I was too heavy. Am I too fat?"

Jazz shrugged. "You're curvy, but you're not, like, fat or anything. Stop obsessing about it. Maybe he just had somewhere else to be, or he didn't have a condom or something."

Sandy didn't point out that she had a stash in her bedside table. Somehow she didn't think that was Troy's reason for walking away. "So what do I do now? Do I say something? Or let it die a quiet death?"

"That's easy. Next time you see him, go into his office, get down on your knees and give him a blowjob that'll have him seeing stars." Jazz took a big bite of her hamburger.

"Can you say that a little louder next time? Sheesh, Jazz."

"No one heard. The place is too noisy." At least Jazz did speak quieter this time, probably because she'd had to speak around the mouthful of burger. She swallowed and continued, "You're the one who said you wanted to get down and dirty, who got turned on spying on Sam and Rosie when they were getting it on in his office."

Sandy glanced around to ensure no one might be listening; at least there was no one in the next booth who might have overheard. "Yes, but that doesn't mean Troy is interested in—"

"Girl, you said you overheard that he belongs to that super-secret sex club, right?"

"Sssh. It's supposed to be a secret, remember? I could get in trouble for telling you that."

"Oh, honey, this is Washington. I'll bet half of D.C. knows about that club. Besides, with Sam's history, it's not like it's a secret that he's into kinky crap like bondage and stuff. The newspapers were filled with that assignment he'd had at that club where his partner got shot when he was with the FBI." Jazz finished her hamburger and wiped her fingers on the paper napkin. "I'm telling you, walk into Troy's office, drop to your knees and blow him."

"Have you ever gone down on your boss?"

"I've done what I've had to do." A hard look flickered across Jazz's face. "Look, you're the one who is always spouting off about not wanting to sit on your ass until you're old and grey, regretting all the opportunities for adventure you let slip past you. This is your opportunity. Have some fun. Just next time you decide to leave with a guy, phone me. That damned text didn't arrive until the next day. I was worried about you."

"I will." Sandy stared at the two uneaten sections of the turkey club left on her plate. "So are you seeing Mitch again? He seemed nice."

"Yeah, he is. He's going to come over tonight. He says he knows how to use that new video editing software and has promised to teach me so I can finally work on those videos we took at the Renaissance Festival."

"Oh, that's great. Then when he's done teaching you, you can teach me."

Jazz grabbed a twenty-dollar bill from her purse and tucked it on top of the bill in the faux-leather folder the waitress left on their table. "So what are you going to do about Mr. Tall, Dark and Mysterious?"

~

SANDY HUNG up her coat in the closet then walked into Troy's office and shut the door.

"Be right with you." Just like before, he didn't even look up from the keyboard again, damn it. What did she have to do to get his attention? Strip naked? Probably not. After all, it hadn't worked completely unsuccessfully last time, had it?

Her resolve firming, she walked around to his side of the desk. Conscious of the hum of voices outside his closed door, of the possibility anyone could walk in and discover her, she pushed him back from the desk. "Why are you avoiding what happened the other night?"

"Because it shouldn't have happened."

"Bullshit."

"I'm serious, Sandy. I'm not good boyfriend material. You know my job and how I'm here one day and gone the next. I'm not a great catch when it comes to stability."

"Bullshit." She folded her arms and glared. "I like you. And more? I trust you. I don't invite just anyone to stay the night with me, you know."

He caught her hand and pressed a fleeting kiss to her fingers in a move so smooth her knees weakened. "You shouldn't trust me, sunshine. I'm not who you think I am."

"Bullshit," she repeated, softer this time. "I know more about you than you think I do. I've read your file, remember? And I know stuff that isn't in those files." She knelt in front of him and stroked her cheek against his knuckles, noticing a trace of gun oil staining his shirt. So he'd not left the building, simply gone to the firing range. "I've seen how you worry about your agents. About Scott. You're a good man. As for you not being here a lot, that's fine with me. I'm not looking for marriage. I just..." *want to come so hard I see stars, the way you made me come the other night.* "I think we'd be good together. I'm not looking for forever."

From the doubt in his eyes, she knew he wasn't buying her explanation. *"This is your opportunity. Have some fun,"* Jazz had said. Wasn't that the whole point of leaving Minnesota?

Troy's eyes widened when she skated her palm along the inside of his thigh and tugged on his zipper. "What the hell are you doing?"

Wasn't it obvious?

"Since you show no sign of taking the initiative, I figure I should show you that you're not the only one talented in the bedroom. Or the office." Not giving him a chance to object, she slid her hand into his briefs and wrapped her fingers around his rapidly hardening cock. His fingers clamped onto the arms of his chair, the knuckles white; his breath quickened to match hers.

With her heart beating as fast as if she'd just run a mile, she licked her lips then lowered her head. A groan rumbled through him when she swirled her tongue around the head of his cock. God, she loved how he smelled, how he tasted of warm, spicy musk. The thick, dark hair at the root of his cock crinkled against her fingers, tickled her nose.

"Sandy." A warning? Or a plea?

She slid her lips down his shaft, her fingers reaching beneath the fabric to cradle his balls. His hips lifted off the seat slightly, pressing his cock deeper into her mouth; his fingers stroked her hair as he curved his fingers around the back of her head. Not a warning then.

"Oh fuck, that's..." His fingers tightened in her hair giving her the bite of pain she loved. She squirmed, pressing her thighs together at the warm moisture gathering between them.

She sucked harder, deeper, rocking until the head of his cock bumped the soft palate at the back of her mouth. What a pity he was still wearing his pants. She'd give anything to see him butt-naked.

Next time. And there would be a next time, she vowed. The

carpet did little to cushion her knees but she didn't care. She pulled back, the pressure of his hand controlling how far she could withdraw. God, yes, she loved a man who wasn't afraid to control her like that. The room filled with the sounds of her slurping his cock, the creak of his chair as he arched his hips, moans and sighs from them both. She lapped the head, savoring the taste of the creamy liquid that leaked from the slit.

"I'm going to blow down your throat, sunshine, and you're going to swallow it all."

He pressed on the back of her head until her nose touched the hair at his groin and thrust up. When his shaft swelled against her tongue, she moaned, thrilled at how she'd made him lose control. The first hot splash of come spilled over her tongue.

"Fuck yeah." His snarl caused her pussy to pulse, wanting to be filled instead of her mouth.

Breathing through her nose, she swallowed each pulsing jet. Once it eased, he released his hold on her. She stayed in place, her tongue gently stroking the sensitive tissues around the softening head, catching the last drops and swallowing them too before she sat back on her heels.

Sweat beaded his forehead and upper lip, his lids heavy as he stared at her. "You have two choices, Sandy. You either stand up and walk out of this office right now and never come near me again, or you accept that you will never date another man while you're with me."

"I told you," she said softly. "I don't casually invite men to stay the night with me. I knew what I wanted when I walked in here. But you should know I'm not looking for a wedding ring or any sort of commitment. And other than in the bedroom, you don't control me."

"You want me to believe you want a relationship based just upon sex? Tell me another one, sunshine." A muscle along his jaw twitched, a sign she knew betrayed his agitation.

"No, I like to be friends with my lovers too. To watch movies on the couch. Or football games, though I warn you I am a die-hard

Vikings fan. And yeah, I like good sex, and what you did the other night? That was fantastic. Incomplete, but fantastic."

"Sandy..."

"I'm not joking here, Troy. No commitment. When this is over, we're both free to walk away, no questions asked."

～

WHAT THE HELL *was her game?* Troy tried to wrap his head around what had just happened. Sandy had surprised him by kneeling in front of him, but when she'd reached for his zipper, she'd knocked him for a loop. She'd given him one of the best—and most unexpected—blowjobs of his life and then that little speech about not wanting a long-term relationship? What the hell was he supposed to think?

A week ago, he'd have bet big money that she'd never go down on her knees for a man she barely knew. Disappointment rippled through him. It took him a moment to realize its source. All those times he'd faced gunfire, or assigned others to face bullets and bombs to protect clients, it had been her image he'd imagined they were protecting. He'd liked that image. Knowing there were things in life worth protecting. Pure. Good. Wholesome.

Now she knelt there, looking up at him like a fallen Madonna. Or perhaps the proverbial cat who had gotten into the cream. As if to punctuate that thought, her tongue darted out and licked a lingering drop of his come from the head of his cock.

I don't casually invite men to stay the night with me.

Before he could say another word, there was a knock on the door that opened immediately afterward and Sam stuck his head in the door. "Hey, Troy, have you..."

His question trailed off, his gaze fixing on Sandy and where she was in relation to Troy. *Aw, shit.*

Sam's eyes narrowed and he shot him a hard look. "When you get a moment, you want to come into my office." Not a question but a command. For an ass-chewing most likely.

"Be right there."

Troy waited until the door closed behind Sam before daring to look at Sandy. The blush filling her face told him that she'd realized Sam knew exactly what they'd been doing.

"Was it worth it?" He couldn't stop the sharpness of his tone. Nor did he want to. "Was it worth losing your dignity?"

Sandy pushed herself to a stand and stared back at him, the blush fading, her gaze calm. "I suppose that depends on you, doesn't it?"

Without another word, she walked out of his office and sat at her desk. While his brain scrambled to keep up, she booted up her computer and calmly pulled out her notebook.

Would he ever figure out what had just happened? Was this something she'd done before? Shit, who else's office had she... *Oh, hell, no!* Troy pushed himself out of his chair, tucked his dick back into his briefs and stomped into Sam's office.

He slammed Sam's door shut and advanced on his boss. "Swear to me that you've never fucked her."

Sam leaned back in his chair and steepled his fingers over his chest. "Strange, that was gonna be my first question for you. Now plant your ass before I knock you on it."

His fingers curled into fists as he stared down at the other man. "Have you ever fucked her? Or had her go down on you?"

"Nope. Sandy's not my type—she's too damned innocent and trusting."

"So you've appointed yourself her guardian? Is she down with that?"

"So I look out for her. The same way I do with any woman I like when a hound dog is sniffing around her. But more to the point she's my employee. Which means hands off. For both of us."

"Rosie works for you but that didn't stop you from fucking her, did it?"

Sam launched himself from his chair. He planted his fists in the middle of the desk. "You better watch your mouth when it comes to trash talking Rosie. Because I will break your fuckin' jaw if you disrespect her. Now sit your ass down and shut the fuck up. And goddamn it, zip up your fuckin' fly, will ya?"

Mother fucker. At least his dick wasn't hanging out in the wind. He jerked up the zipper then sat in the chair opposite Sam with a thump. "There. You happy?"

"Not hardly. I want to know what the fuck is going on between you and Sandy. Before you tell me it's none of my fuckin' business, I'll remind you that it will be my fuckin' company that gets sued if Sandy decides to hit us with a fuckin' sexual harassment suit."

"I'll bet you worried about that when you hit on Rosie."

Sam's upper lip curled. "I did. Now answer my fuckin' question."

"With all due respect, considering what you and Rosie were doing in this office last Thursday night, you don't have the right to tell me, or Sandy, what to do." He sneered at Sam's sharp look. "What? You think that door blocked out the sound of you two getting your rocks off? From the sounds of it, you were fuckin' her right up against the door. So excuse me if I can't take your rules too seriously when you can't follow them yourself."

"I told you before, and I ain't gonna tell you again." Sam's voice got very quiet, his body completely still. "Keep your dick zipped when you're in the office. If you have to, use some fuckin' epoxy. And stay the hell away from Sandy."

"Fine. For office hours. What goes on after hours is none of your fucking business. *Sir.*"

"Damned straight it's my business. This is Sandy we're talking about, not some goddamned faceless woman at the club."

"Fuck you and the horse you rode in on."

"Listen to me, son. Sandy ain't your type. She's straight-up wholesome and deserves someone better than you. Hell, she deserves someone better than me."

If she were so wholesome she wouldn't have gone down on her knees voluntarily, but he'd be damned if he'd say that to Sam. "As I said, what goes on outside of the office between Sandy and me is none of your business."

"Yeah. It is. And this is the only warnin' you're getting'. Leave her the fuck alone." Sam's jaw locked down hard from the way the muscles in his neck strained. He punched a button on intercom. "John, you want to come in now?"

Moments later the IT manager walked in, sliding Troy a glance as he sat down. It's not like he or Sandy had made any noise so there was no way he could have known what they'd been doing. Had he and Sam been yelling loudly enough they could hear what was being said in the office beyond?

Bloody hell, maybe he was imagining things.

John took his seat across from Troy. From the shadows under his eyes, he'd had little sleep in the last twenty-four hours. "We had another hacker try to get in last night."

As he listened to the details of the attempt to break into the company's computers, Troy rubbed his temples in an effort to ease the headache gradually building strength. "What's that make this, the third attack this month?"

"Fourth." John plugged his laptop into the viewer and launched into an outline of the procedures the IT geeks were taking to prevent a breach of their security.

Lost by all the geek speak, Troy stared at the screens of data the IT geeks had captured of the hackers' attempts to penetrate Hauberk security. Yeah, like that helped clarify things for him at all. Show him a blueprint or a timeline of who did what, that he could follow. Even if it were in Russian or Arabic. But this coding gobbledygook? Might as well have been in Martian.

Thankfully Sam looked just as confused and interrupted John's lecture. "Yeah, you're tracking them. Great. What I want to know is do you have any clue of what they're looking for?"

"Not so far. They're testing the firewalls and trying various permutations of passwords and user IDs. It could be a teenager who stumbled upon our system and is poking around to see what damage he can do, or it could be someone attempting to find information on our safe houses or our procedures, but at this stage, it's anyone's guess."

Frustration gnawed at him. The Sig Sauer in his holster wasn't a threat to a hacker hidden behind firewalls and proxies. Nor was the knife strapped to his ankle. Give him a hard target to take out. A building to breach. A person or people to hit or defend others against. Tangibles. Those he could fight.

SIX

AND THEN SAM WALKED IN. WITH ME KNEELING RIGHT IN FRONT OF TROY.

SANDY HIT SEND in the messaging app she'd opened with Jazz as soon as she got home.

MAYB HE WANTED 2 WATCH OR WAS PISSED HE'D MISSED OUT.

Sandy snorted.

ESPECIALLY SINCE SAM/ROSIE WERE OBVIOUSLY GOING AT IT—LOUDLY— IN HIS OFFICE LAST WEEK.

She hit Send and then continued immediately with a second message.

ANYWAY, HE HAULED TROY INTO HIS OFFICE. REST OF DAY TROY WOULDN'T EVEN LOOK AT ME.

He might be playing it slo 2 try 2 fool Sam. Don't read things in2 it. Yet.

Easier said than done.

Hey, how are things going with Mitch?

An emoticon of a girl fanning herself popped up on her screen along with an icon of a blushing happy face.

Great. Oh, BTW, did U look at those videos he helped me edit yet?

Shit. Where the heck had Jazz put that thumbdrive? It took ten minutes but she finally found it beneath three days' worth of junk mail piled on the corner of the desk. She popped the drive into her USB port and loaded the file.

Oooh, they're great. Good job.

Thx. Gotta go. BTW hooking up w/ Mitch l8r, don't head to bathroom naked 2nite n case he's still there.

She clicked on the icon to open the email program to find she had four emails waiting, one from her mother with the details of the party she'd missed and how Ernie's cousin had been disappointed to miss her—sheesh, would she never give up?—two were jokes, and one was a chain letter an acquaintance insisted on sending her. While she was here, she might as well check her work email too. She opened the VPN program that would let her access the Hauberk private network and typed in her password. When she hit Enter the screen cleared then returned with the password screen. That was weird. She typed in her password again and this time she got into the network.

She'd finished clearing Chad's inbox when there was a knock on her door. She peered out the peep hole. Troy. Oh shit, and here she was in her PJs. After a brief debate about whether to change first, she removed the chain and unlocked the door.

His expression heated as his gaze fell to her pajamas. "Funny. I pictured you wearing skimpy teddies around your apartment."

"Sorry to smash that fantasy. I'm all about warmth and comfort." Damn it, why couldn't she have been wearing that sexy little teddy she'd bought at Victoria's Secret a couple months ago? Because her apartment was too freaking chilly to wander around in that type of outfit.

"To be honest, I find this effin' sexy." He toyed with her collar, rubbing the cloth between his fingers. The heat of his hand flowed through the fabric and revived a memory of when he'd touched her skin-to-skin. "I like the glasses too. They're sexy. Gives you a sort of wanton librarian look."

"My contacts were bothering me. How'd your dinner with Senator Brannally go?" Next she'd be showing him the retainer she'd worn. She led him inside her apartment and closed the door.

"Fine." He curled his fingers beneath her jaw, his thumb stroking her bottom lip. "I figured we needed to talk without an audience."

"Just talk?" She sucked his thumb into her mouth, in an obvious imitation of what she'd done for him earlier.

"Yes, just talk. You are a cheeky monkey, aren't you?" He pulled his thumb from her mouth and shook his head, but he couldn't hide the smile tugging at the edges of his mouth.

She wrapped her arms around his waist, enjoying the strength of him beneath her cheek, the lingering remnants of his aftershave and a hint of one of Sam's cigars filling her nostrils. "I was going for sex kitten or siren or something better than monkey, to be honest."

His laugh rumbled deep in his chest. "All right, sex kitten it is." His smile dimmed. "Did Sam give you any grief today?"

"Other than giving me the stink eye when he came out to refill his coffee cup a couple times, he didn't say anything directly if that's what you're worried about. What about you? Did he ream you out?"

"He tried. But I told him given his and Rosie's antics in his office lately, he can't say much."

"I guess we need to be more discreet. Next time I'll remember to lock your door." Though most of the thrill had come from knowing someone might walk in on them.

"That's why I came over. We need to talk about if there should be a next time."

Damn it. "I want there to be, don't you?"

"Things could get complicated." He swept her bangs to the side. Instead of dropping his hand, he toyed with her earring, his fingers occasionally brushing the sensitive skin behind her ear. He might as well have been playing with her pussy from the way it pulsed with each touch.

"I told you. I'm not looking for a long-term relationship, if that's what you're concerned about."

His expression confirmed he doubted her assertion.

"Look, I'm serious," she continued. "That's one of the reasons why I moved to D.C. If I'd stayed in Minnesota, I would have died of boredom. Nothing exciting ever happened there. I don't see myself as settling down anytime soon. So if you think I'm going to tie you down, I won't."

The doubt in his face didn't recede. "What *do* you want, sunshine?"

"I want to explore sides of me I wouldn't have had a chance to back in Minnesota. I'm tired of people thinking I'm nice, quiet Sandy. That I'm looking for the white picket fence and two point five kids. So if you picture a relationship of missionary position with the lights out, then I'm not your girl. I want to live my life on the edge. I want excitement. I don't want to look back when I'm Mom's age and regret anything. Is that too real for you?"

His smile returned, softening the sharp planes of his face. "Getting on your knees and blowing me shouldn't rank very high on the excitement meter. You might want to try skydiving or running a marathon. Maybe running with the bulls in Pamplona."

"I found this afternoon exciting." Apparently he didn't feel the same way. "As for skydiving and marathons, maybe one day I'd like to try skydiving, but running? That's not something I'm into. But you, I could definitely get into you." And she'd prefer he get into her too.

He dropped his hand with a sigh. "So you're just looking for sex."

"Not *just* sex, but yeah, that'll be a start."

Was that disappointment on his face? Weren't all guys looking for the scenario she'd laid out for him? Well, not all guys. Glen hadn't been.

"I travel a lot, sunshine. Which means I may break a lot of dates, and I may not be around for your birthday or when your family's visiting. So if that's going to be a problem..."

"No. It won't be any problem. Believe me."

"If we're going to date, I expect you to date only me, no one else at the same time."

"I can live with that as long as that restriction goes both ways."

"Of course."

"Look, I don't want you to think I'm some sort of skank who sleeps around a lot. I just..." How the hell did she explain? "I have certain expectations. Like I expect you to get me off whenever we have sex, and we don't have to have sex every single night, or have sex be the only reason we're together, but I don't want to be Suzy Homemaker—"

"—like your mother. I get it. And if your experience with sex is that the guy doesn't get you off every single time? Then you've been dating some real losers."

Ouch. True, but still. "Not everyone has been bad. It's not like I've never had an orgasm before. A couple guys—"

He pressed his fingers against her lips, stopping her. "I do not want to know about my predecessors, sunshine. But while we're on the subject, I will want to see your health records. I'll let you see mine so all's fair. But we don't take any chances. Life's too dangerous to play that type of sexual roulette."

His intensity overwhelmed her. In an effort to shake it off, she forced a laugh. "I guess that means a threesome is out?"

His jaw dropped for a second before he snapped it shut. "I beg your pardon?"

"You don't have to sound so surprised." Sandy shrugged, glad to have him off balance again. "I told you I was into excitement."

"Have you really had a threesome before or are you yanking my chain?" She could have spit nails at the suspicion in his voice.

"I had one once." She shrugged. Why was it guys could have threesomes, usually with two girls, with no repercussions but girls—women—were immediately considered sluts for the same behavior? "But it was a double wham-bam-thank-you-ma'am where I was basically a guy's version of a vibrator, you know?"

"You—You did it with two guys, not with another woman? You had a frickin' devil's triangle?" His phantom Irish accent returned in full strength. Obviously she'd totally thrown him.

"I was in college. This guy I was dating and I were fooling around in his dorm room. His roommate walked in on us. One thing led to another. It was sort of fun at first, but it was over pretty quick. As I said, they didn't bother about making sure I got off at all. They were more worried about satisfying their own needs. Now, about my demands." She outlined a shopping list of her fantasies. Everything she could think of, from nipple clamps to floggers to public sex.

Once she'd finished her recitation, he barked an incredulous laugh. "Who *are* you?"

"I'm me. The same person I was yesterday. Now you know more about me. Does that disappoint you?" *Please say no.*

"No. Surprises me though." He stroked her bangs to the side. "At work you're this clean-cut All-American apple-pie-and-ice-cream Miss America. I never figured you'd be—"

"Oh, please, give me a friggin' break. Those pageant divas are anything but virginal. Now are we done with the contractual arrangements?" She walked her fingers down his chest, the muscles firm beneath their tips. "Because I think it's time for us to strip naked and get horizontal."

He caught her hand before it reached his fly. "We aren't done with the discussion yet."

Sheesh. She couldn't stop herself from rolling her eyes. "What else do you want?"

"I want you to agree that whatever happens between us in the bedroom stays between us. We keep our relationship out of the office."

"I can do that." At his questioning look, she crinkled her nose in disgust. "Give me a break. Have you ever heard me talk about my sex life at work? Or even who I'm dating? I do try to keep things professional in the office, you know. Well, until this afternoon."

A possessive look flickered across his face, one of pride and satisfaction. His palm skimmed up her side, his thumb brushing the edge of her nipple, before slipping behind her neck to cup her head. "We don't bring what happens outside of the office to work. That means no more blowjobs beneath my desk. No quickies on the desk either."

"Damn," she breathed. "That was my plan for lunch tomorrow."

Laughing, he bent down and feathered his lips over her forehead, skimmed along her nose then captured her mouth. The warmth sparked a bolt of lightning through her core. She palmed his behind and squeezed. Damn, his ass was taut beneath her fingers. He pressed his hips against hers. Hot damn, his erection pressed into her belly like a goddamned fence pole.

"So how about we seal the deal?" She gave his butt one last squeeze and sauntered toward the bedroom without checking to see if he'd follow.

≈

QUESTIONS FILLED HIS HEAD—WHO had she had sex with who would fail to fulfill her? Just what else had she done? And how the hell had she slid in under his radar all these years?

He followed her into the bedroom, captured her hands and lowered her to the bed. When she tried to touch him, he caught her hands again with a growl. "No."

"What? Why can't I touch you?"

"Because you make me lose control." Her tongue slid over her top lip in a sinuous motion. He found himself staring at it, wanting to trace its path, to taste her lips and make them plump the way they'd been after she'd sucked him off earlier. "You said you wanted to be tied up. Have you tried it before?"

"Of course I have been. It was okay, except that the first guy thought tickling was a form of foreplay. Oh, fair warning? Yes, I'm ticklish but I hate being tickled. You deliberately tickle me, especially while I'm tied up? You'll never see the inside of my bedroom again."

"Noted." The douche had tied her up only to tickle her? What type of idiots had she dated? No, strike that. He didn't want to know.

"Anyway, the next guy I let tie me up thought the only place he needed to pay attention to was my pussy. The—"

He removed her glasses, placing them carefully on the night table. "As I said, I don't need a recitation of all your lovers, sunshine. I get it. If you're tied up, you want foreplay, and to have more than your pretty little pussy."

"I want to be licked and touched and kissed. Everywhere."

"I guarantee you won't want for attention." He unbuttoned her shirt and spread the edges apart to admire her breasts. Unlike some of the women on the D.C. party circuit, her body was luscious, her breasts plump globes that had almost spilled over the lacy cups confining them.

"Oh, and you have to use a condom. Non-negotiable."

"Of course. What do you take me for? A fool?" His tone

softened. He nipped and sampled the length of her neck and over the top of one breast. He kissed his way over the plump mound, tasting and teasing, not just her nipples, but the tops, the sides, the sensitive spot beneath. Only once she was panting and writhing beneath him did he position himself between her thighs.

He nuzzled her belly and tugged the tiny charm at her belly button with his teeth. "Did I tell you this surprised the hell out of me the other night?"

"Jazz and I got them done a couple months ago."

After stripping those ridiculously adorable fuzzy pajama bottoms from her, he caressed the thin strip of hair covering her mound. She was one of the few natural blondes he'd been with. It reflected her whole personality, he realized. Natural. Soft. With exactly the right amount of kink to be interesting.

He placed his hands on her thighs and she opened them with no hesitation. Did she realize how naturally sensual she was? Because there was no way her response was an act. Her folds glistened with cream, her labia plump and cinnamon colored to match her nipples. And her freckles.

His mouth watered as the scent of her arousal assaulted his senses. While some women would have questioned why he was taking so long, Sandy waited, letting him take the lead. Not in submission, but with patience. He wondered how many men understood and appreciated the difference. He rarely needed submission, and there would come a time he'd demand it, but for now, her patience pleased him.

Parting her folds with his thumbs, he swiped his tongue up one side of her clit and down the other. Her essence burst sweet on his tongue, transporting him back to when he'd first allowed himself to taste her.

Her feet wrapped around his back, holding him in place. The movement angled her hips so he had better access to her core. He used the flat of his tongue to tantalize, to tease, then when she thought he'd established a pattern, he'd change the tempo and strength of his attentions.

He breached her entrance with his thumb and stroked the lower wall until her hips lifted off the mattress. He pressed harder and discovered she wasn't a screamer, but a moaner. A tiny grunt escaped her as her entire body tightened and her passage clenched around his fingers. Not an orgasm, but close. Damn, she was responsive.

Replacing his thumb with two fingers, he stroked the front of her passage. Cream coated his fingers with each thrust, let his thumb slip over her clit with little resistance. Her moans grew louder, faster; her skin glistened as he forced her to the brink of orgasm then backed off.

"Troy, please. I need it hard and fast."

He tilted his head as he considered her demand. "Do you use vibrators?"

She gave a quick nod, a blush creeping into her cheeks.

"You're not to use them when I'm not around." At her questioning look he narrowed his eyes. "You have to trust me to please you. Now close your eyes and just let yourself feel what I'm doing."

He could have laughed when she swore at him under his breath. "Trust me, sunshine. I'll make sure you're satisfied by the time I'm done."

Over and over he drove her to the brink then backed off before he finally let her take that leap over the edge.

If he'd thought her sensual before, watching her recover from her orgasm was a work of pure art. Her lids heavy, she lifted them, entrancing him with the promise of more. Not just more sex but anything he wanted. Her voice was husky when she regained her breath.

"Come up here and let me return the favor."

He debated telling her no, that he had more planned to please her, but the idea of being buried in her hot talented mouth was too enticing to deny. Without wasting any time, he ditched his clothes, then positioned himself by her head and watched, entranced, as her lips curled and her tongue peeked out to lap at his cock. His balls immediately drew tight when the moist heat of her mouth enveloped the sensitive head. There was nothing more beautiful than watching his shaft glide over her open lips.

She sucked him down until her nose hit his groin, her tongue lapping and swirling about his length in a tantalizing massage that hit all the right spots. Yeah, so much for the Madonna image he held. She was an angel trained by the devil himself.

The moment he felt that tingling sensation at the base of his spine, he pulled from her mouth.

She licked her lips, made plump from sucking him off the way he loved. "What's wrong?"

"I want to finish in your pussy, not your mouth."

"Oh, well, all right then." Damn it, how could such a sinfully talented mouth curve into such an angelic smile?

He cursed to himself as he fumbled through the heap where he'd abandoned his clothes to find the condom he'd stuck in his wallet only to have Sandy toss one to him. He handed it back to her. "You put it on me."

Moments later he nearly regretted the request. Between the sensual look on her face—the way her lips caught the tip of her tongue as she concentrated on unrolling the latex—and the erotic touch of her fingers along his length, she nearly had him coming right there in her hand. By the time she finished sheathing him, his breath was rough in his throat, and his balls drawn tight to his body, aching with his need to relieve the pressure building deep inside.

Unable to wait any longer, he positioned himself over her. Her passage was so fucking wet there was no resistance at all to his entrance. Buried deep within, he stilled in an attempt to regain control over his body. It wasn't her heat enveloping him that nearly had him shooting off like a schoolboy, it was the soft look in her heavy-lidded eyes. The promise of softness, of acceptance. Of love.

Once his arms stopped shaking, he pulled back in a long slow retreat, her passage clamping around him to hold him in. It took all his strength to thrust back in just as slowly, drawing out the experience of being wrapped in her heat, instead of pumping hard and fast the way she'd demanded earlier.

Her hands trailed over his back, settling over his behind and drawing him closer. She tightened her grip, her nails digging into his skin. Her touch both soothed and incited him.

Her eyes fluttered closed as she whispered to him, murmuring soft encouragement, telling him what she liked. Her breath glided over his skin like a kiss. Fuck, if she kept that up, he wouldn't last another three thrusts.

He pulled out and flipped her over, lifting her hips so her ass was high in the air then sank into her until he was buried to his balls. She pressed back, driving him deeper than he'd thought possible. He held her hips and withdrew slowly, then thrust back in fast and hard. She wiggled when he tried to withdraw a second time. Using the flat of his hand he slapped her behind, leaving a handprint behind. Shit. He'd forgotten who he was with. This was Sandy, not some woman from the Rouge who got off on being manhandled.

"God, yes," she breathed. "Do it again."

Then again, maybe she was. He obliged her, striking the other smooth globe with the flat of his hand.

"Again."

Her body shuddered around him with each slap until both sides were red with handprints and her honey coated his balls. She ground back against him, her passage so hot and tight around his cock he couldn't hold back anymore.

In a frenzy, he grasped her hips and rammed into her over and over again, all thoughts of being gentle driven from his thoughts. Her orgasm triggered his own. His arms shaking once more, he slumped beside her then just about had a heart attack when something heavy landed on his legs.

"Get down, Xander." Sandy waved her arm at the purring furball. Taking it as an invitation, Xander only purred louder and wedged his fat body between them.

"Sorry about him." Sandy rolled from the bed and walked over to deposit the cat in the hallway. "Go on, you silly cat, go sleep on your own bed."

The moment she closed the door, the cat meowed plaintively and began scratching to be let back in. "He's Jazz's cat but you'd think he owns the place."

"He's...cute." If you could call a twenty-pound furball with claws and fangs cute.

"Not a cat lover, huh?" She sat back on the bed and crawled over to him, pressing her backside against him.

"Don't know. I've never had a pet. Always figured I'd be more of a dog lover though. Some of the police dogs are freaking clever." Damn it, he'd lost control after all. He smoothed a hand over her behind, grimacing at the half-dozen handprints he'd left. She made a soft sound, almost like the cat had purred earlier, and snuggled closer.

Down the hall, a key jangled in the lock and the front door opened, making Troy stiffen. A woman's giggle, followed by a man's chuckle floated down the hall.

"Relax. It's my roommate and her boyfriend," Sandy murmured without opening her eyes.

Moments later, the headboard started banging against the adjoining wall, accompanied by moans, both male and female. The thought that the roommate might listen to him making love to Sandy may add to Sandy's need for excitement, he supposed, but being watched wasn't one of his kinks. It wasn't as if he could take Sandy to his place. He had a roommate too. Besides, Sandy wouldn't like his place. It was nothing like this.

A stuffed toy stared at him from the chair in the corner, a teddy so well-loved its ears were threadbare and one eye was perilously close to falling off. Dozens of photographs lined the full length of her dresser like haphazard soldiers. Almost all were of the Hallquist family through the years, a four- or five-year-old Sandy playing with a golden retriever, a teenage Sandy in a cheerleader's outfit, one of a couple who could only be her parents surrounded by three boys, Sandy standing in front of a white frame house, a couple of boys with the same blonde hair wearing football uniforms, several of Sandy through the ages, and a college graduation photo. He smiled at the requisite prom picture of teenage Sandy in a formal gown, an uncomfortable boy with a bad case of acne in a tux beside her.

His smile faded. Had her date been Sandy's first love? Had he been her first lover? If he had, Troy hoped he'd been a gentle and careful lover, especially for her first time. That he'd taken the time to make sure she was ready, and made her feel beautiful.

I'm not looking to settle down. I want excitement. Women like Sandy were raised to seek security, to provide comfort and stability. To have a solid family like the one in the portrait hanging beside the dresser mirror. Yet she'd had a ménage. Obviously he'd pegged her completely wrong.

In her sleep, Sandy shivered. Troy reached down and pulled up the quilt he'd shoved out of the way in his hurry to take her. To fuck her. Upon closer inspection he realized the patchwork quilt had been hand sewn. Probably by her mother or maybe a grandmother.

She had a family who cared about her. Connections. A normal life. Everything he'd lost with the death of his parents.

His phone dinged from wherever he'd dumped his pants on the floor. He eased from her side and felt around until his fingers found his cell. A message from his second-in-command in Africa about a developing *situation* that meant he'd have to go into the office and arrange a conference call. Fucking perfect.

Guess this was as good a time as any for Sandy to get used to the fact he'd not be there most of the time. He stroked the hair off her forehead, pressing a kiss to the spot he'd bared. With a sense of regret he'd not felt in a long time, he dressed by feel, using the label at the back of his undershirt's collar to tell him it was on the right way, the buttons on his vest that it wasn't inside out. Not that it would matter—no one he'd run into between here and his SUV was worth worrying about. But he probably should do a quick wardrobe check before he headed back into the office.

He paused at her door, examining the lock and security of her unit. Security, he grunted. There was none. No alarm system in her apartment for starters. None in the building either. He'd gained access to the building because some asshole leaving had tried to be helpful by holding the door open for him. The deadbolt on her door was laughable. Someone with the right length of two by four could bend the frame and pop the bolt right out of the hole and be into her apartment, no muss, no fuss. There weren't even video cameras in the hallways. Not to mention her apartment was right beside a stairwell, making her target central.

~

JAZZ ROLLED ONTO HER STOMACH. It had been a while since her body ached in all the right places the way it did at the moment. She reached out on her left side, expecting to find Mitch's warm body only to find his spot empty. She fumbled for the lamp on her bedside table. Hadn't that been on before? Huh. He must have turned it off.

"Mitch?" She squinted toward the bathroom. Nope, the light wasn't on. Not that he might not be taking a whiz in the dark, she'd done it after all, but...

Ah, shit, don't tell her he'd crept out without saying good-bye.

She padded out of the bedroom, grabbing her robe from the hook on the back of her bedroom door. "Mitch?"

Mitch sat on her couch, his laptop open, frowning at the screen. "Be right with you, Jazz baby."

"Whatcha doin'? Because if you're watching porn, I gotta tell you, I prefer to be the star in any sex scenes that get you off." She curled up on the couch beside him, only catching a glimpse of the control panel screen.

"I couldn't sleep and didn't want to disturb you. So I figured I'd catch up on some work while I had the time, but I can't get onto the net. Your router's got a password."

"Oh, the password is SandyandJazzrule—all one word—304."

"Thanks." He opened the network connections box and typed in the password, then checked his email. When she snuggled closer, he lowered the lid until it was only open an inch and set it on the coffee table.

"Hey, did your roommate get a chance to download those photos we worked on off my flashdrive? I need it back."

"Yeah, I think so." With a sigh, Jazz unfurled herself from the couch and searched through the papers on the desk.

Mitch joined her, poking through the desk drawer. When he picked up Sandy's notepad and thumbed through it, Jazz snatched it from him. "Yeah, that's not something you need to see."

He shrugged. "Just looked like a bunch of addresses."

"Yeah, and it's not mine." She shoved it back into the drawer and shut it firmly with her hip. "Look, I don't know where your thumbdrive is right now. I'll check with Sandy in the morning and get it back to you when I see you again."

"I guess." he palmed her breasts and tweaked her nipples. "Since we're both awake, how about we try out those nipple clamps you said you'd bought?"

SEVEN

BY THE TIME Troy freed himself from the meeting and headed out to his car the sun was already over the horizon. As he pulled out of the parking lot he hesitated, wondering whether to turn left and head to Sandy's place or right and head home. If he went back to Sandy's, it was likely she'd be late because there was no way in hell he'd be able to keep his hands off her. Of course that meant not seeing her with sleep-heavy eyes and tousled hair. That was almost worth making her late. Except that would get her in trouble with Sam.

He turned right.

The track on his playlist changed from a Corelli sonata to a requiem by Mozart. Where normally it would have calmed him, this morning he found it depressing. He stabbed the radio button and set the system to scan until Jay-Z thumped from the speakers with an obscene amount of bass.

How had Sandy managed to fool so many people, even him, into thinking she was a shy virgin? Well, not a virgin, that might be a bit of a stretch. But she sure as hell had everyone convinced she was demure. Reserved. Modest.

Beneath that façade, he'd discovered a molten sensuality that had set him back on his heels.

She was an enigma. A conundrum. Innocence and artlessness hiding a quicksilvered, sexually charged pixie. A pixie, he snorted at the image. If anything, she would be right at home wearing a dominatrix outfit, complete with leather flogger and thigh-high boots with stiletto heels.

Scott was turning on the coffeemaker when Troy returned to his apartment. His roommate smirked when he snagged a mug and stood waiting impatiently for the machine to finish brewing. "I take it your date went well?"

"She's...surprising."

Scott's smirk widened. "I figured she would be. Some of those farm girls are a lot more adventurous than city girls, you know?"

He didn't. But he was planning on having fun finding out. The coffee brewed, he filled a cup and took a sip. "You could have knocked me over with a frickin' feather. Anyway, according to her, she wants excitement, in the bedroom and out."

"Told ya." Scott shoved him out of the way and grabbed his own mug from the cabinet. "If you bring her here, give me a heads-up and I'll stay out of your way."

Here. Where her walls had been painted in soft pastels and were adorned with pictures of her family, his were unadorned stretches of builders' beige even though he'd owned it for three years now. Strange how he'd never noticed it before. Then again, considering he spent more nights in hotel rooms in other countries than here in D.C., it hadn't mattered.

A whistle from Scott brought his attention back to find his friend looking at him with a bemused expression. "I was saying if she is looking for excitement you could always reserve one of the guest-house suites up at the Rouge. See if that lights her fire."

"That's a thought." Is that what it would take to keep her happy? Playing D/s games. What would she do if he brought out a flogger and tried to use it on her? Although given how she'd enjoyed him spanking her, perhaps she would enjoy it. Despite his exhaustion, his body jonesed at the idea of turning her pretty ass red with the tails of a flogger. Of having her completely obedient to him. His.

Scott waved a hand in front of his face. "I asked how far in advance do you have to book the place?"

"Depends. This time of year, probably a couple weeks. I might be able to pull a few strings to get an earlier date, but considering I'm not a paying member, I doubt I'll be put high on the list."

"A couple weeks is good. It'll give you a chance to find out if things will work between you two."

"Yeah, I guess so." Troy considered his friend as Scott poured himself a cup of coffee. "So how's your newest assignment going?"

Satisfied their friendship had survived, albeit a little bruised, he excused himself and went into his bedroom. Once he'd stripped and was lying in bed, he stared at the ceiling, worrying both about Chad's decision to put Scott back in the field, and his own decision to get into a relationship with Sandy. He hoped both decisions were right and wouldn't end up with either of them hurt.

SANDY GRINNED as she peered through the peephole of her apartment door and saw Troy standing on the other side. Instead of looking back at her he was staring down the corridor, one hand inside his coat on his holster. Was he even aware he did that every single time he'd come over? She turned the deadbolt and opened the door. Two weeks of dating and he'd never once been late. And he'd never failed to complain about the security in her building even after he'd had the alarm people install an alarm system on her doors and windows.

"If you're expecting someone to attack you, I can pretty much guarantee it won't happen here. It's a quiet building with very little drama."

"Drama can happen anywhere, sunshine." Once he was inside and the door closed and locked to his satisfaction, he settled his hands on her hips and drew her against him. "Never hurts to be prepared."

"My brave Boy Scout," she murmured as he claimed her lips. "Always prepared."

Her complaint when he broke off the kiss evaporated as he trailed his lips down the curve of her neck. Her skin broke out in goose bumps, the exact opposite of the heat sizzling beneath.

"You buy extra condoms? Because you're gonna need them tonight." She grasped the bottom hem of her T-shirt and prepared to pull it over her head.

To her surprise, he stopped her. "How about we go out for dinner first?"

She tilted her head, considering suggesting take-out. But from what she'd overheard at the office, he ate out a lot. There was something different about him tonight, a seriousness in the way he looked at her. Come to think of it, he'd been looking at her like that for a couple days now. Why? Was he regretting dating her?

Shit. If he was about to dump her, she'd rather not be dumped in front of an audience. "How about we eat in tonight?" She forced a smile and bounced her breasts in her palms. "Besides, we've eaten out three nights this week. If I eat any more restaurant food, I'll blimp out and I'll be able to smother you with my cleavage. My mom sent me some tomato sauce she'd bottled last summer—I could make spaghetti."

He barked a laugh. "Spaghetti with homemade sauce sounds great. As for your cleavage..." He covered her hands with his and squeezed, his eyes filling with heat. "I'd manage to fight my way out. And enjoy it while I do."

Going up on tiptoes, she recaptured his lips with hers, tasting the coffee he'd probably been sucking back all afternoon during yet another meeting about the latest hack attack. Maybe that's why he was serious. Maybe there was something at work bugging him. "Why don't you sit down while I get dinner?"

He shucked off his jacket and tossed it on the arm of the couch.

Xander immediately jumped up on the couch and stretched out on the jacket.

She grimaced. "I hope you don't mind cat hair. He sheds. A lot."

"Doesn't bother me." Instead of sacking out on the couch as she'd expected, he scratched the cat behind its ears, then followed her into the kitchen. "Why don't I help you?"

"I don't know. Are you one of those guys who uses up every pot and pan in the kitchen and then leaves the mess for someone else to clean up?"

"Mmm, don't rightly know. I rarely cook."

She rummaged through the cabinets, pulling out two jars of her mother's tomato sauce, along with the spices she'd need. "Grab one of the onions from that basket, and dice it, will you?"

For a guy who rarely cooked, he sliced the onion with a speed and accuracy rivaling a Cordon Bleu chef.

"Well, for a guy who doesn't cook, you know your way around the kitchen. Who taught you? Your mom?"

Sadness flashed over his face but he turned away as he dumped the diced onions in the pot. "No. Boarding school kid, remember?"

Shoot. Way to remind him he was an orphan, Sandy.

By the time he turned back, he'd regained control of his expression. "I have a knack with knives. It's come in handy in my line of work."

His line of work. Right. While Sam and Chad had often warned her about asking too many questions about any of the managers' pasts, it didn't stop her from wondering what they had done before they'd joined Hauberk. Troy was no different. In fact, from the lack of details in his file, he was even more mysterious. "I'm glad. Otherwise you might not be with me tonight."

He darted a glance in her direction before focusing too hard on the red pepper on the chopping board. "I'm not sure I follow."

"I know you worked with the Diplomatic Security Service. And of course I've read the reports of some of the missions you've been on with Hauberk." Like the one where they'd rescued the remaining hostages. Dry reports filed long after the blood had dried. "I figure you probably had to defend yourself by any means possible."

"I've done what I've had to."

She'd heard enough talk in the lunchroom, along with sitting in on enough meetings in Sam's office, to know that what really went down—the adrenaline, the fear—did not translate onto paper or pixels. "How did you end up in Diplomatic Security?"

"The State Department recruited me at college. I'm pretty sure Senator Brannally put a word in for me and since I didn't have anywhere else to go—which may have been why they found me a good candidate—I said yes."

"So why did you leave?"

"It was time."

She moved closer, until their hips bumped. "You don't owe me an answer if you don't want to tell me, but I would like to know more about you."

He took a deep breath and carefully set the knife down before turning to her. "The work was good at first, exciting. I got to guard some bigwigs, go places I'd only read about. But then—" he drew a deep breath, "—it got to a point where I started questioning some of my orders, and the decisions the higher-ups were making. I started wondering who the good guys were and if they were any different than the bad guys."

"I'm sorry." Sensing his discomfort with the topic, she wrapped her arms around his waist and buried her nose in his chest. "I shouldn't have asked."

"No." He rested his cheek on the top of her head. "There are some things I'm not going to talk to you about, missions and such. But considering our...situation...I think you have the right to ask me the occasional question."

She pulled back against his arms and looked at him. "Situation."

One side of his mouth quirked up. "You're the one who insisted that we're not into anything serious, that you don't want a long-term relationship, so I'm not sure what we qualify as at the moment. Would you prefer affair?"

She frowned. For some strange reason, hearing her own words used against her annoyed her. "We're lovers, so I guess affair works well enough."

"So do you have any more questions for me, sunshine? Bearing in mind I have the right to ask you questions too."

"Hey, I'm Miss Apple-Pie-and-Ice-Cream, remember? I'm an open book."

"Are you?" His thumb swiped across her cheek. "I don't see the regular Miss Apple-Pie-and-Ice-Cream having a threesome."

"Maybe I'm a banana split, the ice cream nestled between two bananas." She clapped a hand to her mouth and giggled. Her laughter died when she noticed he wasn't smiling. "Come on, it's funny. Haven't you ever fantasized about having one? I thought it was something all guys fantasized about."

"I've had one." From the way he ground out the confession, he hadn't enjoyed it.

"What happened? Was the girl your girlfriend and she decided she liked the other guy better?" Or other girl better, depending upon the threesome.

"It was part of an op I was on." He pulled away and walked to the window, stared out as the wind lashed it with a combination of sleet and snow, their first winter storm. "I prefer to choose my partners. And what we do. But that one? I had no choice or else I would have blown my cover. And the other man—he was a bastard who got off on hurting his girlfriend in front of an audience. From everything I could tell, she got off on it too, and she sure as hell seemed willing, but I came away from it feeling like I'd been part of a rape."

"Have you ever talked to anyone about it?" Somehow she didn't see him sitting on a psychiatrist's couch listening to any touchy-feely advice.

"Once the assignment ended, but..." He faced her, his expression both bleak and fierce. "Tell me the guys you were with didn't hurt you that night."

"They didn't," she whispered. "Oh, Troy."

"Don't get all maudlin on me, sunshine. It was a long time ago and I'm over it."

Despite his assurances, she wasn't so sure. The conversation between them during dinner stayed on the lighter side; Troy's compliments of her mother's homemade sauce, her telling him about some of Xander's exploits. By the time they piled their dishes in the sink and retreated to the couch, the cinnamon from the apple crumble she'd baked for dessert still hung heavy in the air, giving the apartment a particularly cozy, welcoming feel to it.

Over the past two weeks they'd been together, she'd discovered they had similar viewing tastes. Legal dramas over comedies. Having Troy's warm body cuddled up beside her on the couch, his hands toying with the side of her breast made it perfect.

He straightened, removing his hand from her breast when a key jangled in the lock and the door opened. Crap, sometimes Jazz had the worst timing.

"Hey, Jazz."

"Hey, Sandy. Troy. You remember Mitch, don't you?"

Troy stood and shook Mitch's hand, giving him a once-over that had Sandy wondering. Didn't he ever turn off that bodyguard switch?

Mitch flopped into the chair nearest Troy, grabbed Jazz and tugged her onto his lap, openly fondling her breasts. "So I hear you're a bigwig over at Hauberk. You guard anyone famous?"

Troy's jaw tightened as he settled back onto the couch beside Sandy. "Our clients' identities are kept private."

"Okay, yeah, sure. So you guys have to be trained in car chases and how to shoot and everything, right? Because the dudes you protect might have stalkers and stuff, right? Real bad guys, I hear."

"Yup." Troy stretched out his legs, crossing them at the ankle.

Sandy might have bought his attempt to project relaxation if it hadn't been for him fiddling with his watch. She curled her legs underneath her while trying to figure out what it was about the conversation that was annoying him. Was it the conversation itself or the way Mitch was pawing Jazz right in front of them?

He removed his hand from Jazz. "Hey, baby, why don't you go grab me a beer, huh?"

Rolling her eyes, Jazz climbed off his lap. When she returned with the longneck, she handed it to him only to have Mitch frown. "Hey, you shoulda offered my man Troy one too. You want one, Troy? Jazz, go get him a beer, will ya?"

Troy shook his head, his jaw tight. "If I wanted a beer, I'd get one myself."

"Cool." Mitch took a long pull on the beer.

Sandy exchanged a "what a douche" look with Jazz, who shrugged.

Mitch pulled Jazz back onto his lap and stretched out his legs, considering Troy. "So if someone comes to you saying they're in danger, how do you know whether to give them bodyguards or to stash them away somewhere secret?"

"It depends upon what the threat is against them." Troy's voice turned chilly, his words clipped. So it wasn't the way Mitch had been handling Jazz that was bugging Troy, Sandy realized, but something obviously was getting his back up.

"So what do you do with these poor saps? Put them in a hotel room? Have this big secret bunker you keep people in? What?"

"I'm not at liberty to discuss it." Though he kept his voice low, his words snapped out.

"Aw, come on, just between you and me. What type of places do you use for your safe houses? Do you actually have houses scattered in the 'burbs? Or what?"

Troy ran a finger around his collar, loosening it. "I told you, I'm not at liberty to say."

"What's the big deal?" Though his tone remained light, Mitch's fingers tightened around the bottle until his nail beds were white. "Is it one of those macho bullshit 'if you told me, you'd have to kill me' things, big man?"

"Yeah, actually, it is." The thigh muscles resting against Sandy's tightened as if he were preparing to launch himself to his feet.

To Sandy's relief, Jazz stood up and held out her hand. "Come on, Mitch. Let's go to my room. I'm sure Troy doesn't want to spend his time off talking shop."

Mitch's scowl deepened. "Aw, come on, Jazz baby. I want to get to know your friends."

"Actually," Sandy jumped in, "you did sort of interrupt us. I'm sure you won't mind giving us some alone time."

Like I gave you the other day when I walked in on the two of you fucking right here on the couch, she wanted to say but didn't.

From the corner of her eye, she saw Troy narrow his eyes at Mitch and give him one of the looks like Chad used when he was exceedingly pissed off at an agent, the type that cowed even the most macho operative. Mitch blanched and took Jazz's hand and the two of them disappeared into Jazz's bedroom.

"Sorry about that." Sandy watched as the tension bled from Troy.

"Don't apologize for things that are out of your control." He shot a dark look down the hall. "I don't like him. There's something off about him."

"He's not always like that. Usually he's friendly and nice." She rested her head on his shoulder. "It sort of felt like watching two alpha dogs fighting over the territory."

Her head bounced lightly as he relaxed enough to laugh. "Are you calling me a dog?"

Recognizing that he'd thrown her own line back at her, Sandy chuckled too. "No, I'm saying you're protective of your territory."

"Guilty as charged." He wrapped his arm around her shoulder and pulled her tight against him, resting his cheek against the top of her head. "Can't you afford to have your own place? I don't like the idea that he's around you the nights I'm not here."

"This is Jazz's place. She took me in when I first moved to D.C. and was looking for a job. And yeah, I guess I could afford my own place, but I like having her around. We keep each other grounded, you know? But if he bothers you, we could always go to your place."

It wasn't a completely altruistic offer. All their dates had ended up in her bed. One day she wanted to wake up in his. Then again, maybe he was a slob and was embarrassed that he only had one pair of sheets that seldom got changed.

"I've got a roommate too, remember?"

"Oh yeah, Scott's staying with you, isn't he?" Two guys in one apartment. Yeah, she bet it was messy. She jumped to her feet and held out her hand. "You're right. We should take this to my bedroom then."

EIGHT

AS SHE ENTERED THE BEDROOM, she pulled off her top and dropped it on the floor. Two steps later, her bra—a sexy little scrap of black lace—hit the carpet. After he thumbed the button to lock the door, he undid his shirt and let it drop on top of her bra. By the time she stood by the side of the bed she was naked as the day she was born. And so was he.

Before she could turn to face him, he banded his arms around her waist. The skin-to-skin contact had his cock as hard as a frickin' fence pole. She clenched her cheeks when the shaft parted them, providing a friction that caused his balls to draw tight to his body.

Yup, an angel in face, a devil in body and spirit.

"Lie down on the bed. Face up." Damn, his voice sounded like he'd swallowed a goddamned bullfrog.

After planting a light kiss on his nose, she pulled the quilt off the bed then crawled across the sheet, leaving her ass high in the air, taunting him.

When she settled at the top end of the bed, her beatific smile was back in place. His breath stuttered in his throat when she spread her legs and displayed her glistening cleft. All she'd done was undress and she was ready for him. It shouldn't have surprised him when her hand skimmed over that belly button ring that had been such a surprise. It shouldn't have surprised him when her fingers parted the glistening folds and toyed with her clit.

With her free hand, she patted the pillow beside her. "Come on up here, McPherson. Or are you planning on watching me get myself off tonight?"

"Since you mention it, I think I'd enjoy the show." He feathered his fingers down her cleavage and over her belly button but stopped short of her pussy. "Go ahead. Use a toy if you need to."

"I don't need toys." She may not need them but she enjoyed them. Otherwise how did she explain the half-dozen vibrators and other various toys in her nightstand?

He swallowed when she rolled the pink nipple between her thumb and forefinger of her left hand. "Harder, sunshine."

She obliged.

His own hands curled into fists and his body tightened. Only his rigid control stopped him from joining her on the bed, from pushing her hand aside and using his teeth to capture the taut nipple.

What he'd give for a pair of nipple clamps right now. He had a pair that would look perfect pinching that tender skin. He'd order her to kneel so the ball would hang from the chain joining the two clamps and add to the weight. He'd press her down on her hands too, and fuck her from behind.

She worked her nipples and her core until her hips lifted off the bed and her breath changed to gasps. "Come over here."

He blinked at her command.

"God, get over here. Now." With her chin, she nodded to his erection. "Let me suck that bad boy down again."

Oh, he was so down with that. In a flash, he straddled her, his knees on either side of her shoulders, his cock nudging her lips. Her lids heavy, she met his gaze as she licked up the side of his shaft and around the bulbous head. He had to grip the base of his shaft and squeeze to stop himself from coming too soon. His whole body shook when the heat of her mouth surrounded the head, then the entire shaft as she swallowed him down to the root. God, how could she do that and not gag?

Not that he was complaining but her tongue twirling and playing with that sensitive spot beneath the head had his eyes squeezing shut. He withdrew slightly but she lifted from the mattress and followed him up. Oh Christ, the woman knew how to give head.

He grabbed the top of the headboard and let her do whatever the hell she wanted to him. Her teeth scraped down the length of the shaft as she sucked him down again. Suck then withdraw, a swirl of tongue, a scrape of teeth. Lather, rinse, repeat, until his whole body was shaking.

She rolled his balls with one hand—the hand she'd used to play with herself from the slickness of her fingers. Between the attention to his sac and the skill of her mouth, he gave up the fight and let his orgasm rip through him.

Damned if she didn't swallowed every last drop.

"Wasn't supposed to go this way," he managed to choke out between gasps. His heart was certain he'd finished a marathon instead of a simple blowjob. Simple? There was nothing simple about Sandy. "I wanted to come inside you."

Her breath was hot on his ear when she whispered, "The night's still young. Just relax and work on getting your breath back. We've got lots of time."

She was right, of course. He let his head sink into the pillows and closed his eyes, enjoying the way she touched him, trying to figure out the pattern she traced up his side, along his biceps, his wrists.

He must have dropped off because when he opened his eyes, the overhead light was no longer on. She'd lit candles around the room, the soft glow reflecting in her eyes as she lay beside him, watching him.

"How long I been out?" He tried to lower his hand to pull her closer to him but couldn't for some reason. Damn it, his arm must have gone to sleep. He tried again. Shit. He twisted his neck to see what was holding him in place. Handcuffs? What the fuck?

"This was not part of our agreement, Sandy. Get these off me. Now."

"Oh, I will." With a smile, she walked her fingers up his chest. "When I'm done playing with you."

She straddled him and lay over him until she was spread like a blanket. A warm, soft, erotic blanket that covered his cock in a moist cradle. Oh. Fuck. His heart kicked into high gear again and sweat beaded on his forehead as he fought the urge to tilt his hips and press his burgeoning cock into her pussy. "You are going to be in so much trouble when I get free."

"Promises, promises." She scraped the tip of one fingernail down the center of his chest.

When she lowered her head to lay a line of kisses along the line she'd just stroked, he pulled his hands together to explore the handcuffs. Maybe he could find a way to pick them. Though without anything to use as a pick he doubted that would be possible. Unless... He twisted his hands and felt the metal. Not his, these were cheaper metal. Aha, just as he'd thought, they were ones she'd probably bought at a sex shop. Which meant they probably had a quick release button. He felt around until... Yup. He hid his grin. She was in so much trouble.

"You'd better put a condom on me or we could both be in trouble."

"Hmm, good idea."

When she rolled off him and opened the bedside table drawer, he flicked the release button on the cuffs. By the time she'd retrieved a foil package he was free. Except he kept his arms above his head. He waited, watched until she was busy opening the package to surge off the mattress and capture her hands.

"Hey!" Her realization he was free came too late. It took him two seconds, if that, to reverse their positions. "How'd you do that?"

Oh, this was too fucking perfect. No one had ever shown her

the quick-release mechanism. His body lying flat on hers, he used his weight to trap her while he snapped the cuffs around her wrists. "Stay. There."

Not trusting her to pull the same trick on him, he retrieved his own set from the leather holster on his belt. He flipped her facedown and straddled her and switched out her handcuffs for his. "You won't get out of this pair."

When she opened her mouth, he shook his head and covered her mouth with his fingers to silence her. "Nope. You don't get to speak anymore. I'm in charge now."

Her lips moved beneath his fingers so he pressed harder. "I will gag you if necessary. But I would like that mouth of yours available for kisses. And whatever other act I'd like you to do for me tonight."

He knew he'd won once she nodded and let her body relax. Still straddling her, he sat back, careful to keep his weight off her. Presented with the view of her behind, all round curves, pale and unmarked, had his balls aching to be nestled against them. He smoothed his hand over one globe, then ran a finger along the line of her cleft. "You ever been fucked in the ass?"

"Yes."

What was with this possessiveness, this weird clawing jealousy that someone else's cock had been in her back channel before him? He'd never worried about that before.

He'd wanted a night of sweet words and soft kisses. He craved the intimacy this type of sex wouldn't give him. He didn't want hardcore dominance games. He'd discovered he genuinely liked going to sleep with a woman nestled in his arms knowing she'd be there in the morning. And the next morning too. And the one after that.

"Troy?" Her soft call interrupted his pity fest. "I wasn't trying to disobey you."

"Too late, sunshine." Did she even realize it wasn't about obedience for him? "Where'd that condom go?"

After a protracted search, he found it beneath her belly. "Grab the end of the bed and scoot up on your knees."

She hesitated. "Will I need a safe word?"

He shook his head. "No. You say stop. I stop. Plain and simple."

Without another second's hesitation, she followed his instructions and curled up with her ass in the air.

Excitement, he reminded himself. She wants excitement. Here you go, sunshine.

He lifted her hairbrush from her dresser and hefted it. The dark side of him smiled in approval. He swatted it over first one cheek, then the other. It would do little more than sting, but it left a nice red mark on her ass. "Don't ever tie someone up in their sleep, especially if you haven't discussed it beforehand."

God, Scott would have freaked out, flashed back to his ordeal in Colombia.

"Because you like to be in control?"

"No." He flicked his wrist to give the hairbrush enough that it would sting. Her folds glistened and a soft expulsion of air told him she was enjoying the hairbrush more than he wanted her to at this point. He continued until her ass glowed a pretty red. She'd not made a sound, though he'd had to caution her about moving twice. Oh, she wasn't trying to get away from her punishment. The minx kept attempting to press her thighs together to ease the ache he knew was forming deep in her pussy.

He knelt behind her, ripped open the foil package and rolled on the latex. Once he was suitably protected, he sat back on his heels and considered the blooming globes presented for his benefit. He couldn't resist swiping his tongue through them, searching for her clit.

She squirmed, lifting her ass even higher to give him better access. "I like that."

"You like the idea of me punishing you? Or you like what I'm doing with my tongue?"

"Both."

Fair enough. Then his ego kicked in, reminding him about how she'd tied him up earlier. "I will punish you if you try it again. And I won't be using a hairbrush, Sandy. I use a flogger. Not some pansyassed rabbit fur one, but a good leather one that'll leave you sore for a day or two after, I promise."

"Bring it on."

Who was she?

His fingers digging into her hips, he positioned himself at her entrance and buried himself balls-deep in a single thrust. Liquid heat surrounded his cock, forcing his breath from him as he attempted to maintain control. He rocked his hips in a slow rhythm, gradually gaining speed. She met him stroke for stroke, pressing back against him, her pussy sucking him in with an indescribable kiss on each pass. He reached around and found her clit, toying with it to increase her pleasure. Her body tightened about him with the lightest touch.

When the familiar electric sensation started tingling at the base of his spine, he lifted her higher and hammered into her. Once, twice...on the third stroke she screamed into the pillows, her orgasm igniting his.

He sagged over her back, his body pumping all his pleasure, his desire, into her. Eventually he rolled off her and freed her from her bonds. With a soft sound, she snuggled up against him. Her fingers stroked his chest and over his thigh as she nuzzled his neck. After a moment, she squirmed, changing her placement and threw one leg over his hip. One hand slipped between them and guided his half-hard cock back into her pussy.

"Baby, I can't, not so soon. You have to give me a minute." An hour. A day, from the way she'd milked him dry.

"I know you can't, but I like feeling you inside me like this." Her breath was a warm caress on his neck.

He slowly pressed the head of his cock against her front wall, finding the spot that had her eyes fluttering closed. He slipped his hand between them and found her clit, brushing it lightly. Her lips parted and her head rolled back on his arm moments before every cell tightened around him, held him in place as she shuddered through another orgasm. He held still, enjoying the moment. This. This was what he'd wanted when he'd come over this evening. The face-to-face contact, soft murmurs, gentle lovemaking. Sharing their mutual passion.

From out of nowhere, a second orgasm rocketed through him. Goddamn, he'd not moved a muscle and she'd made him lose control like a fourteen-year-old boy. He clung to her as his body shuddered through his release.

She fell asleep in his arms. In awe of the emotions she'd awoken in him, Troy lay on his side, watching her sleep. When she rolled over to face away from him, he followed, tucking his legs behind hers. He buried his nose in her hair, inhaling the fragrance of her shampoo. Of her.

In trying to give her the excitement she craved, he'd discovered his own needs, his own desires.

It would damn near kill him if she decided she was bored, if she walked away now. Somehow he had to convince her that excitement came in many forms.

NINE

WITHOUT A WORD, Troy handed his phone over to the guard at the gate and followed it up by removing his weapons. The Sig Sauer, the backup Glock strapped to his left ankle, the knife strapped on his right.

Once the guard pressed the button and lifted the gate, he shoved the SUV into gear and drove toward the Colonial mansion with its trademark red front door.

The usual twinge of anxiety at being unarmed warred with his restlessness as he parked in the spot reserved specifically for him. Maybe the Rouge wasn't the best place to head. Hitting the punching bag at Hauberk's gym until his knuckles were bloody sounded like a damned good idea about now.

A knock on his window had him reaching for his gun before he remembered the holster was empty. Standing outside his door, Cooper Davis grinned. Even the damned dog sitting beside him looked like it was laughing from the way its tongue hung out to one side.

"Douchebag," he muttered as he pocketed his keys and opened the door.

Cooper stepped back, one hand wrapped around the shepherd's leash, the other toying with a fat unlit cigar. His grin widened at

Troy's snarled greeting. "Didn't expect to see you out here tonight, Colin. You here on business or for pleasure?"

Troy grabbed Cooper's jacket with both hands and shoved him against the Humvee beside his Porsche. "What the fuck do you think you're doing using my real name?"

The dog leapt to its feet, snarling, its fangs clamped around Troy's wrist, but Cooper's grin didn't drop even a millimeter. "Relax, *Troy*, no one's around to hear."

"That you know of," Troy corrected, not relaxing his grip on the other man. The dog's teeth broke the skin; a bead of blood dripped down his wrist and onto the shepherd's muzzle. "Call him off."

With an infinitesimal nod, Cooper gave a command in German. The dog released him and sat back on his haunches, though his hackles stayed lifted and a soft growl continued to rumble from his throat.

Troy released Cooper and stepped back. "What the fuck's your game, Davis? For all you know someone could be listening to us. Who knows who's listening from how far away."

"Relax, we've installed equipment that should interfere with any listening devices. You helped install it if I remember rightly." Once he'd righted the satin lapels that Troy had pulled askew, Cooper pulled a matchbook from his pocket, curled his hand to shield the flame and lit his cigar. The match burned nearly to his fingertips before the cigar glowed to his satisfaction. He blew out a long stream of smoke that dissipated in the crisp breeze. "So what bug's crawled up your ass tonight, *McPherson*?"

Fuck. "I knew it was a mistake to come here."

Cooper cocked the cigar in a Groucho Marx impression. "Coming is the reason most people visit the Rouge."

Unable to find a curse adequate to meet his frustration, Troy snatched the cigar from Cooper's hands and tossed it aside. Sparks showered across the tarmac in a brilliant blaze of orange as the cigar bounced to the far side of the driveway. "Fuck. Off."

"Again, that's the whole purpose of the club." While the grin stayed plastered in place, Cooper's eyes narrowed, the amusement draining from them like a switch had been thrown.

Ignoring the danger signs, Troy balled his fists in preparation to land his first punch. Before he could blink, Cooper grabbed him in a move Troy didn't see coming. He landed face-first and off-balance against his own vehicle, Cooper's arm wrapped around his neck, and Cooper's knee in his back. "Watch your temper. This is not the place to bring that type of aggression."

He had to hand it to Cooper. While Cooper might not work in the field anymore, he hadn't lost any of his training. The chokehold he had him in left no room for movement; he either relaxed or he choked himself to unconsciousness. Strangely, the dog had not moved from his place at Cooper's side. Troy pounded the side of the Porsche with the flat of his hand, signaling his yield.

"What's got you spoiling for a fight?" Cooper released him and stepped back. "Or are you looking to have your teeth shoved down your throat?"

Troy ran a hand through his hair and blew out a breath. "I want to ask you about the guest house and whether I can book it for myself."

Cooper shoved one hand in his pocket in what Troy knew was his way of attempting to appear casual when he was anything but. When Troy didn't say anything more, Cooper gestured to the club. "Let's go inside and we can discuss it over a drink."

He followed the other man through a secret side entrance, Cooper swiping his security card in the reader so as not to set off the alarms. Few members knew this entrance existed. Most of the ones who did thought it led to the hallways used by staff so as not to disturb the members.

Instead of opening the door to the main club, Cooper slid a section of chair railing aside. He pressed the button that had been hidden by the wood and a secret door sprang open. Troy walked down to the landing and waited while Cooper secured the panel back in place behind them.

"Do Sam or Chad know about your bunker yet?" he asked as

they trudged down the two flights of stairs, the shepherd's claws clicking behind them.

"If they know, they've not said anything to me."

At the bottom, Cooper lead him down the plain white corridor. They passed a large room resembling a small army barracks, a half-dozen beds lined up against the wall, their mattresses rolled up at the end of their steel frames. Beyond it was a small kitchenette, and the room with a metal table and two metal chairs where they'd interrogated him after they'd freed Scott and the other hostages in Colombia.

To his surprise, Cooper continued toward the large steel door at the far end of the corridor, a door he'd never been allowed past during his last visit.

He waited as Cooper looked into the retinal scanner mounted on the wall beside the door. At the computer's command, Cooper punched a number in its keypad. A click echoed down the hall before the door swung open to reveal another long, equally bland passageway.

When Cooper gestured for him to precede him, Troy hesitated. "Why are you bringing me here? Why can't we talk in the bar?"

"Because I don't want anyone overhearing what I have to say."

Inclining his head in a shallow nod, Troy stepped through the door. His footsteps echoing off the painted cinderblock walls, he passed another interrogation room, this one a plain room with a large mirror at the far end, a metal chair bolted to the floor in the middle, wires and cuffs hanging loosely from its frame. As he expected, the next room was filled with electronic equipment for Cooper's agents to use to monitor their subject's blood pressure and voice stresses during their interrogations of whoever was in the first room. He'd gotten off easy with his questioning, he realized.

The next four doors were closed, preventing him from figuring out their purpose. Cooper directed him to the office at the end of the corridor. A massive oak desk, piles of papers littering its top, sat at one end of the room. The walls surrounding the desk were covered with screens displaying real-time satellite images from around the world. The dog slid past Troy and headed to a blanket-covered heap in one corner and lay down on it with a sigh.

"Take a seat." Cooper pointed to one of the plush armchairs grouped at the closer end.

He chose the seat that left his back to the corner while Cooper walked over to the wall unit and opened a panel to reveal a bar. "What's your poison?"

"You think I'd trust anything you'd offer considering the last time I did? You spiked my drink and I was out for almost twenty-four hours."

Cooper chose a bottle of what was probably one of the world's most expensive brandies and poured it into a glass. He returned with both the glass and the bottle and sat in the chair opposite Troy. "We had to get you out of Colombia and down here for questioning with the minimum of fuss."

"You could have asked me to come with you." He wouldn't have agreed, but not being given a choice still rubbed his balls raw.

"You wouldn't have agreed, and you know it." He swirled the brandy in the glass, considering it, before he met Troy's gaze again. "So why do you need to book the guest house? Who is your guest?"

Was he really going to do this? If he didn't, would he lose Sandy because she thought him too boring? Fuck it, she wanted excitement in the bedroom. He could do that for her.

"I've been dating someone. She's..." Delicate. Soft. Sensual. "I'm..." Not. He shook his head. He sounded like he was back in grammar school, right down to the short pants. "She has some fantasies I want to fulfill."

"She craves being watched?"

"Amongst other fantasies."

"Is it someone I know?" Cooper took another sip of his drink. "Sandy perhaps?"

How the fuck had he figured that out? Troy schooled his face so Cooper couldn't read anything from his expression, though he wasn't sure if he'd be successful "What makes you think it's her?"

"Because you've had your eye on her since you first met her."

The mask he'd donned slipped for a fraction of a second. "No, I haven't."

"Maybe you weren't aware of it, but you've always lingered an extra second on her whenever she was around. More than any other woman you've been around."

Son of a bitch. "Does it make a difference?"

"Not to me. As long as she's agreeable to our requirements."

"She will be. I don't want to take her somewhere truly public. That's why I'm—" *Selling my soul to you.* He shifted in his seat. "So can I reserve a suite any time in the future?"

"There was a cancellation this weekend. If you're interested, it's yours. But you'd better make sure she understands what's required. Because Sam's assistant or not, if she talks about what she sees while she's here, I will go after her."

TEN

TROY TAPPED on Sandy's desk as he passed, their private signal that he needed to speak with her. Sandy picked up her notebook and followed him into her office, not quite closing the door behind her.

"Do you have any plans for this weekend?"

There was something in the way he said it that told her he wasn't talking about a trip antiquing in the country. "I think I can arrange to free my schedule."

The heat in his eyes was primal, untamed. "I've reserved a suite at a very special resort. I was wondering if you'd be interested in going with me."

A whole weekend together? Uninterrupted by Jazz and her boyfriend. Where did she sign up? "Will you be on call?"

"Nope. I won't even be able to bring my phone with me. Club rules."

A club? As in Club Med? Or the Porte Rouge? How could she ask without letting on that she knew of that private sex club? As much as she wanted to jump up and down in excitement, she forced herself to perch on the chair on the other side of his desk. "So it would just be me and you in a hotel room all weekend. No interruptions?"

He reached past her and shut the door. "It won't quite be just you and me."

"Oh?"

"This resort isn't quite like anywhere else you've probably been. It caters to clients with very specific tastes, where we can explore some of your fantasies."

Holy crap, it was the Rouge.

TROY LEANED one shoulder against the storage locker and watched Scott stripping the Glock. "You got any plans for this weekend?"

"Nope, why?"

"I may need your help. I've reserved a suite at the Rouge's guest house for Sandy this weekend. I'd like you there to make sure her initiation goes off without any interruptions."

Scott looked up, a question—and doubt—clear in his eyes. "Are you expecting me to have a threesome with you?"

"That depends upon what Sandy wants." If that's what she wanted, he'd give it to her, but only on the condition it was a one-time deal because he damned well didn't want to have to watch any other man touching her regularly. "Mainly I want you to make sure that Cooper Davis doesn't interrupt us."

The door squeaked open as Hauberk's youngest agent walked into the equipment room. When the newbie debated over what type of bullet to use, Troy wanted to growl. "Take some of each, kid. Take 'em all. Just make up your goddamned mind."

The tips of Kris's ears flushed bright red, but he grabbed his pistol, and enough ammunition to fight off an entire squadron and stalked from the room.

Once the door to the firing range closed behind him, Troy straddled the bench where Scott had returned to cleaning his gun. "Are you in?"

Scott swabbed the barrel with more attention than it deserved. "Are you sure you want to do this?"

Troy paced the length of the room, not speaking until he reached the end and turned around. "She's always going on about how she wants excitement. How boring it was back in Minnesota and that's why she moved to D.C. It's what she wants." That he was willing to give her anything—even consider letting another man touch her—showed how deeply he was in over his head. "I thought about flying her to Palm Beach for the weekend. Renting a sailboat and teaching her about the joys of the motion of the ocean. Finding a secluded cove and having sex on the beach, but I can't leave right now and I think this is what she wants."

"Is it what you want?"

What did he want? Marriage? The house with a white picket fence? Children? Maybe. The thought of them wasn't as scary as they'd once been. Not that she wanted any of it. So what did he want, he asked himself again and could come up with only one answer—her.

Tied up and blindfolded while he fucked her. Hard.

"Man, you've got it bad, don't you?"

"What are you talking about?"

"You're in love with her."

"No. Maybe." Shit. Maybe he wasn't in love with Sandy. Maybe he was in love with the idea of having someone in his corner. Of holding that brass ring—or in this case wearing a gold one. Of having what Sam had with Rosie. What Chad may have rediscovered with Lauren. "I don't know. We've barely started dating."

"You've known her for two and a half years. It's not a big leap from friendship to love."

"It's not love." Even as he spoke the words, he knew they were a lie.

"So tell her you want to make it exclusive. You don't have to commit any further than that. Yet."

Why was he unwilling to reveal that he'd already taken that step?

"So she can take me home to Minnesota and introduce me to her parents? 'Hey, Mom and Dad, this is my new boyfriend. He used to be an assassin and he was exceptionally good at his job.'" He laughed darkly. "It's all moot anyway. She'll never want to get involved with me long term. I'm just a way to kick up her heels, to have an adventure while keeping things safe."

"From what I've seen of Sandy, she's not the Madonna you're making her out to be. There's a lot of fire inside her. Waiting for the right man to set it free. If she's the right woman for you, she'll accept you for all your flaws."

Or she'd see his flaws and punch him right in the gut.

ELEVEN

"SHIT. I'm running so late. Troy's going to be here in like ten minutes and I'm not anywhere near ready." Sandy grabbed a blouse from her closet and held it up in front of her. "What do you think, Jazz? This one?"

"The color washes you out a bit." Jazz reached across the pile of tops Sandy had already discarded and plucked a blue sweater from the middle of the pile. "I liked this one better. It brings out the highlights in your hair."

"I don't know. Troy likes things he can undo easily." Sandy swiped at the ginger cat hairs clinging to the wool. "The sweater sorta leaves the girls hard to get to."

"Ah, so he's a breast man, huh?" After frowning at the abandoned clothes, Jazz uncurled her feet from beneath her and joined Sandy to stare at the closet.

"Breast man. Butt man. Leg man. He likes it all." Together they went through the remainder of Sandy's wardrobe before settling upon a peach shirt Sandy had folded away for spring. "It's a little thin but with my coat I should be okay."

Jazz crawled back on the bed as Sandy dressed. "You've been seeing a lot of him lately. What's it been now? A month?"

"Just about."

"You getting serious?"

"I don't know." She wished she had the time to flop on the bed and discuss what the heck was happening in detail with Jazz. "I mean, the sex has been great. I told you about the time he had me do him at the booth in that little bar, right?"

"In graphic detail, babe. You also told me about the time he got you off at the theatre. And the time you two did each other in the parking lot later. So what's the matter? You think he's one of those guys who doesn't like to commit?"

"No, that's the problem. I think he might be. I don't know." She lifted one shoulder before dropping it. "I'm not ready to settle down yet. I've got too much I want to do with my life."

"Like what?"

"I want to travel more. I want to take courses at GW. Maybe get a degree. I don't know. Just...do stuff."

"You can travel even if you're in a relationship. Hell, with the way you say Troy travels, go with him on his business trips. And if you want to take courses, hello, why haven't you enrolled already? You're the only one stopping you, babe. None of that will stop you from being in a relationship."

"Yeah, but..."

"Yeah, but? You've got a really great guy interested in you, girl. Don't fuck this up."

Great, here she wanted someone to back her up and Jazz decided to be the logical one all of a sudden. What did they say about the best defense? "What about you and Mitch? I haven't seen him around much lately."

"He's coming over tonight. But I'm thinking of breaking it off with him. He's getting too intense, you know?"

Ha! So she wasn't the only one who couldn't commit. "I thought he was kind of cute."

She must have hit a sore spot because Jazz wandered to the window and stared out. "Yeah, he's cute enough, but he's always on his laptop, you know? And there's something creepy about the way he's always hanging around here. Do you know I found him waiting for me outside the apartment again the other night? We didn't have a date or anything, he was just there, waiting." Jazz pressed her forehead against the glass. "Wow, you should see the size of the limo that's pulled in."

Sandy peered over her shoulder in time to watch the driver open the rear door and Troy emerge. "And there's my cue to leave."

"Mine too. If I don't get my ass in gear, I'm going to be late for work." Jazz hugged her at the same time as someone knocked on the door. "Don't worry about anything this weekend, okay? Just have fun."

Exactly what she'd planned. She dashed out to the entrance and grabbed her coat, Jazz trailing her. "I'm so excited, I can't stand it. Now open the door."

With a laugh, Jazz unlocked the door and swung it open. "Hey, Troy, come on in. Your girl's all ready to go."

Troy's gaze skimmed down Sandy, hardly sparing Jazz a glance. "You sure about this, sunshine?"

Holy crap, he looked hot in leather pants and a black shirt. "You betcha. I can't wait to see what you've got lined up. Let me grab my purse."

"You won't need it." Troy grinned and Sandy's heart sped up at the promise in his eyes.

"I need to bring my phone. In case there are any messages. And to check my email."

"You're not going to have any time to check your email. And where we're going, they make you leave all electronic devices at the gate. So there's no use bringing it."

A thrill went through her as she remembered what she'd heard of the Rouge's policies to prevent blackmail. Whoa, Momma, she'd asked for excitement because she was tired of the usual hundred and twenty volts and he was delivering a sixty-thousand watt experience.

"I like the sound of that." She reached up on her tiptoes to kiss him. "Anything else I need to bring?"

"Just yourself. Come on, the car's waiting downstairs." He took the keys from her hand and led Sandy into the hall. Once Jazz locked the door, he laid his arm across Sandy's shoulder and hugged her.

He didn't say anything in the elevator, and Sandy was too juiced to talk anyway. Her imagination, however, ran overtime trying to come up with the various scenarios they might act out over the weekend.

She stopped when they walked outside and the chauffeur opened the rear door of the limo. "This isn't a Hauberk's car. You went out of your way to rent one? That's so sweet." So extravagant.

"I'm not about to use a work limo for what we're going to do." He leaned down to whisper in her ear, "It's provided by the club. The driver's going to watch everything we do on the ride up. Give you a little experience performing for an audience."

"Oh."

She ducked her head and climbed in. Holy shit. This wasn't just a limo, it was a sex club on wheels.

"No one can see in the windows. There's a special coating on the glass that prevents anyone from seeing in." Troy tapped the glass of the door.

"That's good." Though the danger of being seen at a traffic light might have added a thrill.

She looked around, wondering where to sit. "Um, don't we have any seatbelts we're supposed to use?"

"There are all sorts of restraints. But they may not go around your waist." Troy settled onto the...well, she wasn't sure what it was. Half-seat, half-bed. The damned thing was made for sex. "You can sit here for the moment. After you've stripped, that is."

Wow. He wasn't wasting any time. Her whole body lit up like a Christmas tree. Maybe she should have put that blue sweater on, she could have lifted it over her head in one motion. No, undoing the buttons one-by-one would make it more like a striptease.

Troy made a rolling motion with his hand. "Don't waste time trying to seduce me, sunshine. Just ditch the clothes and sit down before we get going or you'll—" The car lurched into forward motion sending her sprawling across him. "—fall."

"If you say 'I told you so', I won't blow you," she muttered.

Very gently, he lifted her off and sat her on the end of his seat. Couch. Whatever it was called. "No blowjobs. I'm not willing to take the chance on being gelded if this damned car hits a pothole. Now undress. I've got other plans for you."

Less than a half minute later, she was completely nude, her clothes piled in a heap on the seat beside Troy. It's not like she had a lot to take off. She'd deliberately not worn a bra or underwear.

"Turn around and lean up against me."

"All right." She obeyed, wiggling her behind against his erection to taunt him. He wrapped one arm around her waist, cupping her breast with one hand, the other toying with her naval ring.

"Hook your legs over mine."

A glance toward the front and she discovered the driver of the limo had an extra mirror—aimed directly at her.

"Don't worry about him." His palm smoothed down her belly and over her mound. "Now, there are going to be a few rules you need to know about for this weekend. First, I need you to trust me. If I ask you to do something, you need to do it with no questions asked."

"I do." Her eyes fluttered closed, giving into the sensations of his fingers sliding through her moisture, the warmth of his breath and the coolness of the leather against her bare skin. The knowledge that the limo driver was watching in that mirror.

"Once we're there, I'm going to turn you over to a woman who will prepare you for the weekend. You're going to get the whole works, a massage, manicure, pedicure and a couple other surprises."

"Like what?" Her heart rate kicked up a little from uncertainty.

His fingers toyed with the thin Brazilian strip covering her mound. "She's going to get rid of this for starters."

"I would have done that myself if you'd asked."

He pressed a kiss to the top of her shoulder while his fingers resumed stroking her clit. "I know, sunshine. You can grow it back afterward if you like, but for this weekend, I want you bare."

"Why?"

"Because I do. Do you have any other questions? Now's the time to ask." His body was rock hard beneath her, his touch a little less gentle than his voice.

"Will the other people take part? I mean will it be like an orgy where I have to have sex with everyone and their brother?" She wished she could close her thighs together to ease some of the ache gathering there.

"No one other than me will touch you but there will be people watching, and a few may have sex while we're making love. But you'll be blindfolded so you won't be able to see them. It's something I had to agree to when I applied to bring you as my guest."

"So that once you take the blindfold off I can't blackmail any of them because they'll be able to blackmail me, right?"

"That's not how they'd word it but essentially, yes. Now, the question is, do you still want to go?"

"Of course! I'm not going to back out. It's all I've been thinking about ever since you told me you'd made the reservations."

"Okay. Lean back and close your eyes. Let's see how you do in front of an audience."

Her pulse racing, she obeyed him. There was something so wicked about being naked in a car with someone watching as Troy toyed with her breasts and stroked her pussy. The car sped up and from the sounds filtering through the windows she knew they'd merged with traffic on the Beltway. Each bump in the road, each corner the limo took, added a new dimension to the experience. He varied the pressure and speed of his fingers until her body bowed against him, both shaking and rigid at the same time, and her breath exploded from her when her orgasm engulfed her.

"That's it. Let yourself go." His breath was hot against her neck, his beard rasping lightly against the sensitive skin.

His fingers still lightly stroking her, he held her until her breath approached normal. "Lift up a minute."

Blinking, she did as he asked. He unzipped the fly of his black leather pants and pulled out his erect cock. She licked her lips, her mouth going dry at the sight of him palming his shaft. He handed her a condom. "I like it when you put them on me."

Straddling him, she unrolled the latex, making sure to give him some extra strokes as she smoothed it over the length of his shaft.

Perspiration beaded on his forehead when she finally finished.

"Ride me, sunshine."

She lowered herself over him over the bulbous head, over the long shaft until their hips met. He skimmed his fingers over her waist and let them sink into her hips, stopping her from moving when she started to rise.

"Slowly, love. It's not a race."

Yet she was so close to the finish line, and she sensed he wasn't far behind.

He captured her mouth with his, the kiss starting as a whisper. Then his tongue slid past her lips in a tender exploration that quickly became an unquenchable hunger. The blood that had hummed through her veins caught fire when he tilted his hips and pushed deeper within her.

The pressure on her hips eased, granting a subtle permission to move. Liberated, she rode him, drawing his cock deep into her body, pressing her clit against the arch of his groin before pulling away, drawing him out. Tightening her body around that glorious thick head.

Want and need spiraled together as they rocked in unison. His name may have passed her lips when he dipped his head to capture a nipple with his mouth. The vibration of the car on the road added extra stimulation, sometimes helping, sometimes distracting.

Her head dropped back as she rocked against the long, blunt fingertip that slipped between her folds and found her clit. The scent of warm leather, of Troy, permeated her senses, combined with the feeling of the hard, hot shaft thrusting inside her until she teetered on the edge of release.

Speech, thought, became impossible. Her rhythm faltered as the first wave of her impending orgasm fluttered through her. Fingers dug into her hips, holding her in place once more as Troy took over with a series of forceful thrusts. A groan caught in her throat each time he bumped against just the right spot, again and again and again. Her whole body bucked when her second orgasm crashed over her.

Troy's pace didn't slow while she came apart. When she opened her eyes, she was caught by the intensity in his eyes; it was as if he could see into her very soul. She cupped his jaw and tightened her muscles around him only to set off yet another orgasm.

When she opened her eyes again, sweat rolled down his forehead but he still hadn't come. She clamped her hands on his shoulders and lifted herself up then slammed back down. Once, twice more. Tighter. Harder. His head fell back, so she dipped her head and nipped at the spot where his neck met his shoulder. Her teeth had barely touched his skin when his arms banded around her, holding her in place. With a deep groan, he stilled and warmth flooded deep inside her.

He held her there, not letting her move for the rest of the ride, one hand stroking her hair until the limo slowed and turned right, stopping at a gatehouse. The limo driver spoke to the guards for a moment before the massive iron gate swung open. Sandy roused from her languor, remembering for the first time that the chauffeur had watched everything she'd done. How strange that she'd been so lost in Troy's pleasure, and hers, that she'd forgotten they'd had an audience.

Troy reached between them to hold the condom in place as she lifted off of him. When she reached down to pick up her clothes, he stopped her. "You'll only need your coat."

"But my clothes..." The limo stopped beneath the porte cochere of a two-story French-style mansion.

"You'll get them back before we leave." He held up her coat. "Normally in the summer you'd be expected to walk to the door buck naked."

The driver opened the door and stood there, his gaze on the mansion's bright red door. The winter wind quickly stole the warmth from the car and she shivered, though she wasn't sure which was stronger, the fear or excitement.

Troy curled his fingers under her chin until she met his gaze. "Last chance, Sandy. We can still go home."

"I'm not chickening out. I want to do this. Besides, I've always wondered what the inside of the Rouge was like."

Troy's eyebrows lifted. "I'm not going to ask how you know about the Rouge, but this isn't the main house. This is merely the guest house."

"Pffft." She waved away the distinction. "Main house, guest house. There's no difference. We're going to have fun having lots and lots of kinky sex, right?"

Troy shook his head. "Some days I wonder if you have an evil twin. Now put your coat on."

She stuck her arms in her coat. Before she could button it, Troy palmed one breast and placed a kiss above her areola. "Just remember, this is all about fulfilling your sexual fantasies. I won't think any less of you if you want to go home early."

"I told you. I'm not leaving." She placed her palm in the gloved hand the chauffeur held out and stepped from the limo. Instead of Troy joining her, the chauffeur offered his arm and began to walk up the path. She pulled away and stared back at Troy, who now leaned against the side of the limo. "Aren't you coming?"

"You have to ask for permission to enter all by yourself. So you can't say I forced you later."

Oh. Guess they had to be cautious both for their sakes and their members'. Cool.

"Just knock on the door, Miss." The chauffeur set her back in motion and led her to the front door. "Madame Jocelyne is expecting you. If you don't wish to proceed, simply tell her that you wish to leave and she will arrange for a car to take you back to town."

Sandy stared at the wrought-iron knocker for a moment before gathering her wits. Just knock. That's all she had to do. Her bottom lip caught between her teeth, she lifted the black lion's head and let it fall with a resounding thump.

Almost immediately the door opened. A middle-aged woman, her black hair highlighted with a single red streak smiled at her. "Bonjour, and welcome, Miss Hallquist. We've been expecting you."

Sandy stepped into the foyer as the woman closed the door behind them. A vase of day lilies adorned the massive round wooden table that dominated the center of the room. She inhaled their fragrance as it mixed with the beeswax they'd no doubt used to polish the gleaming banisters of the dual staircases on either side of the hall.

"I am Jocelyne. I must ask, my dear, if you are here of your own free will, and if you have been informed of our rules."

"I am. And I have."

"*Très bien*. My staff and I are here to ensure you receive every pleasure imaginable during your stay with us."

"Thank you." Every pleasure imaginable. Until she'd met Troy she thought she'd had a pretty good imagination. Now, surrounded by opulence, she realized he could show her so much more.

"I'll take your coat and then I'll show you to our spa."

Her coat. Right. All right, she could do this. Taking a deep breath that only made the stones avalanching in her stomach larger, she undid the coat and took it off so all she wore were her heels. Jocelyne's gaze skimmed down and back up before she nodded. "Very nice. Now if you'll follow me."

Jocelyne's footsteps echoed off the warm marble floor as she led her through a set of French doors at the far end. She stopped in a room at the back of the house that had Sandy's jaw dropping. Overhead, the ceiling was entirely glass, the overhanging tree branches filtered the weak winter sunlight, accenting the Wedgewood blue walls with their white trim. "This is where your initiation shall take place this evening."

Vases of roses formed a walkway that widened and surrounded a raised dais in the center of the round room. An archway decorated with more flowers had been placed in the center of the dais. Two silk ropes dangled from it while a leather fainting couch and numerous pillows had been placed to one side. Instead of the straight lines of its historical counterparts, this was all bends and curves.

"Wow."

Jocelyne chuckled, a rich throaty laugh. She touched Sandy's elbow, the jewels in her rings catching the halogen lights, scattering a myriad of prisms across the tiled floor. "It is impressive, is it not?"

Impressive didn't begin to describe it. "How many people will be here this evening?"

"Approximately a dozen, give or take a few. If all those who made reservations show up, that is. Some arrive later than others, though most try to be present for an initiation. But since you will be blindfolded, it should not matter, should it?"

"No, I suppose it shouldn't." What if Sam and Rosie showed up? Or someone she knew and would have to work with every day. She pressed her hands against her stomach as the realization of what she was about to do hit her with an iron fist.

"Now has *Monsieur* McPherson told you what is to happen tonight?"

"I'm going to be blindfolded, stripped naked and have sex with Troy in front of everyone, right?"

"*Exactemont.*" Jocelyne led her back to the foyer and tapped on a door beneath the right-hand stairs. "Now, after tonight, you may venture where you will, wear what you wish, and speak freely. But for now, we mustn't waste any more time."

The door opened and a younger woman appeared, her gaze raking Sandy from head to foot with a much more critical gaze. Had she noticed the dampness streaking her thighs? Or the redness where Troy's beard had rubbed her breasts?

"Crystal, Miss Hallquist shall require the full treatment today. In all respects." Jocelyne nodded to Sandy. "If you require anything, just let Crystal know. And in the meantime, enjoy yourself as she prepares you for the festivities."

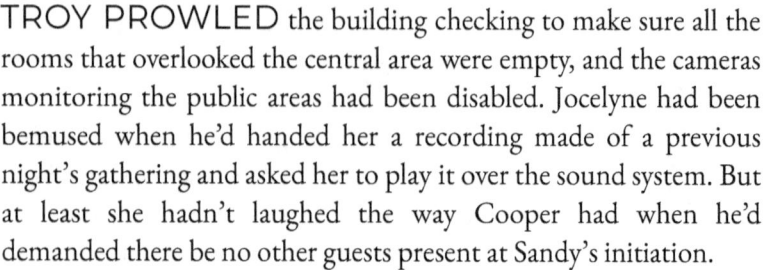

TROY PROWLED the building checking to make sure all the rooms that overlooked the central area were empty, and the cameras monitoring the public areas had been disabled. Jocelyne had been bemused when he'd handed her a recording made of a previous night's gathering and asked her to play it over the sound system. But at least she hadn't laughed the way Cooper had when he'd demanded there be no other guests present at Sandy's initiation.

He stopped in the central hall and checked the strength of the flogger he'd asked Jocelyne to set out. He dangled the tails, then snapped it against the leather couch where he'd make love to Sandy later. The leather whistled through the air, landing with an impressive thwap but it was more sound than fury. It would leave a pleasing redness to her skin but shouldn't cause too much pain. Of course, Sandy might have something different to say about it, but from the way she'd reacted the night he'd spanked her, he doubted she'd object too strongly. Or perhaps she'd be into pain and would demand more.

A shadow in the hallway had him reaching for his weapon only to remember he'd surrendered it, along with his cell at the front gate. Seconds later Scott appeared in the archway. His brows drew together when he spotted the flogger but he only said, "Davis won't be bothering you tonight. He's attending a fundraiser in Baltimore."

"Good. Can I ask you to hang out in case he decides to return early? Or in case he's set something up for one of the other members to intercede."

"You're not, uh, wanting me to stay and watch, are you?"

"No." From Scott's body language he didn't want to be anywhere near there which suited Troy just fine. "Just patrol the perimeter and stop anyone from interrupting us."

"Can do." Scott started to turn, then stopped. "I guess I should tell you—I've rented a place of my own so I'm moving out next weekend. I thought you should know."

"Good." Was it?

Left alone once again, he continued to prowl the room. Sandy wasn't the only one who required more than the standard missionary position. If they were going to continue this relationship, if that's what it was, he needed to free some of his own closely held needs.

TWELVE

THE INITIATION HADN'T EVEN STARTED, Sandy realized, and there hadn't been a part of her body that hadn't been touched. Pity it hadn't been Troy drying her off after her shower—the second one she'd had that day. As nice as Crystal was, having a woman towel her off had been strange. Letting her shave her private parts was no biggie. After all, she got Brazilians all the time. But when she'd been asked to turn over? Well, a little warning might have been nice. Warmer hands might have helped too.

Once she'd been cleaned inside and out, she'd been given a massage that left her a puddle of boneless goo. She'd then been whisked to another room where Crystal touched up her nail polish on both her hands and feet. Another woman had come in and carefully applied her makeup. She was in the middle of asking herself why she couldn't she put on her own makeup so skillfully when the woman asked her to stand up and proceeded to dust a glittery powder all over her body.

Standing in front of the cheval mirror that reflected the image of someone she barely recognized, she tried to convince herself there was no reason why her stomach should be doing flip-flops the way it was. Or for her palms to be sweating. Oh yeah, she was going to have sex in front of total strangers.

"May I offer you a glass of champagne, Miss Hallquist? It might help soothe your nerves."

She took the slender glass flute, needing to hold it with both hands to stop the shaking. What the hell had she gotten herself into?

Jocelyne reappeared and gave Sandy a quick inspection where she expressed her approval. "Now do you have any other questions?"

About a billion. Yet, none of them managed to make it from her brain to her mouth.

"And you're sure you wish to continue with tonight's event?"

"Yes." Wow, were they ever obsessive in making sure she agreed. Although a lawsuit could be pretty embarrassing for everyone. Especially if a list of the club's members ever became public.

"*Très bien.*" Jocelyne held up a black satin blindfold. "Do you wish me to blindfold your lady now, *Monsieur*, or do you wish to do it yourself?"

Sandy's head whipped around to find Troy standing in the doorway behind her.

"I'll do it myself." He walked across the space separating them and took the mask without ever taking his eyes from Sandy. "Thank you, Jocelyne, now leave us please."

He waited until they were alone before he trailed a finger across her collarbone and down her arm. "You're beautiful."

She'd never felt as beautiful as she did when he looked at her. The rocks that had been taking turns tumbling in her stomach slowed. "Thanks. It's just something I threw on at the last moment." She rubbed the lapels of his tux. She'd seen him in it at company functions before, but never when she'd worn so little. There was something erotic about the combination. "You're overdressed. Shouldn't you be naked too?"

"It's part of the initiation." He lifted her hand and kissed her knuckles. He rested his lips against her knuckles, his breath caressing the back of her hand. "Lie facedown on the massage table for me, will you?"

The leather beneath the sheet creaked as she climbed onto the table. His warm palm nestled at the small of her back while something smooth and hard touched her ankle. He dragged it up the back of her calf, and along her thigh.

"Have you ever worn an anal plug, sunshine?"

"No." Her pussy rippled and she knew if he touched her down there his fingers would come away dripping wet. "You're not expecting me to do a threesome, are you?"

His hand flattened over her behind. Though he didn't tighten his grip, she could feel the intensity flowing from his skin to hers. "No. I will not share you, Sandy. Ever."

"Oh." Wow.

"Does that disappoint you?" His voice turned cool.

"No. I don't need another man when I have you."

His chuckle rippled through her, relaxing her. Until he touched her behind and parted her cleft. "Just relax. It won't hurt you, I promise."

"It's not exactly the most romantic way to start this weekend," Sandy said once the mild discomfort of him inserting the plug passed. "I would have thought you would have had Crystal put that in."

"She offered." He used a towel to clean off any extra traces of the lube he'd used. "I wanted to do it for you."

"Because that part of me is your property?" She hefted herself up on one elbow to look at him. Was he this possessive with all his lovers?

"No." His expression was unreadable when he met her gaze. "Because I couldn't bear the thought that it might have hurt you. And if you found it enjoyable, I'd prefer that you think of me instead of a stranger."

"That's kinky. But it's nice too." So what was up with that fluttery "I like that you're so possessive" feeling in her belly? It's not love, she told herself. It's just lust.

He held out his hand and helped her swing her feet to the floor.

Jocelyne reappeared, a pair of five-inch stiletto heels in one hand

and a matching thong in the other. "If you will put these on, Miss Hallquist, then you'll be all done and ready for this evening."

Aware of both Troy and Jocelyne watching her, Sandy pulled on the thong. She took the stilettos and stuck her toes into the glittery silver shoes. The men that would see her wouldn't care less about the height of her heels. They'd be focusing on her boobs and the easy access to her girl parts but if she fell off them she'd probably break her ankle. "I hope I don't have to walk more than a couple steps in these."

"They're mainly for show, of course. Just remember to walk from your hip and it'll give your derrière that nice little swing men love."

Right, walk from the hip. And keep her butt clenched so the plug didn't shift too much. Which was why they'd given her the thong to wear, she supposed. What else did she need to remember? Oh yeah, to breathe.

Her heart pounded as Troy tied the silk-padded mask in place. The blackness enveloping her caused her heart rate to soar until she took a deep breath. *This was all part of the experience, remember?* The room that had seemed so quiet before came alive. The windows overhead couldn't entirely mute the creak of the trees or the hum of the warm air blowing through the heating vents. Her breathing seemed louder, and she was certain he would be able to hear her heartbeat pounding like a bass drum.

She sniffed. He smelled spicy and warm. Male. "You're wearing that cologne I said I liked the other day."

The one he scoffed at when she'd tested it at the mall, saying he didn't care for colognes.

"Just for you." Despite the blindfold she could feel his fingers tracing over her eyebrows. "I knew you were going to be wearing this, so I figured it was important to give you something else to focus on."

God, he'd thought of everything, hadn't he? "Thank you."

Troy captured her hand and laced their fingers together and led her down the hall to the rotunda's double doors.

The murmuring swelled as they walked into the rotunda. Sandy didn't need to take off the blindfold to imagine all eyes focussing on her.

She'd always laughed when her friends talked about having a nightmare of being forced to walk naked down a street. No laughter came to her now. She gripped Troy's arm harder. If she ran down the hallway, could she find her clothes? Not that she had her car here to make a getaway in, but maybe she could find a phone to call a cab?

No. This was one of the things she'd put on her bucket list. She'd not run away like a coward. Besides, as she'd told Troy, he'd make sure she had fun. He wouldn't let anything bad happen.

"Ladies and gentlemen," Jocelyne's voice sounded far away, as if perhaps she were on the stairs or perhaps up on one of the balconies that ringed the room. "May I present Miss S., who joins us for her initiation tonight."

Following Troy's murmured instructions, Sandy walked up the three steps onto the dais and wrapped her hands around the silk ropes. But when she was instructed to place one foot up on the jewelled platform, a woman's laugh floated down from the balcony. Oh God, she was really doing this. In front of an audience.

THE LIGHTS in the hall had dimmed, though a halogen spotlight lit up the rose-bedecked dais where Sandy stood on display. God, she was lovely. The black silk blindfold highlighted the gold in her hair. Her skin glowed beneath the lights, the pose turning her into a living statue. Despite the warmth of the room, her nipples hardened into tight buds that begged his mouth to capture them, taste them.

Jocelyne had tweaked the settings of the sound system until the taped conversations were little more than a murmur, the way it would be if there'd been a real crowd watching. Thank heavens Coop had agreed to close the place to any visitors except them tonight. He curled his fingers into damp palms. Shit, he was sweating like a frickin' schoolboy called in front of the principal while she was so frickin' calm. What the hell was going on with him?

Jocelyne approached, her head tilted to one side. "Are you well, *monsieur*?"

"I'm fine, thanks."

"She is a beautiful woman. Enjoy your stay."

Only after Jocelyne disappeared down the main hallway, did he shrug out of his jacket. He fumbled with the clasp of his cuff link when a petal fell from one of the overhanging flowers and fluttered onto Sandy's shoulder. Her soft intake of breath as it glided down her breast and over her belly highlighted her sensuality.

God, he wanted to do this for her. He wanted to give her everything she desired. He wanted to give her softness and warmth, she wanted more. She wanted excitement. Once he was completely naked he picked up the flogger. "You liked being spanked, didn't you?"

"Yes." The conversations all around her, the knowledge people were watching, or that some were not, should add to her confusion.

He let the strips of leather dangle down her back and over her behind so she'd have a clue as to what he was about to do. "Do not let go of the straps. Or should I tie you to them?"

"I won't let go. I promise."

The first time he flicked the flogger over her ass, she hissed and jerked, but she didn't let go. "Don't come, sunshine. Not until I'm in you."

By the time her ass glowed a pretty pattern of red, her buttocks were rhythmically clenching around the butt plug. Her skin glowed in the light of the halogens, not from the glittery powder they'd dusted over her but from a sheen of perspiration as she struggled not to come. He let the flogger drop to his side to admire her. Not once had she objected to anything he'd suggested, not just tonight but during their relationship. She'd never felt the need to pretend to be something she wasn't. Everything she felt was right there on her face for anyone to see. So trusting and open to anything as long as he was there with her.

She was a surprise. A gift.

She was his.

EVERY NERVE ENDING in Sandy's body felt alive, on fire. Beyond the mask, the voices had continued their quiet chatter, occasionally she swore she heard someone else panting as if they were being pleasured and about to come. The first time the flogger had touched her flesh she'd nearly let go of the straps to protest. The damned thing hurt. The second time was harder, biting into her skin. To her surprise, the sting on her ass faded and spread to the pleasant warmth she'd first experienced when Troy had spanked her.

"Everyone's watching you. Can you feel them? Can you imagine the lust in their eyes?"

Though she could hear voices, she wanted to see their faces as they watched Troy flogging her. Lust, as he'd suggested. Maybe even jealousy.

The flogger fell again, driving the thought from her head, returning it to the warring sensations in her ass and her pussy. Trusting that he wouldn't truly hurt her, she'd soon lost track, the pain turning to pleasure confusing her mind as her body craved more.

The butt plug enhanced the experience of the flogging until her body hovered on the brink of orgasm. Yet he'd told her not to come. Sandy fought the muscles that clenched the plug, tightening her passage until her head lolled on her shoulder and tears gathered in her eyes, her whole body shaking with her need for release.

Strong hands molded around her fingers, prying them free of the straps. "Let go, sunshine."

Where she would have sagged to the floor, he caught her, rubbing the circulation back into her arms. Once she was steady again, there was a gentle pressure on her shoulders.

She sank down and discovered instead of the hard marble she'd expected, a pillow had been placed on the floor to cushion her knees.

Something warm and velvety bumped against her lips so she parted them. Immediately his shaft thrust into her mouth, filling it until the thatch of hair at his groin tickled her nose. She breathed deeply, loving the musky scent mingling with the hint of cologne he'd worn simply because she'd said she'd liked it.

His fingers threaded through her hair and he held her still as he worked his cock back and forth in her mouth. A hot bead of come tantalized her taste buds as his cock swelled and pulsed against her tongue. Her pussy throbbed with each stroke, as if he were plunging deep against her womb instead of her throat.

"Yeah. Just like that." The huskiness of his voice rasped her senses as surely as the sting of her hair as he tightened his grip. Despite the blindfold, she could picture him naked in front of her, his butt clenched with each thrust, his thigh muscles taut, his head thrown back as her mouth pleasured him.

His thrusting shallowed for a moment as he struggled to hold off, then his control snapped and he surged deep, his thrusts wild and rough. Her hips rolled in time with his thrusts, the plug heavy against her needy tissues. A groan rumbled deep in her throat, her body forgetting the plug was not him as she approached her own climax. Too soon his release jetted out in a hot stream; she swallowed the creamy essence, licking the pulsing head until his movements gentled.

She licked her lips once he pulled from her and released his hold on her hair. The extra stroke over her head had her turning to rub her cheek into his palm. He pulled her to a stand, his fingers lacing with hers. "Your turn now."

Was the public part done? Would they end up in a private room or would he fuck her right here in front of everyone?

"Hang on to me for a moment." He placed her hands around his neck then lifted her, carrying her. Cool leather touched her heated skin and her back had to arch...ah, he'd taken her to the curvy piece of furniture. Unhooking her arms, he positioned her over the highest arch and she realized the benefits of the curves and how the couch allowed her to be put on display. The possibilities of the positions they could use on the strange piece of furniture now seemed endless.

Her legs naturally fell open as he knelt on the lower curve. He positioned himself between them and removed her shoes. The rough pads of his fingertips skimmed down the curve of her neck and circled her breasts, his thumb brushing over her areola until it beaded and quivered. They skimmed around the globes then skated across her belly.

"You're so beautiful, sunshine. So responsive." He pressed a kiss to the ticklish spot above her hip. "You should see the looks you're getting. The women wish they were you, while the men all wish they were me."

With each touch, with each murmur he gave, her core grew heavier, the skin of his belly that rested against her mons grew slippery with her juices.

She squirmed when he flattened his palm over her belly and dragged it down to her mound. The heel of his hand pressed against her clit in a tantalizing promise of pleasure. As she lifted her hips to press into his palm, his mouth caught her breast, his lips, teeth and tongue teasing her until she was breathless and dizzy.

"Can you smell your arousal? I can. So can everyone in the front row." He slipped a finger through the wetness of her folds. She squirmed, wishing he'd breach her entrance, allow her to come. Instead he withdrew, causing her to moan in disappointment.

"I know what you want, but you're on my schedule tonight." He traced the curve of her mouth, then slipped it past her lips. "Taste yourself, Sandy."

She licked her own essence from his finger and the scent of her arousal—and his—grew stronger. When he tried to withdraw his finger from her mouth, she caught his wrist and held him there, sucking his fingers deep as her hips rolled, pressing her mound against him. She couldn't resist running her fingers along the ridges of his arms, loving the way the dark hair crinkled beneath her fingertips.

"Such passion." he murmured. "There's a couple watching us—the woman is mimicking everything you do. Does that turn you on? Do you like the idea that you inspire passion in others?"

She'd never thought herself an exhibitionist before, but the idea that others were watching, were getting off on what she was doing made her even wetter. Humming her assent, she sucked harder on his finger, rolling her tongue over it as she had done for his cock before releasing it. "Fuck me, Troy. Please. I need you."

"Not yet. It's not a race tonight. It's never a race." His lips captured hers, his tongue sliding over her teeth, dancing with hers. His body covered hers, the crisp hair on his chest rasping her breasts until they ached for more of his touch. The length of his cock slid through her slick folds and over her clit until she cried out once again for him to take her. Instead he broke off the kiss and drew back, paying homage to her breasts, using his tongue and teeth in an onslaught that left her trembling with need.

Leather creaked as he once again shifted his weight. His thighs pressed against the inner flesh of hers, and the hard head of his cock broached her entrance. He thrust into her with a slow but steady pressure until he filled her completely.

"Oh, God." Between his girth and the butt plug filling her, she'd never been so stretched.

Her body reached a fervor she'd never known before. Her hips lifted, trying to find...something. He gripped her hips and pressed her back against the leather. The angle had changed slightly until the bulbous head scraped along a sensitive section that started her quivering. Once assured she wouldn't move again, he released one hip and moved one hand to toy with her clit.

Her vision removed, her world was reduced to sensation. The wet slapping sound each time their hips met, even the soft breath brushing her neck seemed warmer, more erotic. He groaned, the sound rumbling through his chest into hers. He drove her higher than she'd ever been before, the air seemed to thin, and her chest heaved, each breath more difficult than the last.

When she finally couldn't draw another breath, her body tightened, clenched around his shaft. Against the blackness of the mask, an explosion of fireworks sparkled in her vision. Just when she thought she was done, he drove her up again until she was shaking so hard she couldn't stop.

His breathing ragged from his own climax, Troy traced the outline of her mask. "You are beautiful, sunshine. I am the envy of every man here."

"They're still watching?" It was hard to form the words, her body was so loose and languid.

"They can't take their eyes off of you." His lips caressed hers. "But they can't touch you. Because you're mine."

"I'm yours," she whispered. She reached up until her hand touched his chest; his heart beat a rapid tattoo against her palm. "And you're mine." For tonight.

"Always."

THIRTEEN

HER FEET DRAGGING as she trudged across the parking lot, Jazz nearly missed the dark blue Beemer parked near the entrance. The rectangular shape of a laptop's screen lit the interior, illuminating the driver's face. Shit. Had she made a date with Mitch for tonight? She was too freaking tired to go out. Hell, she was too freaking tired to talk to him right now. Hopefully if he wanted to come up, he wouldn't mind if she fell asleep while he fucked her. After all, she didn't have to be awake. Really. Did she?

Maybe she could sneak past—nope, too late. The driver's side door swung open. "Hey, Jazz baby. I've been waiting for you."

"Hi." She mustered as much enthusiasm as she could for his kiss. "Did we have a date?"

"Yeah, baby. You told me about your roommate going away for the weekend and how we could hang out here together with no interruptions."

Had she? "Look, I totally forgot about it. And I'm really exhausted."

"It's all right, we can order in tonight. Pop in a movie, chill out in front of the TV with a beer or two." He grabbed his laptop and shoved it in his case.

Jazz zoned out as he talked about his plans for the weekend.

From the way he jabbered, her "uh-huh's" and "hmm's" must have been at the right spots.

After disarming the security system that had been installed upon Troy's insistence, she dumped her coat over the back of the chair and kicked off her shoes.

Mitch followed her into the bedroom, dumped his laptop case by the door. "So what do you want to do? There's only the late-night shows on, but maybe we could find a good movie. Oh, do you like that new vampire show? I downloaded it, if you want to watch it from the beginning."

"I don't think I have much of an attention span tonight." She stripped off her top and ditched her jeans. God, all she wanted to do was crawl in bed and fall asleep.

At least Mitch followed her into the bedroom and didn't press her for sex. He turned on his laptop and checked his email before turning to her. "What movie do you want to watch?"

"Whatever. Come on, Xander, off you go." She picked the cat up off the middle of her bed and deposited him on the floor. The cat meowed and tried to jump back up only to be nudged out the door by Mitch.

"Do you want to order pizza now or later?"

"I don't care. I'm easy." For now all she wanted to do was crash and zone out.

"Maybe later then." Mitch queued up the movie then removed the remote from its compartment in the side of the laptop. "I hope the genius who designed these got paid a fortune."

He bounded over to the bed, dropping his clothes to the floor as he stripped naked then crawled onto the bed beside her. The movie was some action flick that had bombed at the movies and involved lots of car chases. Jazz wasn't sure but she must have fallen asleep because when she roused, Mitch was playing with her breasts and he'd moved the laptop to her dresser.

"Wake up, Jazz baby. It's time to play."

Though she wanted to stay asleep, the warmth of his hands was sort of nice. And she liked having him beside her. Without Sandy in the apartment, she liked the idea that she wasn't alone. Without fully opening her eyes, she pressed her breast into his palm. She'd learned early that Mitch didn't need her to be fully awake to have sex.

He moved the remote from the comforter between them and put it on the nightstand before turning back to tweak her nipples harder than he'd ever done before.

Her breast throbbing, she turned her head to see if he'd meant to hurt her. He didn't look angry or anything. More excited, and his cock was rigid against her thigh. He lowered his head and licked then bit the side of her breast. "Yeah, you like that, don't you?"

"Mmm-hmm." Okay, so she liked a little pain with her pleasure, so sue her.

His smile widened. If he'd been anyone else, his smile might have scared her. "Yeah, I knew you were a dirty girl that first night I met you."

Whatever. She let her eyes close and concentrated on the attention he was giving her breasts.

"You like me talking dirty too, my little slut? You like me talking about how I'm going to fuck your cunt? How I'm going to make you scream as I ram my cock into you?"

She didn't particularly care for the slut comment, but the rest of it? Yeah, okay, whatever floated his boat.

"Can I tie you up like we did last time?" His excitement rippled through his tightening grasp on her wrists.

"Sure. Why not?" Besides if she were tied up, he'd have to do all the work.

"Where'd you put the cuffs, baby? They with the rest of your toys?" At her nod, he dug around in the bottom drawer of her night table and held them up, the steel glinting. "I love that they're real and not those stupid plastic ones or the ones with the quick release you get at a sex store. You used to date a cop or something?"

"One of my old boyfriends used to be an MP with the Navy." He was the one who had introduced her to bondage. Pity he'd been the stereotypical sailor with a girl in every port. Not that it had bothered her at first, but then he'd decided they shouldn't use condoms and she'd shown him the door.

Once Mitch secured her, he rummaged through the rest of her drawers and pulled out one of her scarves. "Can I gag you?"

"All right, but we should—"

He slapped it over her mouth before she could suggest they set up some sort of safety signal. "We're going to have so much fun tonight."

Fun? Without a safe word? She tried to speak but the gag muffled her words until they were little more than gurgles. Apprehension curled and wormed its way up her spine to settle in the pit of her stomach.

Without any foreplay, Mitch rolled on top of her, his weight pressing heavy on her belly, making it hard to breathe through only her nose. After he'd positioned himself between her thighs, he shoved himself into her hilt deep. Shit, he hadn't used a condom.

Humping over her like she was a damned dog, sweat dripped from his forehead into her eyes. His teeth latched onto the tender skin of her breasts and bit hard enough to break the skin. With a yelp, she attempted to buck him off, only to be stymied by his weight. The wild look in his eyes as he bit the other breast even harder. The apprehension in her belly roiled.

He pulled out before he finished and sat back on his heels. The smug look on his face did nothing to alleviate her concern. The apprehension clawed her conscience when he flipped her over on her stomach, forcing her to cross her arms. The discomfort in her arms was soon forgotten when he smacked her behind with his belt. "I wish I'd known you liked it rough before, Jazz baby. I can't tell you how much I love dirty girls."

Her "no" disappeared into the fabric, so she tried to turn over, only to have him put his knee at the base of her spine.

"That's it. Fight me, baby."

Fight? She was tied up, gagged. Unable to move, unable to scream. Totally at his mercy. Fight, he'd said. Fine, she'd fight, and when she got free, she'd tie him up. Gag him. See how he liked being totally helpless.

You're not helpless. Keep fighting.

She rubbed her face against the sheets in a futile attempt to dislodge the gag. Shit. That wasn't working. She had to get his attention somehow. Gathering all her strength, she heaved up off the mattress, thrashed her legs to try to keep him away.

"Stop it, bitch." His playful tone changed to irritation, but he left the side of the bed, giving her hope that he'd stop completely. Until he grabbed her right leg and tied it to the foot of the bed with a scarf. Her left leg was similarly tied, leaving her spread-eagled.

Oh God, now she *was* helpless. He could do anything he wanted and there was nothing she could do to stop him.

"You said you liked pain, so here's a little pain for you, Jazz baby."

The sound of leather cracked through the silence, making her jump, but she felt no corresponding pain on her back. Mitch laughed, a twisted menacing sound. "Ha, psyched you out with that one, didn't I?"

The belt once again appeared in her view—the bastard had doubled it up on itself. He flexed it and let it snap again. "I love that sound. But do you know what I love more? How you flinched. Yeah, look at that fear in your eyes. We're going to have fun tonight, Jazz baby."

The next time the belt struck her. She'd had worse. It struck again, this time the prong dug into her hip. Shit, he was using the end with the buckle? This was going to get bad.

Again and again and again, it hit her ass, the buckle biting into her tender, abused flesh until she felt her skin would hang off in raw strips.

Sandy, come home. Please come home. Please.

Just when she thought she couldn't take any more, he shifted his angle. The next strike caught the knobs of her spine.

You told me about your roommate going away for the weekend.

He could rape her for days. Torture her.

Kill her?

Oh Fuck! Panic raced through her veins like wildfire as her imagination supplied images of Sandy finding her dead when she returned. Imagined what else he might do to her. A scream welled in her throat, once again trapped by the fabric.

She fought the handcuffs until her wrists were raw and bloody. Nausea roiled and she panicked even more, fearing she'd choke if she vomited into the gag.

Stop it. You have to stay calm if you're going to get through this. Focus on controlling your breathing. Just get through it. You can survive.

God, she'd *liked* him. Even trusted him. What was it with her choice in guys? Her vision clouded with tears, she buried her face in the bedding and concentrated on just getting through the ordeal.

How many minutes had passed since she'd been so warm, so comfortable with the covers pulled over her? Ten minutes? Twenty? An hour? The room was so cold now. So cold. Her flesh crawled as warmth leaked from her, in slow trickles over her skin to pool under her belly.

Whether it was his sweat or her blood, she couldn't tell.

When he finally set down the bloodied strap, every nerve ending in her back and ass had been touched by the fires of hell. He swiped a finger over her hip and made a feral sound of approval. Fear changed to hatred when his fingers closed around the leather belt and it again disappeared from view.

Fuck him. There was no way she was going to be a statistic on a police blotter. She had to get free. She had to do it herself.

How?

The security system. She had to get free and push the panic button hidden beside her bedside table.

How? repeated through her head. She was tied hand and foot. Unable to move. Unable to speak.

You have to make him want *to release you.*

"Take the gag off me, baby," she mouthed through the fabric, her throat raw. "Let me blow you."

If he understood her, he didn't fall for her ploy. Instead, he started poking around in her toy drawer. With his back turned, she clawed at the metal links, hoping to find a release like Sandy's pair had even though she knew there was none. Her repeated attempts to kick away the bindings at her ankles only served to snarl the knots tighter.

Her muscles seized when he straddled her and his fingers parted her ass crack. Oh God, no. She'd done anal with him once and vowed never again. Apparently he'd forgotten that night. Her ass clenched around the intrusion, the memory of the pain he'd caused before a virulent entity.

Fight him!

Her repeated attempts to buck him off failing miserably, she tried to tell him to use more lube, to use the whole damned tube, to fuck her pussy, anything else. The tissues at her opening burned when he shoved his dick in without waiting for her body to adjust. While he'd used some lube, just like last time he hadn't used enough.

As he pounded into her abused flesh, he whispered a stream of filth into her ear. The control she'd so desperately clung to shattered and the sobs she'd tried to choke back exploded. She screamed until her lungs burned and her throat seized. Unable to draw a proper breath, her vision greyed and she prayed for unconsciousness. A prayer that wasn't answered.

By the time he pulled out of her, she'd lost all track of time, trapped in a morass of pain and loathing, for him and for her. A smidgen of hope flickered that he'd finally untie her. Its tiny ray wavered and died when he wandered out of the room without a word.

From the flickering light, she could only guess he'd turned on the television but the lack of sound confused her until she recognized the familiar click of a keyboard and realized he'd taken his laptop from her dresser. He'd fucking raped her and now was sitting on her couch checking his email or playing some goddamned computer game?

She slammed her head into the pillow, cursing Mitch, herself and even Sandy for going away, for having fun while she was here, trussed up, helpless.

Despair replaced anger, leaching all the fight from her body. She was alone. Totally and completely alone. All because she'd been too tired, too stupid, to tell him to go home. To break it off right then and there.

"Yeah, I told you I'd get it for you. Trust me." Mitch's voice startled her. She lifted her head only to realize he hadn't returned. That he wasn't speaking to her. So who was he talking to? Chills wracked her at the thought he might have invited others to participate tonight.

There was a pause, then he started speaking again. "I understand, but you have to give me some time here. I'm so damned close I can almost taste it." Another pause. Thank God, he'd not invited someone else; he was on the phone. "No, I couldn't get it that way but I found another way in that'll work just as good. Don't worry. I'll get the address. Once I find her, I'll get you the money. I promise."

The room went silent again except for more tapping. Exhausted, she closed her eyes, trying to marshal her thoughts off her pain, focus on devising a plan to escape. She had no idea if she'd slept or fallen unconscious, but she awoke to him untying her right ankle.

She tested her left leg and found it already unbound. Before she could react, he flipped her onto her back. Her breath hissed from her and she arched at the agony of the fabric touching her wounds.

"Jazz baby, you may not have been the woman I intended to pick up at Rusty's that night, but you've worked out pretty good too."

When he started to crawl between her thighs she kicked out at him, catching him in the side of his face with her heel. With a curse, he sat on her legs and swiped his hand over his mouth. He stared at the blood on his fingers. "What the fuck? Why'd you do that?"

She tried to spit out the gag and once again failed so resorted to cursing him out through the fabric.

"Aw, Jazz baby, you're mad at me for leaving you tied up and gagged?" He leaned over and pulled down the gag.

Afraid he might leave her tied up, or worse, if she cursed him the way she wanted to, she forced herself to stay calm. "Undo the cuffs so I can touch you. The key's in the top drawer."

He rummaged around for what seemed like forever before finding the key. Instead of immediately unlocking the cuff, he took his time dragging the metal over her midriff and up her cleavage. "I gotta tell you, you're sexy as hell all tied up like this."

Jazz started trembling when his cock grew half-hard. No way was he going to get another chance to fuck her. To hurt her. "Come on, Mitch honey. Unlock me so I can take care of that bad boy for you."

"I don't know. I think I'll let you suck me off right where you are."

"I'll make it good for you. I'll get on my knees in front of you, be your slave, just the way you like." *Tell him whatever he wants to hear to get out of this.* "I'll deep-throat you. You know I give good head, baby. You've told me I'm good at it. And it's less tiring for you that way. You could sit in the chair if you want."

Come on, let me go. Do it.

After a moment's hesitation, he relented. But he was standing between her and the damned panic button. Fine. There was one out in the living room.

As soon as he freed her, she dragged herself to the edge of the bed and stood. Her legs felt like there were no bones within them, her back as if it were on fire, but she forced herself not to sag to the floor. She staggered to the living room, ignoring his calls asking where she was going.

Just another four steps, maybe five. She could do this. She had to. Her arm trembling, she lifted her hand to press the panic button. Mitch grabbed her arm, spun her around. "What the fuck are you doing? You hit that button you'll have half of Hauberk as well as the police here. What's your fucking problem?"

"My problem? My *problem*? You fucking raped me, you asshole, and you ask me what my problem is?" God, she couldn't stop shaking.

"Rape?" He shoved her against the wall, using his weight to once again hold her in place. "No way. Uh-uh. You said you were into rough stuff. You're the one who suggested being tied up. You could have said no any time. You can't deny you were moaning and writhing and everything. You were into it as much as me."

"How could I say no when you'd fucking gagged me? I never said you could whip me like a fucking racehorse. My back hurts like hell and my ass..." Holy fuck, she was so fucking sore. It felt like he'd damaged something deep inside. "I told you last time, I never wanted anal from you again."

His expression hardened and he released her. "Isn't that typical. Say yes one minute and then when you've had your fun you scream your head off and cry rape. Fucking bitch." He pressed on her shoulders, forcing her to her knees. "You were the one with the handcuffs, not me. You're the one who let me gag you. Face it, you wanted my cock in your ass. So it hurt a little. Big fucking deal. You told me before you like a little pain when we have sex, you just don't want to admit you got off."

"Then why don't you turn around and bend over. See how you feel when I shove one of my dildos up your ass."

He glanced to the side, his jaw clenched. "All right, maybe I pushed things a little hard on you tonight. How about next time we don't use a gag, so you can tell me exactly what you like?"

"No. There'll be no next time. We're through. I don't ever want to see you again. You got that?"

"Yeah, I got it, bitch." He released her and headed into the bedroom.

Unable to stand, Jazz crawled across the room on her hands and knees, past the coffee table to the couch. He didn't know there was another button concealed beneath the side table. "I want you the fuck out of this place. Now."

He reappeared with his clothes, cursing her with each item he pulled on. Once dressed, he stomped into the living room and shut his laptop without turning it off. "Tomorrow when you realize how wrong you are, you'll be phoning me. Wait and see. You're just embarrassed because you got off on it."

"No. I'm not ever going to call you." But the cops would. After she filed her report and pressed rape charges against him. "Now you get the fuck out of my place. Before I call the cops."

He shoved the laptop into his bag and tucked it under his arm. "So call them. I'll play the cops the videos I've made. They'll prove that you agreed to everything that happened tonight. And the cops will know you're the liar. It's not me they'll charge. It's you. It's against the law to lay false charges."

Video? He was lying. He had to be. Except...her gaze dropped to the laptop bag clutched beneath his arm. The laptop he'd left open on the dresser. Oh God. No. He wouldn't. Would he?

"Yeah, that's right." He tapped his bag. "I taped it using the webcam. I won't have to say a word to defend myself. Yeah, you didn't notice my laptop was on the whole time, did you, you stupid bitch? I taped all our other little sessions too. And all those games we played. So don't threaten me, because it's all here, Jazz baby. Once the cops see the video, they'll see that the handcuffs were yours. They'll see you handing them to me. Hear you telling me you liked pain.

"Oh, and if you blab anything about me to any of your bodyguard friends, I'll post the entire video on the Internet for everyone to see. Then I'll set up ads on Craigslist claiming to be you looking for a partner willing to hurt you during sex, talking about how you love pain, how you love to be abused. By the time I'm done, there won't be a person on earth who will believe a word you say. And they'll all know you're nothing more than a whore."

The screams started up in her head—screams of frustration, of anger. "You fucking bastard." He was right. Everything he'd said was true. She had handed him her handcuffs, sat quietly while he'd put them on. Agreed to be gagged. They'd never believe her.

He ran the back of one knuckle down her cheek. "So when I call and ask to see you again? And I will call—you're going to invite me back." Not a question. A statement. The fucker was that sure of himself.

"You're never coming back here, you bastard." She balled her fist, pulled back her elbow and let fly. The satisfying sound of bone crunching, the warmth of his blood spurting over her knuckles, was worth the pain in her hand. "Next time, I'll have more than a fist for your face. I'll have a gun."

~

MUSIC AND LAUGHTER engulfed Cooper Davis when he walked through the Rouge's double doors. "Any problems tonight, Fred?"

"No, sir." The club's doorman helped Cooper off with his coat. "I've notified Miss Delayna that you've arrived, sir. She'll be here momentarily as you've requested."

No sooner had Fredrickson finished speaking than a side door opened and a dark-haired woman joined them. With a nod to Cooper, she shrugged out of the terry spa robe she wore and handed it to the doorman.

"Good evening, Delayna."

With a soft huff, she handed Cooper a leash attached to the leather collar around her neck. "You're late. Did you run into problems?"

"Only that Senator Brannally was long-winded in his speech tonight as usual." He wrapped the leather strap around his wrist. "Did you walk George?"

"Yes, sir. He's asleep in your office."

After Fredrickson opened the double stained glass inner doors leading to the club's common area, Cooper walked down the hall toward the music that mingled with voices and the occasional crack of a whip.

As she'd been trained, Delayna padded after him, leaving the requisite amount of space to keep the leash loose. With her background, she'd never have qualified for admission to the club as a member, which would have been a pity.

"Did tonight's session in the guest house get recorded?"

"Yes, sir. It's burning to a DVD even as we speak."

"Excellent." The noise of the whip, and the moans of the other members grew louder the closer they got to the central hallway. Ah, yes, one of the billionaires from the west coast had planned a public discipline session with his sub tonight. "McPherson didn't suspect the cameras existed?"

"He only checked to ensure the regular cameras were turned off." Obviously he hadn't found the special ones Davis had ordered installed two weeks before when one of their members had hosted a bachelor party with some very interesting guests. Guests that provided him with footage ensuring he'd have access to information his regular contacts couldn't provide.

"Baker phoned from Val Varde, sir. He wants you to contact him as soon as you're in the bunker."

Shit. He tugged on the leash, not enough to pull her off her feet, but she'd get the message he was not pleased she'd waited to impart that nugget. If she were truly his sub, he'd be borrowing the congressman's whip. "Did he say why?"

"No, sir, only that it was imperative that you return his call."

They passed through another set of double doors into the rotunda with its soaring dome. Neither spared the couples in various states of undress copulating in the grotto at the far end even a glance, nor was their passage acknowledged by any of the members. He headed to the marble staircase leading to the Founding Members' wing. They were halfway to his private suite when another member's door opened and a couple emerged, the man dressed in leather chaps, the woman leading him by a leash similar to the one wrapped around Cooper's own hand.

Turning quickly, Cooper shoved Delayna against the wall and captured her mouth with his. His operative tensed until her gaze flickered sideways and found the reason for his embrace. As the couple approached, Delayna relaxed into his hold and accepted the kiss with a moan that shot straight to his groin. Cooper couldn't help sinking into the kiss, enjoying her honeyed taste along with the feel of her skin against his. If she felt his hard-on against her belly, he had no clue, nor did he care. It couldn't be helped. She was a sensuous woman with full plump lips to match her luscious breasts and generous hips. Pity she was his employee and not his lover in truth.

The hallway empty again, he stepped back. Without saying a word, he rewound the leash around his fist and headed to the room at the end of the hall. Once inside Delayna shut the door and unclipped her collar.

He crossed the room and opened the secret panel leading to the stairs down to his group's bunker, not waiting for her to don the sweat pants and camouflage tee she'd left at the door.

Moments later, he heard her steps light and quick on the stairs. "May I ask why it was necessary for this charade? Why didn't you head straight to your office when you arrived?"

"Because it was necessary for me to be seen in the common areas. If I am not seen coming to my rooms on occasion, people will start asking questions as to where I am." He paused on the landing and fixed her with a look that had her stopping half a flight above. Her caution pleased him. "We've been through this before. If you do not wish to accept your role, then you may leave the Brigade."

A flush rose up her neck though stopped short of her face. "I have no desire to leave the group, sir." Her lids dropped, hiding the expression in her eyes, though not on her face. Interesting. It wasn't embarrassment or even anger, but lust she sought to hide. "Sometimes it is difficult for me to be...submissive."

"Noted. But it is necessary for the roles we play." He continued down the three floors until they reached the sub-basement, wondering how he could use Delayna's attraction to his own purposes, as well as those of the Brigade.

FOURTEEN

HE DIDN'T REMEMBER FALLING asleep but he must have for he woke up to Jocelyne shaking him.

"*Monsieur*, I am sorry to disturb you but there's an important call for you. You may take it in my office."

He carefully extracted himself from the tangle of Sandy's limbs and climbed from the bed. Though she frowned, Sandy snuggled in his spot and stayed asleep. Muttering to himself that the phone call had better the hell be important for taking him away from a night with Sandy in his arms, he grabbed a robe. Without saying a word, Jocelyne led him to her office then left him alone. The display showed it was an internal call. Which meant it could only be one person.

"McPherson."

"Garcia's arrived in Val Varde." Cooper Davis's clipped speech shot out of the receiver.

He forced himself to concentrate on the implications of Davis's announcement. "I thought that fucker was planning to stay in Colombia for another week."

"Plans changed, I guess. Which means we've had to change ours. We take off from Andrews in ninety minutes with or without you."

Shit, that was going to cut things close. "I'll be there."

He got an outside line then dialed Sam's private number. Sam answered on the second ring.

"A situation has come up in Kinshasa." While they had clients in Africa, he could only hope Sam wouldn't ask for more details. "I need to fly out this morning. I'll be gone for at least forty-eight hours, probably more like seventy-two."

Silence filled the connection for a long moment before Sam's deep voice rumbled over the line. "Take care of yourself, you hear?"

He stabbed the button, ending the connection, and dialed his backup. "Heads up. I'm going to be out of the loop for at least two days." He quickly ran down the outstanding issues and made sure his own agents could handle their assignments.

TROY UNLOCKED his apartment but stalled opening the door. He was pretty sure Sandy hadn't seen Scott in the parking lot when they'd left the club, nor would she have any reason to check that Scott's engine would still be warm where it sat in the parking lot. He should have sent her home in a limo but the thought of sending her off alone felt wrong. Like she was a one-night stand, which she definitely wasn't. "I'm sorry about bailing on the weekend. But this situation in the Congo can't be put off."

"It's all right." Sandy squeezed his hand. "We can try again another weekend."

He pushed open the door, blocking it until he made sure Scott had already arrived. "Don't mind the mess. The lady I have come in and clean up after us only comes once a week. She's due in tomorrow."

Sandy's lips firmed but the tips of them twitched as if she were trying not to smile. "I forgot two guys living in one apartment equals frat central."

He snatched up the empty pizza boxes from the coffee table. And the half-dozen Starbucks cups. And the discarded Mrs. Fields cookie box and wrappers. The dirty socks got kicked under the couch. "Um, yeah, pretend you didn't see these. Let me give Scott a heads-up that I'm back."

Leaving her in the living room, he headed to Scott's bedroom door and knocked, reminding himself that he had to pretend Scott had been there the whole time. "Hey, Scott. You awake?"

At Scott's answer, he opened the door and found Scott shrugging out of his jacket. "Look, I was wondering if you could do me a favor?" He kept his voice louder than he normally would so Sandy would overhear. "Something urgent's come up over in the Congo. I have to head to the airport right away. Can you drive her home and make sure she's not thinking I've run out on her." He lowered his voice. "Thanks for getting back here without her seeing. I owe you one."

Scott didn't bother hiding his smirk. "Yeah, you do. Man, you've got it bad for her, don't you?"

"Fuck you." Yet as he headed back to the living room, Scott's taunt became an earworm. Yeah, he had it bad. For a woman who didn't want any long-term relationship with him. How fucked-up was that?

Sandy was waiting right where he'd left her, her eyes still heavy-lidded and sleep filled. Damn, what he would have given to have woken up to her in the morning looking like that. To wake her by thrusting into her while she was all sleep soft. To wake up every day beside her.

Lost in the depth of her eyes, the curve of her jaw, the softness of her skin, he rested his forehead against hers. Sandy was self-effacing and down-to-earth. She was also sexy and funny and sensual as hell. She didn't crave the spotlight like some of the women he'd dated.

Dated. No, somehow that seemed wrong for her. Courted, as outdated and archaic as that word was these days, suited her better. She deserved to be pampered and feted, placed up on a pedestal.

The words "I love you" hovered on his tongue but he swallowed them. If he said them out loud, she'd think he'd want to tie her down when he wanted to show her how she could fly beside him. How they could have adventures never leaving their bedroom. How he could show her things she'd dreamed of seeing, take her places she'd always wanted to go. But if he didn't say them, if something happened to him on this mission...

While he was debating whether to take that leap, she lifted her face and captured his lips. He sank into her kiss like she was oxygen and he was drowning.

We take off from Andrews in ninety minutes with or without you. Damn it, that window was closing and too damned fast. Hating that he had to leave her, he ended the kiss. God, he hated the idea of leaving her. "I have to go."

She followed the curve of his ear with one finger. He marveled at how provocative she could be with such a simple touch. "Promise you're not going to be in danger and you'll come back in one piece?"

No one had ever asked him to do that. Not because they cared about him.

"I'll be fine." Why did Garcia have to choose this weekend to leave his hideout? Why couldn't he have stayed where he was another forty-eight hours? Was that too much to ask?

Sandy covered a yawn with her hand.

Damn, he'd worn her out. "Why don't you sleep here tonight? Scott can drive you home in the morning."

Her nose crinkled, no doubt wondering whether his sheets were clean or not. Given the state of the living room, he couldn't fault her for her hesitation. "The bedding was changed on Wednesday." Two days of him sleeping in it shouldn't be too bad. Should it? "I like the idea of you sleeping in my bed. Waking up in it, even if I can't be there."

She yawned again, then nodded. "All right. Scott'll probably prefer not having to leave his warm bed to go out in the cold to drive me around anyway."

"He will. There's fresh linen in the closet if you want to change it." He raised his voice. "Hey, Scott. You can go back to sleep; Sandy's going to sleep here for the night."

"Geez, get dressed. Don't get dressed. Make up your mind, man," Scott grumbled from the bedroom in a good imitation of a man just awoken.

Removing his arm from Sandy's waist was an almost physical pain, but he needed to pack. He settled for holding her hand and leading her into his bedroom. Shoot. He should have at least made the bed before he left. And maybe picked up his clothes. He grabbed his duffel bag from where he'd left it from his last trip. Sandy sat cross-legged on the bed, staying quiet as he packed.

Neither of them spoke until he zipped the case and put it on the floor. He knelt on the bed beside her and pulled her into a hug. Damn it, he didn't want to leave her. Not right now. "I shouldn't be gone more than a couple days."

"Promise you'll call me to let me know you got there safely, or at least when you're coming back?" She seemed to be having the same problem he did disentangling herself from him.

"I may not have phone service. But I'll call from the plane on the flight back, I promise." He hefted his bag and walked to the front door.

Her, "I'll miss you," made the thirty-foot walk to the elevator feel like a mile. Especially the way she stayed in the doorway, watching him.

Don't look back. If you do, you won't be able to leave.

FIFTEEN

WATCHING Troy walk away made her stomach jump in ways Sandy wasn't used to. It wasn't as if she hadn't watched him leave for missions before. But this time...this time it was different. She'd read the reports, both the private Hauberk ones and the newspaper accounts, of all the turmoil going on in Africa. The risks he took were suddenly so much more real, so much more dangerous.

When the elevator arrived and he hesitated, looking back at her for a brief second, she clutched the doorframe to stop herself from running down the hallway and jumping in his arms.

"He'll be all right," Scott said. "Don't worry."

His reassurance might have had more strength if he hadn't sounded doubtful himself.

She wandered back into the apartment. *I couldn't bear the thought that it might have hurt you. And if you found it enjoyable, I'd prefer that you think of me instead of a stranger.* There'd been something different about the way he'd held her after they'd finished, gentle yet fiercely protective. And then there was how he'd paused to look back at her before he got on the elevator. Did that mean anything?

"You know, you're the first woman he's ever brought back here. Try not to screw him over."

That might not mean anything. It might just mean he hooked up with whoever was there at the time. "He brought me here because he was short on time. And what do you mean about screwing him over? What makes you think—"

But Scott had already disappeared into his bedroom and shut the door.

Left alone, Sandy felt more confident in examining the condo. Other than a couple pairs of discarded socks under the couch, there was nothing personal in the living room. Oh, sure it had the requisite couch and chair, along with one of the biggest flat screens on the market. A stack of games had been piled haphazardly beside a Playstation, but there were no cushions on the couch, no pictures on the wall. Not even a rug covering the hardwood. Nothing that gave her a clue about who lived there. Okay, so she could tell that a guy lived here from the socks and the Playstation but heck, Jazz often left her socks on the floor, and they had an Xbox. But their place felt like a home. This didn't. It didn't even feel like a hotel. It was a box with furniture.

The bedroom was no different. She stripped off her clothes and crawled into the middle of the king-sized mattress tucked into the corner of the room. He didn't even have a proper bed frame for the thing. It was like walking into a college kid's first apartment.

Maybe that's why he traveled so much. Kate, the accounting manager, had often complained about Troy's travel expenses, citing the ability to videoconference these days. Maybe he wanted to travel because he didn't feel comfortable here. Maybe she could do something about it. Make him want to stay around longer. She lay back on the bed and stared at the ceiling, plotting.

WHILE COOPER HAD FALLEN asleep before the plane had taken off, Troy had fidgeted until they were halfway across the Caribbean.

What if Sandy decided she wanted to go back to the Rouge? It wouldn't be a total disaster. Lots of couples enjoyed themselves in the privacy of their suites. And if she liked having people watch, he could live with that too. He supposed.

Shit. She'd said she'd miss him and he hadn't said it back. What if she thought he wouldn't? He pulled out his phone then shoved it back in his pocket. Fuck, he was behaving like an insecure teenager mooning over his first crush.

Focus on the mission. He opened his laptop and pulled up the blueprints for the villa Hunter's people had rented. The plane had begun its descent before Cooper roused.

After a trip to the head, Cooper stopped to glance at Troy's monitor. "I've got an update to that. And a list of people we think are staying there"

The seventy-degree temperature change wasn't as bad as the wall of humidity that slapped Troy in the face. Sweat dripped down his back and beaded in places sweat shouldn't gather. The arrival of a brand-new air-conditioned Jeep had him breathing a sigh of relief. If the gods were kind, they'd knock the temperature down about twenty degrees by the time the attack Cooper had outlined started.

He regretted not forcing himself to nap on the plane when Cooper took him to the Brigade headquarters and immediately launched into yet another briefing. Even though he knew it was critical that he focus on the discussion, he found his mind wandering back to his apartment, imagining Sandy lying in his bed. Would she sleep in her bra and undies? Or would she sleep buck naked the way she did in her own bed? Or maybe she'd pull on one of his T-shirts.

He liked the idea of her wearing his clothes.

"McPherson, you mind joining us here?"

A dozen men and two women stared at him, with Cooper frowning from the far end of the table.

Shit. "Sorry, I didn't get any sleep on the flight down."

The man two to his right snorted at the excuse. Cooper's frown turned into a scowl. "You pay attention and get the details right. Because if you fuck this up for us tonight, your ass is mine."

At Troy's nod, Cooper pulled up the floor plans. "Now, we've got someone on the inside who will leave this side door unlocked. Team A will go in there and proceed to the suite Garcia is supposed to be occupying. Team B will go in through the kitchen area and secure everyone there. Our source says there will always be at least six workers in the kitchen, another four scattered throughout the other rooms."

"Add to that the dozen men Garcia's brought with him." A grizzled vet the others called Sarge and who Troy had learned was Cooper's second-in-command used a laser pointer to highlight their positions.

Troy forced himself to focus on the rest of the briefing. A loss of concentration could cause the death of one of Cooper's team. Or his own. Or worse, it could provide Garcia a weakness to exploit and make an escape. He owed it to Scott, and to Devon, to take Garcia down.

SANDY SET the roller in the paint tray and stepped back. "There, that's a lot nicer, isn't it?"

"I guess." Scott put down his own brush and nodded.

"We can always paint over it if he doesn't like dark green." Jazz looked up from where she'd been painting the baseboard. Well, maybe painting was the wrong term considering she'd been at the same spot for the past hour. What was up with her anyway? She'd been quieter than she'd ever been and she kept disappearing into the bathroom for ages yet claimed she was fine.

"True." Her conscience nagged that she'd guilted Scott into helping pay for the new drapes and the bed frame she'd coaxed him into setting up in Troy's bedroom. "Oh, and Scott? Thanks for helping us do all this instead of kicking me out and protecting Troy's space. If he doesn't like it, we can take everything back. And I promise I'll pay you back either way."

A grin softened the grim expression he usually wore. "I'll admit, your threatening to paint my room pink and plaster Hello Kitty logos all over my stuff was a hell of a motivator." He glanced at the walls they'd already finished painting and scratched the side of his nose with the handle of his brush. "I think he'll like it, although it's sort of hard to tell. I can't remember him ever bothering to decorate any of his places before."

"Never?" Jazz stood with a groan as if she were an eighty-year-old man. "This place was a mausoleum before. How can you live without color?"

One shoulder lifted and dropped. "He's on the road a lot. I think he just uses it as a place to crash. And don't worry about the money. Troy will pay me back. Or he will if he doesn't want me raggin' on him in front of the guys about all his frou-frou cushions."

Sandy shoved him, and to her surprise Scott let her. "Leave my cushions alone. They brighten up the place. Make it more homey."

Once it was dry, she and Jazz could hang those photos she'd framed earlier. She'd spent at least an hour hidden in the bedroom after she'd accidentally found the bag containing dozens of photos. Snapshots of Troy as a baby in the arms of a woman who had to be his mother from the shared hair and eyes. One of a man, perhaps his father, or maybe an uncle standing beside an eight-year-old Troy who looked uncomfortable in an ill-fitting suit. Probably his first communion from the way he held his hands in prayer. Others of him as a teenager, his arm hung over Scott's shoulder, both of them wearing military-school uniforms. Troy had brushed off her questions about his family each time she'd broached the subject. Would Scott?

"So you went to school with Troy, huh?" Was that casual enough?

"Yup." He dipped his brush in the paint and stroked it along the baseboard. "Let me guess, you want to know what he was like as a kid?"

"I'm that obvious, am I?"

"Nah, it's a usual question from girlfriends." His brush stopped moving, and he looked up, eyes wide for a moment. "I mean, it's not like he's, I mean... Shit. He's a guy. He's dated. So have you. Live with it."

Laughing, Sandy held her hand up to stop his explanation. "It's all right. I want to know more about him. Did he like going to the Academy? I mean, I know it was probably better than an orphanage."

Scott resumed painting, letting the quiet stretch for at least five minutes. The brush paused again. "Troy hated the Academy at first. He was good at the drills and keeping his kit neat and stuff, but he hated having anything to do with guns or mortar."

"You'd never know it from the way he handles a pistol." He'd always been cool and confident at the practice range. And from what she'd seen of his silhouettes, an expert marksman.

"He's mighty good with a knife too. Doesn't come easy to him, you know. Not after watching his father murdered in front of his eyes."

She sat cross-legged on the floor. This was what she'd wanted to know but she'd never felt comfortable asking for details from Troy. "What happened?"

"You know he and his parents lived in Northern Ireland, right?" She nodded.

"He's never talked about it, even to me, but the word at the Academy was that his dad was working undercover for the SAS, trying to find those responsible for bombing a British barracks the year before. Somehow his cover got blown. Some locals associated with the IRA ambushed him on the road. Troy was right there when they shot his father in the head point-blank." He dropped the brush back in the jar and stared at it. "He blamed himself for a long time. I think he still does."

"But he was only ten. What could he have done against them?"

"I think he knows he couldn't have stopped them from shooting him. It's more because Troy convinced his father to take him to a friend's house out in the country. His father hadn't wanted to go, but he took him anyway. Turned out the boy who had invited him was the son of one of his father's murderers. Anyway, from what I've heard, the senator was over there on some peace talks between the Brits and the IRA. I always got the feeling he saw Troy as a good publicity opportunity. American senator saves a poor orphaned boy, gets him out of a dangerous situation. You know how these political types like to spin the facts."

"What happened to his mother? Did the IRA kill her too?"

Scott's forehead frowned as he tried to remember. "I think she'd died in a bomb blast a couple months earlier. It may have been longer, I'm not sure. Troy never talks about it and I don't like to ask."

Maybe that's why he seemed so alone. Losing his mom and then watching his father murdered because a friend he'd trusted had betrayed him. No wonder he was so protective of Scott. And so isolated from others.

With a groan, Scott pushed himself to stand and checked his phone. "It's getting late. We should clean all this crap up so you ladies can get home and get your beauty sleep."

"Why don't we both stay here tonight?" Jazz suggested. "That would give us an early start on painting the living room tomorrow instead of wasting time driving back and forth." She glanced between both Scott and Sandy. "Scott, you wouldn't mind the company, would you? We could order pizza and drink beer and watch movies. I can sleep on the couch. If that's all right with both of you."

That would also give them more time to work tonight, but Sandy had been hoping to talk privately to Jazz. Something had been off with her all day.

Scott, you wouldn't mind the company, would you? From beneath her lashes, she watched Scott. Troy had invited him to stay at his place because Scott had nowhere else to go. Now that she thought about it, she'd never once heard Scott talk about family members, and no one other than Hauberk people ever bothered to visit him in the hospital. And Troy had said he still worried about leaving Scott alone. "If it's all right with you, Scott, Jazz can sleep with me in

Troy's bed. It's big enough to sleep six." Yeah, that sounded right. Putting a hand to her aching back, she stretched in an effort to play it casual. "What do you say, Scott? Do you mind if we hang out here with you tonight?"

Scott shrugged. "Yeah, I guess. But we'll have to order dinner in or we'll have to take a trip to the grocery store because we've got zip in the way of food. Hell, we're even out of coffee for tomorrow morning."

Jazz scrambled to her feet. "Tell you what, you order the pizza and I'll pick it up after I've hit the grocery store and bought coffee and whatever else you need."

"All right." He gave her the address of their usual pizza joint, along with a list of the necessities they'd need. "And when you're choosing the coffee, buy French roast, none of that caramel vanilla hazelnut crap."

She was out in the living room and out the front door before either of them could say a word.

Huh. Something was definitely up with her roommate. Oh well, if they were sharing a bed, she was sure she could get Jazz to spill the deets.

"So what's her story?" Scott leaned against the wall then cursed when he remembered it was still wet.

"Jazz?" So she hadn't been the only one to pick up on Jazz's weird mood. "I'm not sure. Did she say anything to you while I was changing this morning?"

"Nope. She stared out the window and didn't say a word." His forehead crinkled. "Sometimes I got the feeling she wanted to say something then she'd change her mind. And now she's all bubbly." He shook his head. "No, that's not the right word. Something's off with her."

"Yeah. I'll talk to her when I get her alone later." Jazz was a lot of things, but he was right, bubbly wasn't the first word that sprang to Sandy's mind either.

~

THE HUMIDITY HADN'T EASED with the setting of
the sun. Sweat trickled down his forehead and leaked into Troy's
eyes. He blinked, trying to lessen the stinging while not losing sight
of the team leader as another member picked the lock to the
compound's kitchen door. Fuck Cooper for placing him with the
secondary team. He'd wanted to be with the primary squad set to
capture Garcia. Instead here he was, skulking around the back of the
estate, his objective to secure the door to the fucking kitchens.
Secure the perimeter his ass. They'd tranquilize any workers they
encountered to prevent them from sounding an alarm, while the
primaries busted into the meeting and got to use the big fucking
guns on the bad guys.

Oh sure, Cooper had promised he'd get to verify Garcia's
identity but only after the fucker was secured.

Big-fucking-whoop.

The team leader dropped his arm and kicked open the door.
The pop of the first tranq sounded quickly, followed by a second,
third and fourth. By the time he made it into the kitchen, the area
had already been secured and the servants, all but one of them
women, were unconscious. Fuck. They'd not even left him a chance
to use his own weapon.

"Hey, new guy." The team leader gestured to him. "Get the
pantry door for us, will you? The rest of you, grab a body and let's
get them locked away before the tranq wears off."

Stalking across the tiled floor, Troy threw open the door to the
pantry. Surprise, surprise. The pantry wasn't empty. A young
woman lay bent over a sack of produce, her skirt up over her hips,
her ass being reamed by none other than Garcia himself.

Ask and He shall deliver. Sorry, Coop. He's mine.

Before Garcia could pull out his dick, Troy squeezed the trigger;
the tranquilizer dart smacked into the woman's buttock. Even as her
eyes glazed, he aimed the gun at Garcia.

No. No tranquilizer for this motherfucker. In the time it took
him to toss his tranq gun aside and unholster his 9 mm, Garcia
grabbed a knife from a nearby shelf and threw it at him. The KA-

BAR whizzed by Troy's head, ruffling his hair as he ducked. It buried itself in the doorframe with a thunk.

"Missed." Troy raised his weapon. "But I won't."

He squeezed the trigger twice. Two holes appeared in Garcia's chest and his eyes widened as he slumped onto the woman's body then slowly toppled to the floor.

Troy walked over and used his foot to turn him over. Blood burbled at the edges of Garcia's mouth. "That's for Devon King and Scott Phillips and for all the others you've tortured and murdered over the years, asshole."

As the light dimmed in Garcia's eyes, Troy placed the barrel of the gun a centimeter away from the man's forehead and pulled the trigger.

The team leader and two of the others crowded the doorway. "What the fuck are you doing? We were to take him alive."

"That was your mission. Not mine."

Leaving the team leader to deal with the body, Troy walked out of the pantry. His footsteps echoed on the slate floors through the kitchen; the rest of the team silently parting to let him pass. As the team leader radioed Cooper to report Garcia's death, Troy opened the door and walked into the night.

He lifted his head and took a deep breath as he stared at the sky. "I got him for you, Scott. Sleep well tonight, buddy."

SIXTEEN

"DON'T WORRY, SANDY." Chad muted the television mounted on his office wall. Not that Sandy needed the sound, the images of the burning cars and dead bodies in the streets of Kinshasa had done their damage. "Troy's smart. He'll lay low and stay out of it."

"How come he's not carrying his satellite phone?" Crap, that made her sound whiny and needy. Three days of silence and she was ready to install handholds on the wall she was about to climb.

"I don't know. Maybe it lost its charge or got busted somehow. Don't read anything into it. Their communications have been shut down by the military." Chad rubbed his shoulder where he'd been shot the previous month. "It's none of my business, but how serious is it between you two?"

Good question. Would she be feeling as queasy if they hadn't been dating? No. She'd been worried about him when he flew to Colombia to rescue the hostages, the whole office had been on edge, but this was different. "I don't know how to answer that. We're dating. We agreed not to see anyone else but neither of us are looking for something long term."

Well, she wasn't. At least she didn't think she was. Troy, she wasn't so sure.

"You realize this is part of his job, Sandy. Part of who he is. If you can't live with it, then it's better to find out now than to expect Troy to change."

She started to say she knew all that, that she didn't want Troy to change when Sam loomed in the doorway, his thick brows drawn together. "Sandy? Can you come in my office for a moment? Chad, you'd better come too."

Oh God, maybe he'd heard something. Chad must have sensed her worry. He wrapped his arm around her shoulder. "He'll be all right."

"You don't know that. You're just saying that."

"He's a survivor. Now let's go into Sam's office and find out for sure, all right?"

Once she was seated in his office, Sam sat at his desk and glanced between Chad and John Lake, his IT manager and fellow Minnesotan, his frown deepening. "First off, Sandy, I want you to know that I consider you a valuable part of this company."

Oh shit. This wasn't about Troy. If it was, John wouldn't be in on the conversation.

"I've never had a problem with your work," he continued. "You're conscientious and you keep this office running better than any previous executive assistant I've had."

"Thank you." Oh, God, this didn't sound good. There was a *but* coming, wasn't there? Was Hauberk having financial difficulties? Was she about to be laid off?

"I know you're trusted with a lot of private information but there are some things in this office that you have no need to know. That's why some files are not open to you."

What was he getting at? "I know."

His brows drew together so hard a line formed between them. "You know John has a program set up to alert us if anyone tries to get into the secure files, don't you?"

"Of course."

"Did you also know we monitor all attempts to access those files?"

"Yes." She shook her head. "What's this about?"

John handed her a printout. "Your ID is shown as trying to access protected files numerous times throughout the weekend."

She flipped through the printouts. Most of it was gibberish but her username had been highlighted in fluorescent pink. The first attempt was Friday night at 11:35 PM, the last Sunday at noon. "There must be some error in the program. I wasn't online at all this weekend. I wasn't even home."

"Sandy, the system logs the IP address of everyone who logs in." John pointed to a number following her username. "Each connection on your ISP is assigned a unique number. And that's the number that comes up every time you log in from home. We checked. Your user name. Your IP number. They all match."

"We need you to be honest with us." Sam pressed his thumbs together as he leaned forward. "We can tell you were looking for the location of our safe houses, Sandy. If that information gets out, that puts our clients and our agents at risk. Are you prepared to accept the responsibility if someone gets killed?"

"This wasn't me, Sam. Honest. I didn't even take my laptop home this weekend. It was sitting right here in the office. You can ask Scott. He'll vouch for me."

"Do you have a password on your router?" John asked.

"Yes, of course. One of your guys set it up for me when I started working here."

"Have you changed the password lately? Or given it to anyone else?" John took over the questions.

"Jazz knows it—we share the apartment—but she doesn't know either my VPN password or my Hauberk passwords. So I don't think it could be her. Besides, she was with me both Saturday and Sunday."

"Is Jazz short for Jasmine? And what's her last name?" Chad tapped the screen on his tablet, Sam ready at his computer.

"Jazz is her nickname. Her real name is Jessica Guidry, but she couldn't have done this. I told you, she was with me all weekend."

Okay, not Friday night but that shouldn't matter, should it? The logins were the entire weekend, not just Friday.

"What does Jessica do, Sandy? Is it possible she needs money?"

Shoot. They'd find out if she lied. "She tells people she works at a call center for a pizza company but she's really an exotic dancer at a place named The Blue Angel off Woodmont. I know she's got money in the bank—she's saving up to go back to college." She leaned forward in her chair. "She doesn't think I know about it though, so please don't tell her."

Sam snorted. "Why the hell do you need to live with a stripper, Sandy? We pay you enough that you could rent your own place."

"Because when I moved here I needed somewhere to live. She was my friend and she offered. And she's still my friend so I don't see why I need to move out. I like having someone there, all right? Holy cow, Sam, I can't believe you're judging her like this. She's trying to find another job but she doesn't have many skills other than being able to dance so it's not like there's a lot out there, especially in this economy."

"I'm not judging her. But why the deception, Sandy? Why lie to you about it?" Sam asked.

"You'd have to ask her, but I've always assumed it's because she was embarrassed about it."

"How long have you known her?" Chad asked this time.

"In person, since I moved to D.C. three years ago, but we'd been chatting online a couple years before that. She's a good person and I like her a lot. She gets me."

John cleared his throat. "Do you write your passwords down, Sandy?"

Thankful that he was getting the conversation off of Jazz, Sandy held up her spiral-bound notebook. "Do you have any idea how many passwords I have? I have the laptop's power-on password, which is different from my VPN password. Then there's my email password, the password to Sam's email for when I have to check it for him. Not to mention Chad's password, and Troy's. And all my personal email addys. I can't keep track of them all. They change every month, and none of them make any sense. I can't remember passwords that are nonsense like Tm79Bx3. It's impossible to remember them all."

"Where was your notebook this weekend?"

"On my desk at home. I went out Friday night, came home to pick up a change of clothes on Saturday morning and Jazz left with me. The apartment has been empty and the security system turned on since then. So unless there was a burglar—which your security system should have registered—no one could have used it." Damn, now she was getting pissed. "Look, I really think you're barking up the wrong tree here."

"We're hoping we are." John's patient manner only served to tick her off more. "Does anyone else have the password to your router? Because they could access it without actually getting into your apartment."

Oh. All right, now she saw what he was getting at, she calmed down. "Jazz's boyfriend has used our system to check his email. Well, he was her boyfriend but they broke up Friday night." Something big must have happened but Jazz had refused to say exactly what. She wondered if perhaps it had something to do with this. But wouldn't Jazz have told her? "His name is Mitch Young. He's a fund manager at some financial firm in Silver Springs. I don't know anything more about him, but Jazz could tell you."

Chad tapped Mitch's name into the search box and pressed Go. "We'll check him out. How about any other friends who've stayed over and needed to check their email?"

"Maybe a couple friends." She gave John their names. "Jazz may have told a couple of her friends too. But that only lets them get on the router not into the Hauberk system, right? Because I swear I've never given my Hauberk passwords to anyone. And if someone did get in, they wouldn't have to do it from my apartment, would they? They could be in Asia or Europe and send out some false signal making it look like they're in the area, couldn't they?"

"They could, but they aren't," John said quietly. "We've tracked the hacker and every single time we've traced him back to your location. I'm sorry, Sandy, but we use state-of-the-art tracking systems. They're not wrong."

Oh crap. There had to be some other explanation.

A moment passed, and another before Sam broke the silence. "Is there anyone else who has a key to your apartment and would know the code to the security system?"

"Just Jazz knows the code, of course. And I'm assuming the landlord has a key. And I guess someone here at Hauberk probably knows the security code?" Troy had it too, but since he was out of the country, there was no need to mention him, right?

"Is Jazz home right now?"

"No, she said she's got a doctor's appointment this afternoon."

"All right." Chad looked between Sandy and Sam. "I want to send Scott and Andy and one of John's technicians over to your place to check out the system. Maybe one of her neighbors is piggybacking off the connection." He looked directly at Sandy. "They'll check your router's security and set you up with another system."

"Of course. Let me get my key."

Chad held up his hand before she stood. "One other thing, who else knew you were going to be away for the weekend? It's possible that whoever you were with deliberately invited you so they could use your system without interference."

"Scott invited me to stay at Troy's place so we could paint it while he was away." It wasn't a lie. Exactly.

"Chad, why don't you get started on checking on Miss Guidry and her boyfriend? John, have your guys look into Sandy's work laptop." Sam locked his gaze with hers. "I want to talk to Sandy alone for a moment."

Once the door closed behind them, Sam sat back in his chair. "You may have been with Scott and your friend Jazz on Saturday and Sunday but you were with Troy Friday night. I find it interesting that you failed to mention that detail. Anything you care to tell me?"

"That's really none of your business."

His jaw jutted out for a second before he nodded. "Just tell me he didn't force you to go there."

There was no use asking where *there* was. But how did he know?

"Of course I wasn't forced to go. Troy wouldn't do that." Oh God. What if Sam had been one of the members who had been watching them? Her cheeks burned red hot. Damn her father for passing on his fair skin. "You weren't there, watching, were you?"

A strange look crossed his face and he mouthed *watching*. "No, I wasn't *watching*. I wasn't even in the damned house—no one was allowed in until after midnight. But I did see you get out of the limo and walk up to the front door."

No one was allowed in? But that couldn't be right. There had been people there. She'd heard them.

"Damn it, Sandy." Sam tossed his pen onto the desk. "I hope you both know what you're doing, because if this whatever you have with Troy goes sour, I don't want to lose either of you."

"I have no plans to leave Hauberk, but again, not your business. And you have no right to judge considering you're dating one of your employees."

"Fine. You've made your point, now why don't you go back to your desk? John's people need that key to your apartment."

Sandy stood, wanting to say something more, but Sam had already picked up his phone. Fuck it. If he didn't like that she was seeing Troy, that was his problem. If he didn't like the idea of them going to the club, that was his problem too. She returned to her desk to find one of the computer geeks in the process of unhooking her laptop from its docking station.

"I'll only be a minute. We're switching it out with a new one so we can run diagnostics on yours and make sure the hacker didn't leave any password programs behind. Make sure you don't download anything onto the new one, will you?"

∼

HIS TRICEPS BURNING, Scott flexed his fingers around the barbell and finished the last of his reps. Where the hell was Troy? He was damned sure he wasn't anywhere near the Congo as he'd told both him and Sandy. But where was he? And why the hell hadn't he at least texted Sandy to let her know he was all right? Damn it, the man hadn't a clue about communication some days.

"I tried to reach you Friday night. Where were you?"

Scott glanced at Andy as he set his barbell back on the rack. "I was busy."

"I didn't have to be a cop to make that assumption." Andy lowered his voice, "I figured you were up at the club since you weren't answering your phone or your texts."

Shit. All he needed was Andy digging into his whereabouts. The cop could be like a pitbull some days. "What did you want?"

Before he could answer, Chad appeared at the gym's door. "Scott. Andy. Hit the showers then come into Sam's office for a minute, will you? We've got a job for you."

Less than ten minutes later, Scott followed Andy into Hauberk's management sanctum. He slowed as he passed Sandy's desk, concerned about the way she avoided looking up at them, instead of greeting them with her normal bright smile. "You all right, Sandy?"

"Fine." Except she didn't raise her eyes.

If there was someone less fine, it was the woman in front of him. What the hell was going on? Shit, had something happened to Troy?

"Sandy?" He crouched down beside her and softly asked, "Come on, honey, what's wrong?"

"I'm fine." Tread carefully. He'd learned long ago that when women said they were fine, they meant the opposite. From the way she snapped out the words, something definitely wasn't fine in Sandy's world.

"Scott? You coming?" Andy called from the doorway to Sam's office.

"Yeah, in a minute." He stayed squatting in front of her. "Come on, Sandy. Talk to me."

Her eyes rose to meet his gaze. Instead of the tears he'd expected, her whole expression blazed with anger. "Someone hacked my Hauberk account. They've been using my system to look for Hauberk's safe houses. If I get my hands on the douchebag who did it, I'll cut his balls off."

Shit. At least it was something containable, not that Troy had been hurt or broken up with her or anything. "It's okay, beautiful. We'll cut them off for you. And look at it this way—it could have been worse. They could have gotten to you."

"Yeah, I know you're right. I feel violated."

The mood inside Sam's office was grim. There were no chairs left so he and Andy stood by the closed door. Chad was already there, looking just as pissed off as Scott felt. The IT manager, John Lake, occupied the other visitor's chair, his grey hair sticking up on end, bags under his eyes from too many long nights from the looks of it. Frustration radiated from Sam as he stared out the window, his fists balled on his thighs.

"Gentlemen, we believe we have a possible suspect as our hacker. One Mitch Young—he's been dating Sandy's roommate Jessica Guidry. Scott, I understand you've met her? And that she was with you and Sandy this weekend?"

"Yeah, though I was told her name was Jazz. As far as I know, she was in the apartment alone when I was there Saturday morning. I guess it's possible someone was in her bedroom but I didn't see anyone."

"How'd she act when you arrived?"

Guilty, now he looked back on it. "She was jumpy. She didn't want to get near me. Kept her back to me and stared out the window until Sandy mentioned she wanted to go back to Troy's and paint. All of a sudden Jazz was all 'hey, I want to help' and next thing she was packed and pushing Sandy and me out the door as if she couldn't get out of the place quick enough. Rest of the weekend, she was hard to judge. Sometimes she was real quiet, others fidgety. Come to think of it, it was like she was nervous. Sandy figured it was probably because she and her boyfriend had had a fight but now I'm wondering."

Sam withdrew the cigar he habitually kept in his shirt pocket and toyed with it. From the teeth marks on the end, Scott wondered if it was the same one he'd kept in his pocket for the last six months, ever since he'd promised Rosie he'd give up smoking. "D'you think she was trying to distract Sandy and used that as an excuse to keep her away from their place?"

He lifted one shoulder for a second and let it drop in a half-hearted shrug. "Could be."

"All right, then for now we'll treat them both as suspects." Chad thumbed the button on his phone. Both Scott and Andy pulled out their notebooks to take their own notes. "Here's what we've found out so far. Jessica Ann Guidry. Twenty-eight years old. Single. Never married. No criminal record. No outstanding warrants or arrests. A couple speeding tickets over the period of five years. Not a registered voter. According to Sandy, she's currently employed as a dancer at the Blue Angel out in Alexandria."

Andy hissed in a breath. "That's a rough joint. Or it used to be back when I was on the force."

"Dancer?" Scott leaned forward, glancing between his partner and his boss. "Am I right in thinking by dancer you're talking exotic?"

"Yup, the Blue Angel is G-string and pasties optional. We busted quite a few of their girls for their extra services—" Andy curled his fingers and made air quotes, "—while I was in Vice. Bouncers didn't enforce the no-touch rules. Owner didn't care either. I've heard that the owner sold out last year so I guess it's possible they've cleaned up their act."

"When Sandy introduced us, she said Jazz works at a call center and Jazz didn't correct her." Then again, would a woman volunteer she was a possible hooker to someone like him?

Chad's scowl deepened. "Apparently Ms. Guidry prefers not to tell her best friend her real profession and Sandy lets her get away with it."

"So we're keeping her on the list of suspects," Sam added. "If she's lyin' about that who knows what else she's lyin' about."

Chad turned back to his report. "Parents are divorced. Father's last known address was in Richmond, Virginia, dropped off the radar approximately twelve years ago. Mother currently resides in Ocala, Florida, and works as a housekeeper at a no-name motel. From what we've been able to dig up so far, until she started working as a dancer four years ago, she was habitually late paying her credit cards. She's now got over twenty grand in a bank account and her credit cards are at a zero balance. Mostly cash deposits from the looks of it, so there's no way to check if she's making her money from more than just stripping."

"Maybe she wants to get out of the dancing business," Andy speculated. "If someone offered her enough money for access to the router and Sandy's accounts."

"Talk to her and see if she'll tell you anything." Chad dragged his thumb across his phone's screen. "Our other suspect is Ms. Guidry's former boyfriend. Goes by the name of Mitchell Young. But he's lied about his name–the Mitchell Young who works at ITF is African American. The guy we're after is Caucasian."

"Maybe that's why Jazz broke up with him. Maybe she found out he'd lied to her." Or maybe she'd tried to blackmail him and he'd broken it off. Or maybe he'd simply decided to move on to the next chicky.

"Sandy got any pictures of him? Of either of them?"

"We have one of Ms. Guidry—I'm forwarding it to your email —but nothing for our alleged hacker, even on social media. Sandy's given us a description of him so we'll have to go on that for now. " He consulted his notes. "Five-ten, maybe five-eleven, around two hundred pounds, Caucasian. Mid thirties."

"Maybe Ms. Guidry's got at least one on her phone."

"Here's hoping."

"So the question is," Scott interrupted, "is *Young* working on his own or for someone else?"

And had Jazz helped him? It cheesed him off that she had sat there the entire weekend, pretending to be Sandy's friend, when the whole time she'd been using Sandy's connections.

"That's what we want you two to find out." Chad held up a key. "Sandy's given us a key to her place. I want you to go over there and see if you can lift some fingerprints and perhaps find anything else that might be of interest while Miss Guidry is working." In other words, toss Jazz's room for evidence she was in on the plot. Although all she'd had to do was copy Sandy's list of passwords, so unless they found that, Scott doubted they'd find anything incriminating.

"Dan Bridges is going to go with you to check out Sandy's router," the IT manager added. "We need to make sure her security password is changed on her router and he's also going to check to see if there are any network extenders hidden anywhere nearby. Who knows, maybe it's one of her neighbors."

"How do we know it's not someone spoofing the IP address?"

John went into a long explanation that lost Scott within the first five words but Andy seemed to follow all the geek speak. From the way John responded, his partner was asking intelligent questions. Huh, who knew the former cop was a closet geek?

Twenty minutes later while Andy drove a plain white van, Scott scrolled through the files on Jazz.

Andy checked over his shoulder at the tech then lowered his voice. "I saw Sandy's roommate at the bar. She hit on Kris. He liked her. Said he wouldn't have pegged her as the type to use her friends."

Scott grunted. "What about you? Did you peg her as being a stripper and possibly a hooker?"

"No, and, not all dancers earn their money on their back. A lot of them are students trying to pay for college."

"If you say so, but I'm not ruling anyone out. It says a shitload about her character as far as I'm concerned." Shit. Had she snooped around Troy's place for info? What if she'd been snooping around, letting them think she was going to the bathroom?

What type of agent was he that he hadn't picked up that she was no good? A fucking useless agent. Just like he'd been to Dev in Colombia. "It pisses me off that she lied to Sandy. That she may have used her."

"Look, this guy lied to her, and to Sandy, even to Troy. If Troy didn't suspect him, why would she? Besides, Sandy said they'd broken up. Maybe she found out something and dumped his sorry butt. First rule of investigation is don't assume. So don't judge her guilty yet. Not until you've heard her story."

"You can pamper her all you want, but I'm not buying her shit."

"I guess that means I'm playing the good cop today."

Didn't he always?

Never had he been so glad to arrive at a potential crime site as he had when Andy pulled into Sandy's parking lot. He grabbed the fingerprint kit and headed up to the third floor, Andy behind him. Who gave a fuck if they'd left the tech to struggle with his equipment by himself? Being on the move, having a mission, helped him focus and let him shove his ire at Jazz aside.

Upon reaching Sandy's door, Scott bent down to examine the brass casing around the lock. The brass gleamed bright compared to the dulled finish of the other apartments' locks. From the security report Chad had given him, the alarm system in Sandy's apartment had only been installed a few weeks before, and the new deadbolt had been installed at the same time. Troy's doing, no doubt. "Doesn't look like it's been picked."

The geek shifted his case from one arm to the other. Whatever the tech carried had to weigh fifty pounds. If he didn't think to put it down while he waited, that was his own damned fault. Laughing to himself, Scott ran a hand along the metal framework. "Hard to tell if someone used a 2x4 to pop the frame but it doesn't look like it."

Probably wouldn't work. He'd bet the new deadbolt would be a good two inches long.

"Of course, they could have used a bump key," Andy helpfully suggested. From the way he choked out the suggestion, Andy had realized Scott's delaying tactics and was equally amused by the tech's cluelessness. "That wouldn't leave any mark."

"I suppose that's true." He stared down the hall and scratched his nose. "Maybe we should interview the neighbors to see if they've noticed anyone hanging around."

"We should interview the superintendent too. Maybe see if there's any security cameras or anything around?" Andy made a studied inspection of the ceilings as if he were searching for cameras. It was the tech's own fault for not noticing his partner's shoulders shaking in his futile attempt to stop himself from laughing out loud.

"All right already. You can make love to the doorframe all you want, and I can tell myself there aren't any security cameras," the tech groused. "Just let me get in the damned place and put this damned equipment down, would you? It's fuckin' heavy."

Scott unlocked the door and stepped inside to disable the security system. While the tech unpacked his equipment, the two operatives set to work dusting for prints. Scott concentrated on the area around the lock and the frame; Andy dusted the router and the modem.

"Probably wasting my time," the tech grumbled. "I bet they don't have the WPA turned on, so whoever's in the neighborhood can steal her bandwidth."

"You'd lose the bet, kid." Andy held up his phone. "I already checked. The security is activated and password set."

"Big deal. I'll bet she's used 'password' as her password. People think they're so fucking clever."

Scott tuned him out as he lifted the prints off the inside of the door. The prints scanned and emailed to the office, he finally investigated the apartment. From the knickknacks on the windowsill to the quilted pillows to the photos on the bright freshly painted walls, the place screamed *Sandy was here*. No wonder Troy had been spending more time over here than he had been at his own place.

By the time he'd finished dusting Jazz's room for prints, he was ready to punch a hole in the wall. How dare she lie to Sandy? Use Sandy to earn money or whatever the hell her motivation was. Worse, he'd bought into her act hook, line and fucking sinker. When the fuck was he going to learn that you couldn't trust anyone?

Finished lifting prints from its case, Andy examined the router and read out the model number.

"Yeah, that's a wireless N router." The tech opened a case and withdrew an electrical wand to check for electrical devices. "Company claims you can get a signal from about fourteen hundred feet away, unobstructed of course."

"So it's possible our guy could have sat in the parking lot right below and accessed it?"

"Yeah, it's possible. There may be an extender to boost the signal that may have given him an even wider area. That's what I'm checking for now. But I'm betting whoever it was sat right there on the couch." Dan waved the device over the desk. When he didn't get any reaction, he started scanning around the door to the balcony.

"What the fuck are you doing in my place?" An extremely pissed Jazz Guidry stood in the doorway, her hand in her pocket as if she were clutching a can of Mace. Possibly a taser? If she were really smart, she would have walked right on by and contacted the police without them knowing, instead of confronting them. The color drained from her face. "Oh my God. Scott! Is Sandy okay?"

She was either sincerely worried about Sandy or she was a helluva good actress, Scott had to admit. He bet on the latter. "Sandy's all right. But we need to ask you a few questions about your relationship with Mitchell Young."

"Mitch?" Her voice was thready and her color hadn't returned. "He didn't come back and hurt her, did he?"

Hurt her? Shit. Just what the fuck type of person was this Mitchell if that was her first question?

SEVENTEEN

"WHERE IS SHE? I want to see her." If Mitch had come back, if he'd hurt Sandy...oh God. Two seconds before her mouth had been dry, now she had to swallow convulsively or throw up. She clutched her purse as her knees wobbled beneath her.

"Whoa, hang on there, Miss Guidry. Sandy's fine." The other guy—not Scott—caught her arm and led her to the couch. "Put your head between your knees and breathe in nice and slow for me."

He pressed her head down before she could object, then crouched in front of her as she gulped in air. "Slow down or you'll feel worse. Just inhale, then exhale."

"Oh, for fuck's sake. It's all an act," Scott snarled. "She copied Sandy's passwords and gave them to her boyfriend and is now pretending to be all upset to try and throw us off."

He stomped off to the bedroom. Her bedroom, not Sandy's. Why was he going in there? And what was his problem with her all of a sudden. He'd been so nice to her over the weekend. She lowered her head to her knees again, wondering if she'd ever learn not to trust guys.

"Come on, Jessica, don't worry about him." His partner touched her knee to get her attention. "Look at me, honey."

Her head fuzzy, she raised her eyes to meet his. He was kinda cute in a rough sort of way. There was a scar over his left eye cutting through his eyebrow, and his goatee had a lot of red in it while his hair was a sort of sandy brown. Just like the guy... "Hey, I know you."

"I've seen you at Rusty's a couple times. I'm Andy Walters. Now take a deep breath for me, Jessica." She did and he smiled. He had a nice smile. The type that probably made people tell him secrets without thinking. Which meant she had to be on her guard.

"It's Jazz. I hate being called Jessica."

"All right, Jazz it is then." He picked up Xander, who wound around her feet. The traitor of a cat began purring at the first scratch behind his ears. "Who's this?"

"Xander. I named him after the guy in Buffy the Vampire Slayer because he's only got one eye too."

"Can't say I've ever seen that show. What night's it on?" Andy's obvious attempt to put her at ease worked.

"It's not on anymore." She was just starting to breathe normally when Scott reappeared with her laptop under his arm.

He set it on the kitchen table and hit the power button. "What's your power-on password?"

"I don't have one." Was she supposed to have one? It's not like she had any state secrets on her hard drive. Shoot. They'd find that damned video clip Mitch had sent her the next morning. Oh God. Had Mitch posted it somewhere like he'd threatened? Maybe sent it to Sandy? From the snippet she'd managed to view, she'd looked like she was consenting. That she'd enjoyed what he'd done. Maybe Sandy had shown it to her boss and they'd done a credit check on her. Her employer would show up on a credit check, wouldn't it? Fuck. "Look, I can explain..."

"You don't need to. We figured it out. Either you showed your boyfriend where Sandy keeps her passwords or you copied them yourself and gave them to him. All we haven't figured out yet is what you're looking for."

"I never gave—" *You showed your boyfriend where Sandy keeps her passwords.* Crap. She *had* shown Mitch where Sandy kept her passwords. And he'd always booted up his laptop as soon as he'd arrived after that. Crap. Crap. Crap.

"Yeah, okay, he knew about her notebook but I didn't mean to show it to him. He was teaching me how to create videos with this new software I got. We'd put some pictures we'd fixed on a flashdrive and Sandy left it somewhere on the desk. If he used the passwords to hack into your system, I didn't know about it."

Still holding Xander, Andy exchanged a glance with the geek who was waving some wand straight out of Ghostbusters over the top of the bookcase. "A flashdrive? Do you know if Mitch ever used it on his computer?"

"Yeah, it was his." Oh crap and a half. He'd played her for the sucker she was. God, what a fucking idiot, she'd been.

"He probably had a password collecting program on it then. He wouldn't have needed the list at all if that's the case." The ghostbusting geek put down his wand and started searching the desk.

"He may not have captured the passwords he needed," Andy suggested. "Maybe Sandy didn't log onto the network while he was collecting them or maybe she didn't check Sam's email or whatever it was he was looking for. Or maybe she changed her passwords because the thirty days were up. After all, he didn't get into her system until this weekend, right?"

"No," the geek said with exaggerated patience. "We didn't notice that someone was using Sandy's access until this weekend. For all we know he could have been using those passwords for days. Weeks. Months, even."

"Excuse me," Jazz raised her voice over the lecture. "Will someone please explain what's going on?"

"As if you don't know. Why don't you tell us what he's after, sweetheart?" Scott snapped.

"Okay, I get it. Someone's been accessing confidential files within the Hauberk network using Sandy's ID. But what makes you think it was Mitch? For all you know, it could be someone over in

Europe or China or somewhere who guessed her password." Even as she said it, she knew it was Mitch.

"Because the connection was traced to this router's IP address."

"Can't that be faked?" Damn it, she should have paid more attention to that computer course she took at night school. And the computer geeks who were always pestering her for a date.

"It wasn't. Our IT guys checked it out," Andy said. Shit.

"Since you're the only one who lives here with Sandy, you're in the perfect position to steal her passwords, wouldn't you say?" Scott set the laptop aside and walked over to her, bracing a hand on the couch, his knees on either side of hers, boxing her in.

Jazz couldn't stop herself from shrinking back. Damn it, what was it with guys bullying her? Did she have a sign on her forehead or something? "I didn't steal anything."

"We've figured out your game, sweetheart. Now why don't you make it easy on everyone and tell us what you or your boyfriend want from Hauberk's database?"

Her mouth went dry. Crap, he really did suspect her. "I told you. If Mitch hacked into the system, I didn't know about it and I don't know why."

His expression hard, Scott leaned down until his mouth hovered less than an inch away from her ear and whispered, "I don't believe you."

"Scott. Back off. You're scaring her."

"No. He's not scaring me. He's pissing. Me. Off." Jazz flattened her hands over Scott's chest and pushed. Although she hadn't expected to move him, he dropped his arm and stepped back with a scowl.

"Jazz," Andy said softly, "what we need to know is if you have any idea what your boyfriend might be looking for."

She shifted so her back didn't touch the couch anymore. She hadn't needed to see the welts and bruising in the bathroom mirror to be reminded of that night. Her shirt rubbing against her skin did that for her. "I have no idea. And he's not my boyfriend anymore. As I told this asshole on Saturday, I broke up with him and kicked him out of this place Friday night. He's history." Except he hadn't really left, had he?

"Yeah, yeah, cry me a fuckin' river." Scott rubbed his thumb and forefinger together. "Enough with the violins and tell us the truth for once in your goddamned pathetic life."

Andy turned to Scott with a scowl. "Did you ever consider that maybe she is telling the truth?"

"Oh, give me a fucking break and don't buy into her shit, Walters. She's a hooker. She's not about to tell you the truth. Look how she's been lying to Sandy about what she really does for a living."

Oh, fuck. They did know about her stripping. She'd known it was only a matter of time before someone found out. "I'm not a hooker. I'm a dancer."

"You take your clothes off for money and give people lap dances. I'm betting for a couple extra bucks you let them fuck you too."

"Yeah, I take my clothes off for money and let guys watch. You know why? Because it pays me a helluva lot more than I'd make as a waitress." Fuck this. He wasn't the only one who could play domination games. She stood up and strode over to Scott. With her heels on, she was almost as tall as he was. "And do you know what else? I like it. I like knowing that guys get off watching me dance." She skimmed a hand down her belly. "I'm proud of my body. I'm not ashamed of what I do, and you're not going to change that. But the guys who get to watch me, don't get to touch me. Ever."

"If you're not ashamed, why did you lie about it to Sandy?"

Damn it, she wanted to wipe that smug sneer off his face. "Because not everyone gets that stripping isn't hooking." *Like you, asshole.* "And when Sandy moved to D.C., I thought she was this prairie princess that would move out if she found out she was living with a stripper."

She knew better now, but once the lie had been told, she hadn't figured out how to un-tell it.

Andy wedged himself between them. "We all tell lies, Scott. This one didn't hurt anyone."

How did such a reasonable guy deal with being partnered with such an assho—oh crap, that's what this was. They were playing good cop/bad cop on her.

"Look, Mitch was always on his computer while he was here, I admit, but he never once said anything about it. All he told me was he had stock indexes in Tokyo he had to keep an eye on."

"Can you describe him for me? How tall was he? How much does he weigh, what color is his hair, that type of thing."

"I don't know. Five foot eleven, maybe. A hundred and ninety, two hundred maybe. But he's strong." Too strong. "He's got short brown hair. He said he was thirty-three."

"Do you know where he lives?"

"He said he has a condo in Silver Springs but I've never been there." Why was that? And why hadn't she wondered about it before? "He works as a fund manager with some financial group there too. ITF Group? ITR maybe. Something like that. That was a lie too, wasn't it?"

As Andy nodded, Scott pulled out his phone and walked into the hall, speaking into it in muted tones so she couldn't hear.

Andy touched her knee, bringing her attention back to him. "You said you broke up with him Friday night?"

Even though she knew it was probably an act, Andy seemed gentler. Safer. Which was strange because he was so much bigger than her. Bigger than Mitch. Who had hurt... *God, no, don't remember that night.* Jazz closed her eyes. "He was sitting in his car waiting for me when I got home from work." Shit. She looked up at him, eyes wide. Had he been hacking into Hauberk even then? "He had his laptop out. But I didn't see what he was working on. He always closed the top whenever I was around." Which should have tipped her off Friday night.

"Don't worry about it for now," Andy said softly. "You came home, he was waiting for you and then what happened?"

"He said we had a date but I don't remember making one with him. I'd told him last weekend I'd wanted to slow things down. He was starting to crowd me, you know? He was always over here. I needed space." And he needed her connection to Hauberk. Not her.

"Okay. Keep going."

God, she'd been so blind. Should she tell them what he'd done to her? No, they wouldn't believe her. Scott already thought she was a hooker. "I let him in for a while, but then I realized I was right about breaking things off, so I kicked him out and said I never wanted to see him again."

Scott had returned. "But you saw him again, didn't you?"

"He was in the parking lot on Saturday." Maybe he'd never left. But seeing his car parked right there beneath her balcony had made up her mind when Sandy had returned to pick up some clothes. "Wait a minute, he made a call Friday night after..." *He hurt me.* "Before I kicked him out. I only heard his side of the conversation so I don't know who he was talking to, but he mentioned something about getting an address and then the money. He seemed worried, like there was a deadline and the other guy wasn't being reasonable."

After sharing a look with Scott, Andy placed Xander on her lap. "Okay, that's good. That tells us a lot."

It did?

"Now we need you to tell us about any conversations you've had with him. His background, if he mentioned any family or legal problems, anything that may tell us what he's trying to find in Hauberk's system."

"WE GOT a match on the fingerprints we took from Sandy's apartment."

Sandy stood when Andy and Scott walked into Chad's office but Chad waved for her to keep her seat.

Andy pulled out his notebook. Considering all the electronic equipment Hauberk issued their agents, Sandy found it amusing he kept his notes on an old-fashioned spiral-bound pad similar to hers.

"Mitchell Young is actually Michael Rowlands, the soon-to-be ex of Janice Rowlands."

"So he's looking for our safe-house locations." At Sandy's questioning look, Chad explained, "Janice Rowlands is one of our clients. She left her husband when he was named a person of interest in an investment swindle. Turned out, he'd put all his assets in his wife's name, including an off-shore account where he stashed his money. He was threatening her to try to force her to sign it back over to him so he can pay off some of the more important clients."

"So the whole thing has been about money?" Sandy knew she shouldn't be surprised, but damn it, having her privacy violated should be for something important. National security or something. Instead some investment banker with no sense of morals and his greedy wife were battling over the money he'd stolen. The bastard had been in her home. Eaten her food. Listened to her and Troy making love.

"It's more complicated than just money, Sandy. From what a little dicky-bird in the D.A.'s office told me, one of Rowlands's victims had a strong *familial* connection if you catch my drift. The D.A. couldn't assure us her location wouldn't leak from their office, so we've given her an alias and kept her in a safe house until it's time for the trial. That's why you don't recognize the name."

"Oh Christ, he ripped off the Mafia?" Scott formed his thumb and finger into an L over his forehead. "No wonder he's so anxious to find his wife."

Chad fiddled with his gold pen. "So now we know what he wants, how do we reel him in?"

"Why couldn't you leave a file open with a fake address for his wife that he can find next time he hacks into the system?"

"Oh, we'll do that. Trouble is considering how he's not been able to find the information before, he may realize it's a trap and not fall for it. So we need to have a contingency plan."

The discussion ended up involving the IT manager as well as Sam Watson, so Sandy returned to her desk when the meeting moved to Sam's office.

EIGHTEEN

THE BRIGADE'S team crowded the old wooden table, some standing, all of them shooting him dark looks. Troy hung back. He wasn't part of the team, his input wasn't needed. And hell if he wanted to be. The humidity slapped him like a wet towel as he stepped from the entrance of the ancient Quonset hut the Brigade had appropriated as their headquarters. He'd grown soft living in London and Washington.

He pulled out his satellite phone and dialed the area code to his home then stopped, unable to recall the number. It took thumbing through his call history to find where Scott had phoned him from home to find the number. Partway through the second ring, the beautiful Minnesotan voice he'd needed to hear answered with a breathless hello. Sandy was at his place? Maybe sleeping in his bed? God, he was so down with that. "Hey, sunshine. How you doing?"

"Troy? Are you okay?" There was an anxiousness to her voice that hadn't been there when he'd left.

"I'm fine. Why? Did you miss me?" *Please say yes*.

"I was worried when I saw the news reports this morning. They said there are hundreds of people dead, that they're calling for air strikes to quell the rebels. When you didn't phone, I thought...I was afraid you'd been hurt." Or worse.

News reports? Hundreds dead? Shit! There must have been an uprising against the latest regime. Served him right for being out of the loop and not checking his cover before phoning home. "I swear I'm fine. Not a scratch on me. Just haven't had cell service, that's all. I didn't mean to worry you." Here's hoping she didn't realize he was on his satellite phone.

"Good. I was really worried about you. Are you going to be home soon?"

Home. Huh. Strange how he'd never thought of Washington or even his flat in London as home. But knowing she was there, waiting for him, thinking of him made him hope that perhaps, for the first time in decades, maybe he did have a home. "I'm flying out in a couple hours. I'll be home tonight."

There it was again. Home. Fuck that felt nice to say.

"What time does your flight come in? I want to meet you at the airport."

She did? He'd never had anyone meet him before. "You don't have to do that."

"I want to. Are you flying into Dulles or Reagan?"

"I'll text you with the details when I know them."

"Good." There was a long pause. "Where are you right now? Somewhere safe?"

As safe as could be given the circumstances. He wandered over to a bench beneath the spreading branches of a monkeypod tree. "I'm outside of the city at a private airstrip." *Stay as close to the truth as you can when lying.* "I'm sitting under a tree, watching the sunset. It's beautiful."

He closed his eyes and pictured her. Wished she were with him. Not in Val Varde but on a secluded beach. Hawaii or the Virgin Islands perhaps. "Where are you? In my bedroom?"

Her soft laughter floated through the connection and lightened his mood. "You betcha. You want to guess what I'm wearing?"

Phone sex. Over thousands of miles and who knew how many satellite connections. God, he loved her. Loved how she made nothing else matter. How she could make him smile when five minutes before he didn't think he had it in him to ever smile again. "Let me guess—you're completely naked. Wearing only your belly button ring."

"Lucky guess."

What he'd give to be there right now. "I'm a lucky guy."

"What would you do if you were here?"

He'd hold her. Bury his nose in her hair and know there was something good in the world, something clean and innocent. "I'd kiss the tip of your nose."

"Oh." She sounded disappointed. "Is that all?"

"Oh, no. That's just the start. After I kissed the tip of your nose, I'd offer you some wine and then after you'd had a sip, I'd kiss you."

"Red or white wine?"

Interesting that she'd ignored that he'd kiss her. "A chardonnay."

"Full bodied?" she suggested.

"They're the best."

Light spilled across the compound when someone opened the hut's door. Davis. Who headed straight for him. "I'm sorry, sunshine. I have to go. I'll see you soon."

JAZZ PEEKED through the security hole before unlocking the door.

One hand shoved in his pocket, the other holding a backpack, Andy Walters grinned. "Good job on checking me out first. Troy teach you that?"

"No." Not wanting to let Mitch back into her apartment taught her that. Instead of inviting him in, she kept her arm on the door and her body blocking the entrance. "Sandy's not here. She stayed at Troy's last night."

"I know. I'm not here to see Sandy. I thought you'd like to know what we've found out about Mitch, and to ask a favor of you."

He wasn't going to go away unless she let him in, was he? With a sigh, she closed the door so she could remove the chain then opened it again and stepped aside to let him in. "I don't see how I can help."

"Let's sit down and I'll tell you what we've got planned. How's that sound?"

Oh great. He was still playing the "good cop" role. "Sure, why not?"

After setting his bag on the floor, Andy moved aside the pile of magazines and perched on the edge of the coffee table in front of her the way he had earlier. Xander, the traitor, jumped down off his perch on the couch to rub against Andy's leg.

"I thought you would like to know what we found out since we were here earlier." Without looking down, Andy scratched the cat's ears, setting off Xander's loud purr. "First off, Mitch's real name is Michael Rowlands and he's in trouble with a lot of people."

Oh crap. "I didn't know that—"

"I know. He fooled a lot of people. So don't you worry about that."

Had he hurt anyone else the way he'd hurt her, she wondered. "So what's he done?"

"He and a business partner ran a Ponzi scheme that ripped off a lot of people for millions of dollars. He's facing charges as well as threats from various sources."

By the time he finished his recitation of what Mitch had done, and why he had used her—and Sandy's passwords—Jazz was confused. "So why are you here? It doesn't sound like there's anything I can do."

"We were hoping you'd help us set up a sting so we can catch him. All you'd have to do is invite him over here. Make it sound like Sandy's left for the evening and you're home alone. Maybe say you need more help with editing those videos."

"I don't think he'd buy me asking him over. Not after I told him I never wanted to see him again. Besides, I don't want to see him again. Ever. So if you're planning on using me as bait, I don't think I can help you." She'd probably throw up if she had to see Mitch again.

Despite the genial expression on his face, his body went on alert and his eyes searched hers. Yet his voice was gentle when he spoke, "He might wonder at your change of heart, but I'm betting that he'll buy into it hook, line and sinker. I think he'd jump at a chance to get inside Hauberk's system again." He dropped his eyes and focused on the sleeves falling over her knuckles. Even though they covered the marks left by the handcuffs, she fought the urge to pull the fabric down farther. "These types of guys, they're on a power trip and they think they pull all the strings. I've seen it before."

So had she. "I am not crawling back to him to save your company."

He placed his hands over her knees without touching, enough to stop her from jumping up but not spook her. "Hang on. I didn't say you would be crawling back. All you have to do is invite him over. You won't have to see him. In fact, we don't want you staying here until he's caught."

Jazz choked back a laugh. "Where do you expect me to go? A hotel? I am not one of your rich clients. I got fired yesterday so I can't afford to spend money on hotel rooms.

Despite the other girls' attempts to cover the bruises and welts with their heaviest makeup, they hadn't been able to disguise the damage. Walt had blown a gasket and fired her on the spot when she'd asked for a week off. "I have some money saved up but it won't last long."

Not if she was going to be able to pay for her tuition at GW. For four long years. Those dreams of being able to graduate with no student loans, of doing something other than dancing after she'd graduated, had probably flown out the window.

"It's not going to cost you a cent. You're going to be staying at one of Hauberk's safe houses free of charge. Bodyguard included."

"Let me guess, you?" Despite her sneer, she half hoped it would be him. With his sleeve tattoo, and the way he treated her, she felt safe. Of course, he was cute too, in a rough-edged sort of way. But then she'd always liked guys who didn't feel like they'd be at home sitting beside her in the salon having their nails buffed.

"Nope, not me." His cute smile that softened his edges and put her at ease appeared. "Your CPO—your close protective officer—will be a woman named Holly. I'll be here, staking out your apartment."

"Oh." She rubbed her arms. "All right. So when do you want me to phone him? Now?"

"Yup. And see if you can slide in that you're using Sandy's computer while yours is being fixed. It'll let him think he can get back into her VPN."

"Okay." She tapped Mitch's number into her phone. She'd deleted it from her contacts list after...well, after. So what sick part of her brain decided it was worth remembering? Her thumb hovered over the connect button as her stomach did flip-flops. *Fuck you, Mitchell, Michael, whatever the hell your name is. I hope they haul your ass to jail and some guy named Bubba wants to make you his bitch.* "What time should I say for him to come over?"

"Does he know you've been fired?"

"No. I never told him what I really did."

"Okay, then tell him to meet you here tomorrow night at eight. That way our cover story fits and we can get all our people in place and the cops and the D.A. on board."

"Right." She pressed the little green connect key. On the second ring, the asshole answered. Her stomach acids burned the back of her throat at the smarmy sound of his voice.

"Hey, Mitch. I've missed you, baby." Oh, gag.

Sweat broke out when Andy leaned over her shoulder as they waited for Mitch's—Michael's response. She covered the microphone on her phone and clasped her free hand in her lap to hide how much she was trembling. "Look, can you back off please? I know you want to hear what he's saying but..."

To her relief, he immediately straightened. But instead of moving away he pulled up a chair from the kitchen table and faced it in the opposite direction but still right beside her. Strangely it worked and some of her fear subsided. She put the phone back to her ear and realized Mitch was speaking, "—didn't figure I'd be hearing from you again."

His voice was cautious. *That's right, buddy. You need to be cautious of me.*

"Yeah. I'm sorry." Oh God, did she really have to say this? If it got him a taste of his own medicine, she could. "I guess I over-reacted the other night." Under-reacted was more like it. "I was wondering if we could get together so I could make it up to you. Maybe tomorrow night? Around eight?"

There was a long pause before he replied, "All right. Is your roommate going to be around?"

"Nope. We'll have the place all to ourselves."

She stiffened when Andy touched her knee. He leaned in and whispered, "Breathe."

She forced air into her lungs and out slowly, before trusting her voice. "Maybe you could edit some more videos? Then afterward, I could thank you properly? I got some new toys we could try."

Say you'll come over, you bastard. So they can arrest your sorry ass.

"All right. But I can't make it until nine."

"Okay, that's still good. See you then. I c-can't wait." *For them to arrest your sorry ass.* Without waiting to hear Mitch's—Michael's—response, she ended the call, clapped a hand to her mouth and dashed to the bathroom. She fell to her knees in front of the toilet and vomited.

Cool hands gathered her hair and held it back from her face until her retching stopped. They smoothed the hair down her back, then disappeared. The faucet turned on and a glass of water appeared in front of her. "Here, rinse your mouth out."

God, how pathetic she must look. Her hands trembling, she accepted the glass and rinsed out her mouth. "Sorry about that."

"Don't worry about it." He helped her to her feet and probably would have carried her back to the living room if she'd let him.

She didn't. She straightened and, holding her chin high, walked on her own.

Once she was seated on the couch, he took up his usual position on the coffee table. "Do you have someone you can talk to about what he did?"

"It's that obvious, huh?"

"You flinched when I touched you, honey. And you're jumpy as hell, especially when anyone's behind you. For all your bravado, when Scott was leaning over you this afternoon? You couldn't hide the terror in your eyes. Something—some*one* put it there. And then there are these." He took her hand and straightened her arm, lifting her sleeve to expose the angry marks around her wrists. "Your cuff fell down when you were holding the door. Sometimes rookies wouldn't tighten the cuffs enough and guys would try to get out of them. They'd rub themselves raw like this. I'm guessing you weren't in them willingly either."

"Then you'd be wrong. They were my handcuffs. I got them out of the drawer and handed them to him and even told him how to put them on me." She bit the words out, but she didn't look away.

"But he went further than you expected, didn't he?" He pulled her sleeve higher and exposed the five dark circles where Mitch— Michael— had held her when he'd been fucking her. Andy gently wrapped his hand around her arm, judging the distance with his own fingers. "It doesn't take a rocket scientist to guess what happened. You like things a little rougher than some women, but he went too far. I'm guessing he went way over the line. I'm guessing you told him no and he didn't stop."

She lowered her head and stared at her toes. Strangely enough the tears she expected didn't come. But then she'd cried enough after he'd left Friday night so she doubted she had any tears in her system.

"Did you file a complaint with the police?" He was so quiet, so controlled. So unlike Mitch. Or so many of the men who catcalled or tried to manhandle her when she danced.

"Why bother? They wouldn't believe me."

"Because you work as a stripper?"

"Got it in one."

"Strippers get raped too. Cops know that," he said quietly.

"It doesn't matter. He'll just claim he's sorry, that he thought it was what I wanted and walk away scot-free."

He traced the outline of the thumbprint on the inside of her arm. "Did you tell him to stop?"

"I tried, but—"

"—But he didn't stop. It's not your fault, Jazz. Stop blaming yourself."

"No. You don't understand. He filmed it. He got the whole thing. Including me telling him I liked rough sex. And me handing him *my* handcuffs to tie me up with. Mine. I handed them to him and sat there helping him put them on me. I agreed to be gagged. We never worked out a code word or anything, so he can quite rightfully claim that he didn't know I wanted him to stop. Don't you see? They'll tell me I deserved it, that I brought it on myself. He'll walk."

His eyes searched hers. Eventually he nodded and released her arm. "Have you seen a doctor and been checked out?"

"Yeah." At least her birth-control shots were up-to-date so she wouldn't get pregnant. The HIV tests and the cloud that hung over her for the next six months wouldn't be so easy to ignore.

"Good." Damn, he was being so nice. "Did they set anything up with a counsellor? Because if you need someone to talk to, I know a couple good people."

God, he thought she was a headcase or something. Wonderful. "Thanks but I can't afford a shrink."

"Considering this guy targeted you to get at Hauberk, I think Sam might see clear to footing the bill." He lifted his hand as if he might touch her face but dropped it before making contact. "We're going to get him for you, Jazz. He'll never be able to hurt you again. Now why don't you go pack a bag and I'll take you somewhere safe until this is over."

NINETEEN

THE CAB HAD BARELY STOPPED when Troy tossed the fare to the driver along with an extra twenty. "Keep the change."

He should have texted Sandy to let her know he'd returned early, but he needed some time to decompress before he saw her. Killing an unarmed man tended to make him itchy. He hefted his pack over his shoulder and headed for the elevator. Scott would understand, even be angry at not being able to watch Garcia's eyes glaze as the life drained from him, but would Sandy? Would she understand that sometimes death was the only way to mete justice? He was still pondering that as he got off the elevator and headed down the corridor. After unlocking the door, he stepped inside, the smell of fresh paint hitting him first. "Son of a bitch."

While Scott had mentioned Sandy had cleaned the place up, the asshole hadn't told him that cleaning included painting the walls. He opened the door again to verify he'd entered the right apartment. Yup. It was his unit, but now the stark beige walls were hunter green on two walls, a fresh coat of some almost-white color, bone or eggshell or some fancy name women loved, covered the others. Even the baseboards gleamed with fresh paint. Heavy curtains hung on his windows over sheers that filtered the mid-afternoon light. The pattern in the curtains picked up the colors of the walls and of the new oval rug with its geometric splashes of dark red. A massive photograph of D.C. at night hung on the wall between the recliners. His flat screen had been mounted on the opposite wall, the DVD, cable box and video console wires had been neatly coiled and hidden.

He shouldered his pack and wandered into his bedroom. "Holy fuck."

The walls here had received similar treatment, though the curtains were plain deep green. A quilt he'd seen stored in her linen closet covered his bed. She'd even framed some of his photographs. She'd turned the condo into a home.

Maybe he wouldn't have chosen that particular color for the towels in the bathroom but for the first time—ever—he felt like he'd walked into a home. When the front door opened, he headed back to the living room.

As he'd expected, Scott smirked when he saw Troy. "Surprise."

"Did you do this?"

Scott snorted. "Think again, buddy. Your girlfriend turned into Martha-Freaking-Stewart once you walked out that door. And you'd better tell her you like it whether you do or not because I am not painting it again."

"It's..." Different. Colorful. Welcoming. "Nice."

It wasn't him. Or not what he was used to. Yet, he liked it. Because she'd done it perhaps.

"Yeah, well, considering it's your birthday and Christmas presents for the next year or two."

"What do you mean?"

"Do you think she had the money to buy all this crap?"

"You paid?"

"She was so excited about making this place into a home. For both of us. So I offered to pay. She says she's going to pay me back but I won't take it."

"Fuck that. I'll pay for it."

"Nah. It's good. As I said, Happy Birthday and Merry Christmas." Scott stretched his shoulder. "At least you didn't have to do any of the fuckin' painting. What are you doing back? Sandy said you weren't arriving until tonight."

"Caught an earlier flight, that's all." Though his actual return had been in question for a while, especially when Davis had threatened to dump him out over the Caribbean. "I figured I'd shower and shave and then head over to the office and pick up Sandy. Take her to dinner."

Scott checked his watch. "You'll have enough time for a shower before Sandy gets here."

"She's coming here?" Troy looked around the place. "Don't tell me she has more decorating to do."

"No. We thought it best if she stayed here until we catch Rowlands."

"Rowlands? Who the fuck is Rowlands?" Shit—what had he missed? And why hadn't Sandy said anything about any trouble when he'd talked to her earlier?

"Her roommate's boyfriend. Went by the name of Mitchell Young? You ever meet him?"

"Yeah, just in passing." Went by? What the fuck? "His real name's Rowlands?"

"Yeah, he's the hacker. We're setting up a sting to catch him tomorrow. I didn't figure Sandy should stay at her place until we've got him." Scott's shoulders slumped and he rubbed his hand over his hair. "Rowlands raped Jazz while we were at the club. He videotaped it too, used it to threaten her. The techs found it on her computer. It doesn't show all of the rape—he's edited out the worst part, of course. But I've seen the report from the doc Sam sent her to. She got hurt real bad."

"Fuck." He'd talked to the fucker, watched television with him. Why the hell hadn't his radar gone off? It had. But he'd been so intent on Sandy, he hadn't listened to it. "Is Jazz okay?"

"She'll recover. She might have a couple scars, but he whipped the crap out of her. Probably the worst damage is how he's fucked with her mind. He convinced her a good defense attorney would get the video introduced into evidence as proof she agreed to have sex with him. Which they probably would." Scott cursed himself. "I wasn't much better. I was so fucking convinced she'd screwed Sandy over that I treated her like shit."

"You can apologize."

"I have. But it's not enough." He blew out a breath. "Anyway, I didn't want either of them going back until we caught him. So we stashed Jazz in the safe house over in Alexandria. Andy's keeping an eye out for her. She's tough though. When we told her about our plans, she was all in, you know? Didn't shy away at all. Even after I'd been a total asshole to her."

"Tell me Sandy isn't going to be part of the bait."

"Nope. And neither's Jazz." Scott filled him in on their plans, ending with, "I told Sandy I'd feel better about her staying here and figured you would too."

"Yeah, good thinking. Thanks." Uncomfortable with the emotions surfing through him, Troy wandered back into his bedroom and shrugged out of his shirt.

To his surprise, Scott had followed him and now stood in the doorway, his head canted to one side. "You love her, don't you?"

"Yeah, I think I do." He stared at the quilt she'd folded at the end of his bed. He recognized it as one her mother had made. "I want more than her coming over once in a while. I like the idea of her sleeping here. In my bed. Waking up beside me in the morning. I want her living here with me. Permanently."

"You talking just living together, or marriage and the whole deal?"

"I don't know. I can't picture myself with anyone else but..." *She doesn't want to commit.* Shit, wasn't that what women usually complained was the guy's issue?

"So what's the problem? Ask her to move in."

"She's not going to stay. She's said over and over again she's not looking to settle down or anything." *Especially if she finds out who I am. What I've done.* Any woman in her right mind would run screaming.

"No? Then how do you explain this?" Scott picked up the edge of the quilt and brandished it at him. "Look around you. She's made this place into a home. It wasn't before. Now it's somewhere that welcomes you. She did that."

"It's only paint and fabric. It doesn't mean she'll want to settle down." He had a closetful of two-thousand-dollar suits that allowed him to project a professional image that made people trust him, but at the end of the day he had to take them off. Underneath he was still the same murderer he'd been all along.

"You didn't see her shopping for this stuff," Scott insisted. "We must have hit every mall between here and Baltimore and back again. Including a few I didn't even know existed. She wanted to make sure she got exactly the right colors and the right pictures, the right pillows. She knew exactly what she wanted and wouldn't settle for anything less. I don't think she would have done that if a) she didn't love you, or b) she didn't have settling down in the back of her mind. I think she'd stay if you asked, and I think that's what's scaring you."

"That's not what I'm afraid of." More like terrified she wouldn't stay.

"She's not going to run out on you. Not Sandy. She may say that she's not interested in marriage, and maybe she doesn't need the piece of paper, but she wants a home. She wants stability whether she realizes it or not. She needs someone she can count on to be there for her. But next time you lie to her? You'd better listen to the damned news and phone her, text her, even send her a damned email to let her know you're okay because I gotta tell you, man, Sandy was fucking worried about you when she saw the news report about the riots in Kinshasa last night."

Shit on a stick. "What tipped you off that I wasn't in Africa?" More importantly, did Sandy suspect he'd lied?

"You told her you were watching the sunset. It would have been almost midnight in Kinshasa when you talked to her."

Damn it, talk about a goddamned rookie mistake. "Did Sandy catch it?"

"Nope, not as far as I know. So where'd you really go? And what was happening that dragged you away from an entire weekend of sex with your lady?"

Showtime. "I was in Val Varde."

"Val Varde? What the fuck's in Val Varde?"

"Garcia." The blood drained from Scott's face. "He's dead. I got him for you. And for Dev."

Scott's expression didn't change but he released a breath in a long slow blow. "You should have told me that's where you were going. You should have let me come with you."

"You couldn't come. It wasn't my op. I had to pull a few strings to go myself."

"You should have tried harder. I wanted to kill him. To watch the life drain from him the way I watched him kill Dev." Scott's voice gradually rose until he was shouting. "It was my right to kill that fucking bastard. Mine."

Shit. This was degrading. Fast. Keep things calm. Matter-of-fact. "I told you, it wasn't my op."

"Fuck that." Sweat beaded on Scott's forehead and his cheeks turned bright red despite the stark pallor of his skin. "Fuck. That. You could have found a way. I could have flown there myself and met you. You could have told me what you were planning. You owed me."

Troy braced himself when Scott shoved him. "I couldn't. Everything was done on a need-to-know basis, and kept compartmentalized. I wasn't allowed to tell anyone. Not you, not Sandy, not even Sam."

"I wanted to do it. I wanted to be the one to pull the trigger." Scott's voice fractured. "I wanted that fucker to know it was me killing him. I wanted to watch him die."

If he'd been in Scott's place, he'd have demanded the same right.

At Scott's second attempt to push him, Troy caught Scott's hands and twisted him around, using his whole body to restrain him against the wall. "Listen to me. Who pulled the trigger, whether it was you or me, doesn't matter. All that matters is that the bastard's dead. He'll never hurt anyone again."

"Tell me it wasn't a quick death." Scott's voice was so fucking rough, betraying the pain tearing him apart. Damn it, Garcia's death was supposed to stop him from hurting, not make it worse. "Tell me he suffered like he made Dev suffer. Like we all suffered."

Troy stayed silent.

"You should have shot him in the knees. Then cut off his balls. Gutted him. Hurt him the way he hurt us. The way he hurt Dev. Oh God, Dev!"

As Scott's body heaved with his sobs, Troy held tight. "Garcia's fertilizer now. And you're alive." Thank God.

Scott shoved himself from the wall, out of Troy's hold. "I have to...I gotta go. I need to get some air."

"I'll go with you." Troy snagged his jacket from the bed.

"No." Scott swiped his hand over his face. "No. I gotta go. Alone."

"Scott." Shit. Alone was not good. "Let me come with you. Let me drive you to Doc Hayes's."

"No. I'm not gonna off myself, all right. I gotta think about this. Without you. Without shrinks. I hafta...I gotta go."

Troy followed when Scott hurried from the bedroom, nearly running into Sandy who stood in the hallway, her eyes wide and face pale.

"Scott?" Sandy caught Scott's arm as he passed.

"Sorry, Sandy. I gotta go. I can't explain, I have to get out of here."

"Call me if you need to talk to someone or need a ride or anything, all right?"

The wan smile Scott graced her with gave Troy heart. "Thanks. You're a sweetheart, you know that?" He glanced over his shoulder at Troy and the smile died, replaced with a blank stare. "I'll see you later."

Before Scott moved, Sandy hugged him. "Remember, you've got friends who will do anything for you. Who care about you and worry about you."

"Thanks." Scott disentangled himself and opened the door.

Divided between greeting Sandy and following Scott, Troy hesitated. He settled for calling out, "Scott. Call me if you're thinking of..." *killing yourself.* The door slammed shut before he could finish.

"Fuck." Troy scrubbed his hands over his face. "I should go after him."

A strange expression on her face, Sandy stared at him for at least ten seconds. She called Andy, giving him the details on Scott's retreat. "Andy will find him and make sure he's okay."

"Thanks, but it's not the same."

"Andy will look after him. And before you thank me, you should know I didn't do it for you. I did it for Scott. Right now, I wouldn't lift a hand if you were lying on the floor bleeding."

Fuck.

"I heard you talking. You lied to me about being in Africa. You lied on Friday night when you left and you lied again this morning when we talked on the—" Comprehension reached her eyes. "When you phoned here, you weren't phoning to talk to me, were you? You didn't think I'd still be here. You were expecting Scott to answer."

Shit. There was no use lying. "Yes."

"You let me think you wanted to talk to me."

"I didn't have to *let* you think anything. I was glad you picked up. I liked talking to you."

"You lied to me about where you were, and yet you let me continue to think you were in Africa. You let me worry about you when you were safe the whole time."

Not safe exactly. The op could have gone very differently if Davis's source had been discovered. "I didn't lie this morning. I told you I was safe. What more do you want from me?"

"Lying by omission is still lying." She shook her head in disbelief. "You could have said, 'I'm not in Africa.' Instead you told me about being out in the country, watching the sunset."

He could almost see the wheels in her head turn as she replayed the conversation, see the moment she realized his error.

"It couldn't be helped. I wasn't allowed to say where I was, or anything about the mission." *I'm still not supposed to.* "It's part of my job, Sandy. It's what I do and who I am. You know that."

"Look, I know you can't give me details when it comes to stuff with Hauberk. I get that." She took a step back when he moved toward her. "Okay, maybe I didn't get that, exactly. But do you know how scared I was when I thought you were in the middle of that coup? And you let me think you were still there." Damn, her eyes were glistening. He'd done that to her. Yet here she was standing so proud, so strong, refusing to give in to the tears.

If she was going to be part of his life, she'd have to learn to deal with it. He pressed the heel of his hand to his forehead and sighed, knowing she was about to walk out the door. Out of his life. "It's part of the job, sunshine. If you can't deal with it, you know where the door is."

The sadness in her eyes, the pain in her voice tore through him. She reminded him of a puppy dog someone had kicked to the gutter and abandoned.

Unable to face her any longer, he walked into his bedroom and stopped beside the bed. He smoothed his hand over the quilt. Even if she left, she'd still be here. Long after her scent faded from his sheets, she'd still be there in the quilt. She'd be in the pictures she'd so thoughtfully framed and hung on the wall. Anytime he saw that dark green she'd painted his walls, he'd be reminded of her.

The shadow in the doorway betrayed her presence seconds before she spoke, "I don't like that you can lie to me so easily. I need to be able to trust that you're telling me the truth. Even if it's just to say, 'I can't tell you where I'm going or what I'm doing.' I could take that."

She said that now but soon she'd be throwing it back in his face. "I thought you were leaving."

"Do you want me to leave?"

No. But she'd leave anyway. She should leave. "I can't change who I am, Sandy."

"I'm not asking you to. I feel like I don't know you. That you don't want me to know you. I learned more about you talking with

Scott this weekend than you've ever told me about you." She caught his hand. "I'm simply asking that you let me in. That you trust me enough to be honest with me."

"You don't know what you're asking. You haven't a clue who I am, or what I've done. Scott doesn't even know."

"So tell me. Who are you, Troy? What have you done?"

For such a simple question, the answer was so complicated. Yet it wasn't, was it? "I'm an assassin. Oh, a government-sponsored one, but I killed—kill— people for a living. And I'm very good at my job." He faced her. "Last night I put my gun barrel to the forehead of an unarmed man and pulled the trigger. I put two bullets in his chest to take him down, and then I walked over to him and put another in his brain just to make sure the fucker was dead." He finally looked her in the face and found compassion, along with tears, filling her eyes. "I'd do it the same way if I had to do it over again. Is that honest enough for you?"

"You did it for Scott. And for Dev. I heard what you told Scott, remember?"

"Why I did it wouldn't make a difference to the courts. He was unarmed and I shot him anyway. Face it, I'm a murderer."

"I've read the reports both from our people and from the newspapers. Garcia was responsible for dozens of deaths." Her voice was soft but sure. "You probably saved dozens if not hundreds more. He was the murderer."

"So am I." He'd killed so many times he'd lost count. No. That wasn't true. He knew each and every kill he'd made. He may not have known their names but he could tell her their hair color, their age. He could still see the looks on their faces when they'd died. Surprise. Shock. Anger. Hatred.

She grabbed his forearms and shook him, surprising him with her strength. "You are different than him. You killed people who deserved to die. He killed innocents."

So have I. The trust in her eyes, the softness of her voice forced him to look away. His gaze landed on a picture she'd framed and set on his dresser. The one of him and his father, taken a week before he'd died. Before he'd been murdered. Not that his father was innocent, but his father's death, and his part in it, had been the start of that slippery slope.

"Let me in, Troy. Tell me who you are. What you want, what you think. Your hopes. Your dreams."

"I don't have dreams. I am who I am, Sandy." He held out his arms. "What you see is what you get."

"I don't believe that." She wasn't lying; she didn't see what he really was. How could she? You had to have evil inside you to understand evil. There wasn't an ounce of evil in her body.

"Trust me on this. I'm not the type you take home to introduce to the folks." Shit. That wouldn't help him convince her to stay now, would it? Guess he'd given up that dream the minute he'd left for Val Varde.

Sam was right. He never should have gotten involved with her. Because now he knew what he could have had, what others had. And he'd never have it again.

"I'm not leaving, Troy. I'm not."

No one had ever stuck around long enough to care.

"Please. Talk to me. Let me in."

"Why?" he shouted. "I lied to you about where I'd gone. I can guarantee you I'll lie to you again."

"As you said, it's part of your job, Troy. I should have remembered that."

Jesus fucking Christ. He speared his fingers through his hair at her steadfastness. "You don't get it. Troy McPherson's not real. He doesn't exist. I'm really Colin. Colin Fitzgerald. And I'm a murderer, Sandy. I kill people for a living."

"You kill people the government's asked you to kill. People who deserve to die. You wouldn't hurt me. I know that." She took a step forward, and another, until she was inches away from him and laid her hand flat on his chest. "Please, Troy. Colin. Let me in."

Shaken by her implicit trust, he stared at the photos once more. The one of Scott and him at Buckner Academy, of his mother and father with him as an infant. "What do you want to know?"

"I don't know. How about we start with simple things like what's your favorite color? Or your favorite dessert? What's your ideal vacation?"

"Navy. Sherry trifle, and snorkelling in the British Virgin Islands." Oh Christ. He couldn't do this. "What do you really want to know, Sandy? Cut the bullshit circling around. Just ask me what you want to know straight-out."

She lowered her voice to a whisper, "Do you still blame yourself for your father's death?"

She knew about that? Ah, yes, she'd spent the weekend with Scott. Who had told her the sanitized, official Brannally version. She deserved the truth about him and all his ugly secrets. She needed the truth, if only to open her eyes as to who he really was.

"His death is *entirely* my fault. Oh, I may not have pulled the trigger but he's dead because of me."

"You were ten years old. You believed your friend when he said you should—"

Was he really going to do this? "It didn't happen that way. I knew I was taking him to his death. I may not have consciously realized they'd kill him right there in front of me, but I think I suspected it."

"I don't understand." He touched her cheek, loving and despairing that every emotion she felt was right there for him to read with not a trace of subterfuge or denial. She would never have made a good mole, he realized. She was too open. Too honest.

"There was no friend I was to meet at the park; there never was. I deliberately betrayed my own father and led him to his slaughter." And still she looked up at him, so trusting. God, she killed him. "Da was a member of the IRA. He made bombs for them. Bombs that killed people. Innocent people. One day, my da and his mates decided to place a bomb in a room above a shop where a group of the loyalists were meeting later that day. But they hadn't told my mum about it. She was there picking up some fish when the bomb went off.

"I heard him talking about it with some of his friends a couple nights after her funeral. They were talking about how the bomb had gone off prematurely and what he'd done wrong. I hated him, Sandy. I wanted to kill him myself. But I didn't think I could have done it. He wasn't a big man, but he was on guard, you know?" He could still hear his father's thick accent, feel the weight of his father's hand on his head. *Stop your whining, boy. It's sorry I am that she was there, but your ma knew we do what we have to to get these feckin' Brits out of our land.*

TWENTY

SANDY DOUBTED Troy realized his accent had thickened. Or that his voice was cracking, or that tears glistened in his eyes. She'd lived such a pampered existence, while he'd grown up surrounded by violence.

He was silent for a long moment, lost in his memories. She was about to prompt him when he took a deep breath and continued, "So one day on my way home from school, I overheard some loyalists chatting. I stopped to talk to them. Told them what da had done, told them he was planning to bomb a market where there'd be more innocents killed."

Most ten-years-olds still idolized their fathers. How hard it must have been to know your father was a murderer capable of coldly planning the death of innocent women and children.

"They asked if I'd bring my father to meet them at the park around the corner from our house." He'd lapsed into a monotone recitation, as if he were deliberately stuffing all his emotions away. Which he probably was. "They said they wanted to try to convince him to be an inside man for them. I agreed. To this day I don't know if I consciously knew they'd kill him right there. At that point, it didn't matter to me. When he was lying at my feet, his blood draining into the gutter, all I could think was that justice had been served. That he deserved to die for killing Ma." His harsh laugh didn't fool her into thinking he wasn't feeling guilty. "What does a feckin' ten-year-old kid know about justice?"

More than his father, though she didn't voice the thought.

"After Da's death, all his friends came 'round the house. Told me how they'd avenge him, promised they'd find the fucker who sold him out and make him pay. They promised that when I got older I could join them, that they'd teach me to shoot and make bombs so I could get my vengeance against the bloody Brits. That they wouldn't let Paddy's boy grow up thinking his father died for nought.

"The next day Senator Brannally showed up at the door along with four security guards and the press. He said that he'd been in contact with an uncle of my ma's in New Hampshire. That as my nearest living relative, my uncle had appointed the senator as my temporary legal guardian and he was to take me back to the States with him." He shook his head. "Next thing I knew I was on a plane flyin' over the ocean with the senator telling me he'd make sure the IRA never bothered me again."

"What happened to your uncle?"

"He died a few months later in a car accident and left my guardianship to the senator. There wasn't much money but the senator stepped up and made sure I wanted for nothing. He paid for my education both at the Academy and later at Boston College."

He lay on the bed and draped his arm over his eyes. "Turned out I'm my father's son after all. I learned how to make bombs and how to shape them so they'll kill the people on one side of a room but not the other. How to disguise them so people wouldn't find them until it was too late. How to kill people in hand-to-hand combat without making a sound. I know what parts of the body can be hurt causing maximum pain with minimum effort. I was good at it, Sandy. I still am."

She crawled on the bed beside him. "If it didn't bother you, you'd still be in the Diplomatic Service." And he wouldn't be telling her this as if it were a confession. No, despite his denials that killing didn't bother him, she bet she could see the face of each one of his victims. And that each one of them had deserved to die.

He dropped his arm. "I'm a killer. Don't make me into something I'm not. After I killed Garcia? I slept as if I hadn't a care in the world."

She took his hands in hers and squeezed. From the dark circles under his eyes, she doubted he'd slept as well as he'd claimed. "You did what you had to, Troy. You slept because the world is a better place, a safer place, without him in it."

"I'm no different than him. No matter what type of spin you try to put on it. I killed him in cold blood and it doesn't bother me a whit. Is that the type of lover you want?"

Yes. "You are different than he was because you're sitting here having this conversation with me right now. You're worried about what I think about what you've done. He wouldn't have cared what anyone thought."

"You keep telling yourself that." He rolled onto his side, away from her.

After a brief debate whether to leave him alone, Sandy undressed, crawled onto the bed and snuggled against him. Though his breathing evened out she knew he wasn't asleep, but he obviously didn't want to talk about it, or anything, anymore.

As much as she complained about her family and her mother interfering in her love life, she still loved her family. Troy—*Colin*— had to live with the knowledge his father had killed his mother, and others. Would she have been capable at ten of dealing with that knowledge? Probably not. Yet at ten years old, he'd come up with a plan, albeit a flawed one as it had left him orphaned. Thank heavens Senator Brannally had gotten him out of Ireland. But he'd lost all family after that and had been alone.

She pressed a kiss to the spot between his shoulder blades. "You're not alone anymore, Troy. I'm right here with you."

TROY AWOKE, immediately noticing three things. First, he had to piss like a goddamned racehorse because he hadn't hit the can before he'd fallen asleep. Second, his stomach was gnawing its way to his backbone because he hadn't eaten since before he'd left Val Varde almost twenty hours before. Third, and much more enjoyable, Sandy lay snuggled against him. This was what he wanted to wake to every morning. Not the bladder and hunger issues, he amended, but Sandy's warm body soft and pliable against his.

He shifted to his side so he could watch her sleep. Her hair had fallen across her face so he brushed the strand that had stuck to her bottom lip. Without waking, she rolled onto her back. The sheet fell away at her movement, baring her breasts. They were every man's fantasy. Curvy and luscious, the nipples a soft pink matching her lips.

His stomach growled at the same time his bladder sternly informed him that any thoughts of waking Sandy with a morning woody would be out of the question. He eased from her side and padded into the bathroom, closing the door before he turned on the light so he wouldn't wake her.

The face looking back at him in the mirror was the same he saw every day. Yet it seemed different today. Oh sure, there was two-days' growth of beard that he seldom sported, and the circles under his eyes were a bit darker thanks to the damned jet travel. But telling her about what he'd done, who he really was?

"What's she done to you, mate? You're goin' all soft over her."

And he liked it. Leaving his reflection to ponder the changes, he stripped off his clothes and took care of the most pressing matter, then turned on the shower. Feeling invigorated, though his stomach still grumbled, he toweled himself off and walked naked to the bedroom where Sandy still slumbered.

She'd sprawled out since he'd left the bed, taking up not only her side but half of his too. Damned if it didn't bother him a whit. He crawled back into the bed and hefted himself up on one elbow to look down at her. With the winter weather, her skin was whiter than normal, her freckles standing out against her milky skin. He kissed the bridge of her nose, half expecting to taste cinnamon. Her forehead was similarly given a kiss, followed by her chin. He worked his way down her body, placing soft kisses and caresses along a meandering path.

She was soft and pliant, warm. Inviting. Her breathing changed from its regular slow breaths of a deep sleep, telling him she was awake even though her eyes hadn't opened.

Though he knew she expected him to go straight to her pussy, he took his time, continuing his exploration of her body, kissing his way down one long limb. He paid special attention to her toes, his thumbs rubbing her sole, careful not to tickle. His trip back up the other leg was just as slow, taking extra special time at her knee and the tender skin of her inner thigh. Once again he knew he surprised her when he bypassed her mound and headed back up her body.

Her fingers threaded through his hair, tightening in a futile attempt to stop him when he approached the ticklish spot above her hips. He lifted his head and watched her eyes open. Oh yeah, this was exactly the way he wanted to wake up every morning. Moving ever so slowly, he touched his lips to the tender skin of her belly. "Morning, sunshine."

"Someone woke up full of ideas." With a tiny wiggle, she lifted her hips, adjusting the angle so his erection slipped through her folds. Heaven couldn't feel any better than it did to be nestled in her moist heat, her breasts pressed against his chest, her lids sleep-heavy over smoky blue eyes that promised more than great sex.

"Couldn't help it." His hips retreated and thrust, so his shaft pressed against her clit in an erotic caress. "Woke up and you were right here beside me, all pink and soft and inviting."

He dipped his head and caught one of her nipples, laving and nipping at it until she was panting. When the head of his cock accidentally brushed her opening, she frowned and pushed at his shoulders. "Condom, big boy."

"Yup, in a minute. Got to do this first." Instead he moved down her body and licked the smooth skin over her mound.

Something had changed yesterday with his confessions. The

intimacy of her opening herself to him, accepting him despite knowing who he was, what he'd done, left him humbled. A sense of worship enveloping him, he parted her labia and indulged in a long slow sweep with his tongue.

She'd started off stroking his shoulders, but with each pass of his tongue, her fingers slowed, digging into his arms, her hips lifting to meet his mouth. He reveled in each gasp, each tremor he brought her. Her thigh muscles tightened around him and her back bowed. Still he drove her up, losing himself in the essence that coated his lips and his tongue. Her essence. He craved it like a crack addict, would never get enough.

Despite the sharp pain when her nails dug into his biceps as her orgasm crested, his cock ached and his balls drew tight to his body, wanting to be buried inside her, to share that completion. To feel her heat surround him with no latex barrier. To be completely with her, part of her. Not just today. But forever.

AS HER ORGASM FADED, Sandy stroked Troy's hair. Her heart rate spiked when he lifted his head to look at her. No trace of the smugness she'd expected to see filled his eyes. The heat was there, but so was something else, something she couldn't define.

God, he looked so sexy with that two-day growth of beard, and his hair all spiky and wild. Instead of the bright pink she would have turned under Val Varde's sun, his skin had darkened to a tawny color. Not tanned exactly but darker than her pasty white. Healthy. She couldn't resist running her fingers along his forearm, loving the way the dark hair crinkled beneath her fingertips. He even smelled like the ocean and its salty breeze.

She stretched over to his nightstand and plucked a condom from the box. "I'm not done with you yet."

To her surprise, he hesitated. "You'll be late for work."

"Yeah, well, I can always claim I was in negotiations with one of my managers." At his frown, she winked. "Come on, we've still got time. And you owe me for leaving me alone on the weekend. You'd promised two days and three nights of non-stop sex, remember?"

He rolled to sit back on his heels. "I'm sorry I wrecked your weekend but I had no control over when the op went down."

Damn it. She'd spoiled the mood. "Hey, I know that. I'm not complaining, all right?" She tore open the package and held out the condom. "I intend to make up for lost time."

"Sandy."

If he wasn't going to put it on himself, she would. She scooched down the bed and kissed his cheek while her hands wrapped around his still-hard shaft. "Ssssh. Let me."

Once he was properly sheathed, she clamped her arms on his shoulders and straddled him. His shoulders and arm muscles tightened and his breath caught as she impaled herself on his shaft.

Now she had him where she wanted. "Question for you, big boy. Sam said there was no one allowed in the guest house until after midnight but he was wrong, right? He meant only invited guests were allowed, right?"

His expression froze into his standard bland mask. She tapped his lips with her index finger. "Nuh-uh. No deflecting on this one. Were there or were there not people watching us?"

"No. There was no one else there but us."

"Why did you lie about it?"

"Consider it a misdirection." He pulled her down on top of him and kissed the freckles on the bridge of her nose. "I prefer to keep certain things—like our lovemaking—private. Since you like the idea of people watching us I figured that you'd be as excited if you believed people were watching us. So I asked Jocelyne to help me create the illusion."

"Huh."

"It worked, didn't it?" He arched his hips, driving his shaft deeper inside her as if to encourage her to drop the subject.

"Yeah, but..." She wiggled on top of him trying to decide how she felt about his deception.

His eyes closed as he pressed his face into the crook of her neck, his breath warm against her skin. "Sandy, you enjoyed it."

"Okay, okay, I admit, I was turned on thinking people were watching us." Bracing herself on his shoulders, she ground her hips against his. Her already-sensitive tissues stretched around his shaft, welcoming the intrusion. Though he hadn't said as much, she was certain he'd never told anyone else about his father or what he'd done. That type of trust overwhelmed her. She needed to show him he could continue to trust her, that she trusted him. Except she didn't know exactly how to show it other than by such intimacy. Maybe one day she'd find the words, but not today. "God, I love how you feel inside me."

She paused when she realized what she'd said. She more than loved how he felt inside her. She loved falling asleep in his bed and waking to him beside her. She loved curling up on the couch and watching movies with him, even if he did prefer documentaries over her beloved action movies. She even loved how they'd fought the day before, how he'd listened to her, opened up to her.

She loved him. Shit. No. This couldn't be happening. She was happy being single. No ties. No responsibilities to anyone else but herself.

Stop over thinking this. Neither of them had said the L-word yet. Who knew how he felt, but guys didn't fall in love as easily as women, right? So this was containable. This was sex. That's all it was. They were just scratching each other's itches.

At that moment his breath hitched and he held her still. "Oh, God, Sandy. You feel so fucking good."

Right. Fucking, that's all this was. Not lovemaking, just sex. As his fingers dug into her hips, she gripped his shoulders and withdrew until only the head of his cock was inside her, then dropped. She set a fast pace, grinding her hips against his, driving them both to the edge until her whole body shook with the ferocity of her climax. Before she'd finished she was flat on her back, staring up at the ceiling.

Troy lifted her hips and drove into her, the new angle providing a delicious friction against both her clit and her inner tissues. She reached between them and found her clit, flicking it until pleasure flooded her once more. He thrust harder, his face contorted. When his climax hit, his body vibrating while his cock pulsed deep inside her, she could have sworn she'd heard him say, "I love you."

Oh shit. He'd said it. Guys never said *I love you* first. Okay, so she'd heard it before, but look where that had led her. To a damned proposal and an expectation she'd become her mother's clone and pop out babies while riding a damned tractor or milking the cows.

She *so* wasn't ready for this.

As soon as his body relaxed, she lifted herself off him and headed straight for the bathroom. "I've got to run. I'm really running late now."

"You can be late. We need to talk," he raised his voice as she closed the door.

Oh shit. She glanced at the shower thinking how she really needed to have one but if she did, he'd probably join her, which would lead to another session of sex. Which she was totally up for, but she didn't want to encourage him. Who knows, if she gave in, he might get down on one knee and ask her to marry him. Her reprieve lasted only until she stepped out of the bathroom. His back was to her as he stepped into a pair of track pants affording her a lovely view of his ass. And a fine ass it was.

"There you are." His whole face softened when he noticed her ogling him. "Come over here and let's talk."

"Can't we do this tonight?" *Please don't get all mushy and expect me to say I love you.* Which she did, but that would take things to a level she wasn't prepared to go. Not yet. She bent to gather the clothes she'd ditched on the floor during the night. "I need to get dressed and get out of here."

"Sandy, all I want to talk about is what you failed to tell me was going on while I was away?"

What she'd failed to tell him? "Oh, you mean about Mitch being the hacker? I was so relieved to hear you were okay yesterday, it went straight out of my head."

Shoot, she probably shouldn't have admitted she was worried about him. He'd read things into it. Things that were true, but she wasn't ready to say those three little words yet. Not for a long while yet. But at least he wasn't getting mushy and going down on one knee.

She laid out the pile of clothes and took stock. Dress slacks. In need of an iron. Crap. Ah well, they'd have to do. Blouse. Equally wrinkled. Double crap. Underwear. Check. Pantyhose. Check. She was missing something but she couldn't think of anything other than getting away.

Troy dangled her bra by one finger. "Looking for this?"

"Yeah. Thanks." She snatched it from him and wrestled it on. "So anyway, I wasn't trying to keep anything from you. I simply didn't remember until we'd hung up. They've come up with a plan to try to catch him though."

"So Scott said, but I'm not talking about that douchebag."

He wasn't? "You aren't?"

"No. I'm talking about all this." He waved his hand over the bed. "The walls, the bedding, all the little touch-ups you've done around here?"

"Oh, that." And here she'd hoped he'd like it. She finished dressing as she considered whether she should be upset that he didn't like what she'd done to his place. "All right. I'll take the quilt back, and you can take down the pictures. You can always paint it some other color. Nothing's permanent."

"I don't want you to take anything back. I like it. It feels warm in here now. Like your place." He reached out and caught her wrist, tugged her onto his lap. Curling his fingers beneath her chin, he stroked her jaw. "As for nothing being permanent. How about we change that?"

Triple crap. He was about to propose.

"How about you move in with me?" He continued, unaware of the double backflips her stomach was doing. "Or if you'd like we could move back to my flat in London and set that up as international headquarters. It's only a hop, skip and a jump to anywhere in Europe. Wouldn't you like that?"

Okay. Living together wasn't a proposal. She could deal with that. London, however, meant quitting her job. *That* was permanent. Too permanent. Holy shit, what part of "not wanting to settle down" had he not understood?

He frowned. "Or not."

She wiggled out of his hold and speed-walked to the front hall. Where the hell had she left her purse? "Look, I have a ton of things I need to do."

Her purse turned out to be on the floor beside the couch. She snagged it and then dodged Troy, who had followed her out and grabbed her coat from the closet. "I have to call Jazz and see how she's doing. And I promised to pick up some fabric for Mom at this quilt shop she found last time she was in D.C."

"Sandy, wait. Please."

"Yeah, so...um...yeah. I'll see you later, all right?"

She must have set a speed record racing down the hallway and out to her car. Ignoring her phone as it rang, she stabbed her keys into the ignition and started the engine. She should never have looked back when she got into the elevator. The sight of Troy standing there, watching her, would haunt her forever.

TWENTY-ONE

WHAT THE HELL had happened this morning? What was he thinking asking her to move in like that? Troy yanked his tie tight and stared at himself in the mirror. *Fuckin' idiot. You knew she was scared of long-term relationships and what do you do? Tell her you love her and then invite her to move in with you.*

"Face it, mate, you lose your brains after sex," he told his reflection, who nodded and agreed with him.

So he hadn't intended to say the L-word quite yet, but fuck it all, it had hurt to see that damned deer-in-the-headlights expression creep over her face. Her race out of his condo could have set an Olympic sprinter's time, and if she continued that speed while driving, she'd qualify for the next pole position at Indianapolis.

When his phone rang, he grabbed it "Sandy?"

After a pause, Sam replied, "Nope. Sorry."

Shit bloody fuck. *Are you about to hand my ass to me on a pike? Because Sandy beat you to it.* He scrubbed his hands over his face. "What's up?"

"I figured you'd want in on the op to catch the hacker, considering it involves Sandy." Irritation filled Sam's voice. "If you do, meet me at the safe house in McLean." Sam cut the connection before he could reply that he was already out the door.

A sense of foreboding plagued him as he jammed his car back into first gear within the first mile after merging into traffic on the Beltway. One of these days he was going to buy himself a fucking tank and be damned with the bumper-to-bumper traffic. He'd plow his way across whatever road, whatever field stood in his path. If anyone tried to get in his way, he'd use the tank's fucking big gun.

A full fucking seventy minutes later, he parked his car half on the curb on the side street in front of the house, barely managing not to hit Sam's brand-new Range Rover. Wouldn't that have been the cherry to top off the fuckin' morning?

The door opened as he approached and Sam scowled out at him. "Took your time, McPherson. We expected you a half hour ago."

"Pileup on the Beltway." He stalked into the house, resisting the urge to flip Sam off as he passed.

Inside he found Andy and Scott, along with Kris Campbell—he needed to stop thinking of the kid as a newbie. He'd worked for Hauberk for nearly two years according to Scott, not to mention spending two full hitches in Afghanistan.

Beside one of their female operatives—what was her name again? Vanessa? Deidre? Damned if he could remember—Jazz sat at the end of the couch, her arms hugging her knees to her chest, her jaw set and her eyes hard. He recognized the look. Grief. Anger. A sense of betrayal. All wrapped into one potentially explosive package.

As he approached he noticed the mascara smudged beneath her eyes, the whites that were more reddened. "Hey, Jazz. How you doing? You hanging in there?"

"They won't let me cut off his nuts when they catch him."

The female operative—Holly! That was it—nudged Jazz with a smile. "He probably won't have any left by the time we get done with him, hon."

An hour, three cups of coffee, and a big-assed headache later, Troy headed for the door only to be stopped by Sam.

"Hold up a minute. You and I need to have a talk."

Right here in front of everyone? Fuck it all. "If it's about me and Sandy, you can save your breath. I screwed it up this morning. I doubt she'll want to see me again."

Sam hissed in a breath. "What d'you do?"

"I asked her to move in with me. I may have also said I love her." He lowered his voice and rushed the last two words, hoping Sam wouldn't understand them and no one else would hear.

From Sam's bellowed laugh, no such luck. "Man, that is so righteous." He slapped his hand on Troy's back, pitching him forward a half step. "Welcome to the club, son."

"What are you talking about? You got your girl, remember? You and Rosie are getting married next month."

"Yeah, but not until I'd done a shitload of groveling. Man, I had to buy a new pair of pants 'cause I wore holes in the knees chasin' after Rosie."

"Point is you won her. I don't think I can with Sandy. She's not into commitment. You should have seen her this morning." He slumped against the wall and shook his head. "You'd think I'd told her a bomb was about to go off in the building. She couldn't get away fast enough."

"She's afraid," Jazz said. "She thinks marriage means staying home and popping out babies. Not having a life."

"Yeah, I know. But I don't know how to get through to her that I don't need kids or for her to give up her job or anything." Shit, was he really standing here talking marriage and crap? Yeah. He guessed he was. "I told her we didn't have to stay in D.C., that if she wanted I could work out of London and we could move there."

"Yeah, but she's heard all that before. From Glen. Turned out he liked the idea of her working until they had kids, but he wanted kids right away."

"Glen?" Who the fuck was Glen? And why was this the first he was learning about him?

"Her fiancé." Her eyes widened a second after his jaw dropped. "She hasn't told you about him?"

What? She'd been engaged? How could she have not mentioned that? Closing his mouth, Troy shook his head.

Jazz scratched her nose. "Oh. I'm not sure I should have said anything then. Just forget it."

"No." He touched her arm before she could turn away. "Tell me about what happened between Sandy and this Glen."

"There's not much to tell. They'd gone together in high school and planned to get married in the summer between high school and college, then they'd rent an apartment in Minneapolis and go to college together."

Was this the same jerk who had suggested the threesome and cared only enough to get himself off?

"Anyway," Jazz continued, "a month before they got married, Glen's grandpa had a stroke and couldn't look after his farm anymore. He and Glen's father told Glen that he could have the farm if he'd move in and help him out. Glen expected Sandy to give up college and everything and move back to help him out. He also found out that she wasn't..." She lowered her voice to a whisper and leaned in. "That he wasn't her first, if you know what I mean? I guess the douche said something like 'he'd forgive her for it', like it was some big concession on his part, you know? From what she's said, he sucked in the bedroom too. Anyway, everyone and his brother was pressuring her to marry him, so she called off the wedding and hauled ass to college alone. The year went by and I guess Glen found out she wasn't dating anyone exclusively. I mean, she had a couple boyfriends while she was there, but nothing real serious, you know?"

"Yeah. I know." The asshole who'd suggested the threesome and then ignored Sandy's needs.

"So whenever she was home he'd show up at her parents', even told her parents that they were still dating. That they were back together. Her mom totally bought into the douche's act and kept pressuring Sandy to stop dawdling and marry Glen. By then, Sandy's brothers were getting married and, well, her family and the douche ambushed her. Her mom told her they were going to a Thanksgiving party and it turned out to be a *surprise* wedding with everyone and their brother there expecting Sandy to be all happy-happy joy-joy *of course I'll marry you*, you know?"

"So that's why she doesn't like going home." That made sense.

"And that's why whenever someone talks about getting serious, she bolts."

Usually he was the one easing out of relationships. Figured that the first time he got serious, the woman he'd fallen for would be the one to have cold feet. "So what do I do now?"

Jazz shrugged. "Beats me."

As she disappeared up the stairs, Troy turned to Sam. "Laugh it up, big guy. Must be funny as hell to watch your prediction come true."

Strangely, Sam didn't smile. Instead he clapped a hand on Troy's shoulder and squeezed. "Just hang in there. You'll figure out somethin' to win her back."

He sure as well hoped he would. If he didn't, that move to London might be in order. Because there was no way in hell he could face going into the office and having to watch Sandy dating others day after day after day, knowing what could have been.

SIPPING HIS GLASS OF BRANDY, Cooper Davis considered the report Delayna had given to him the week before and weighed the consequences of his plan. It could be risky. The senator had almost as many contacts who could make him disappear as he had. Of course, if he didn't co-opt the senator, the bill might fail and the Brigade's funding would evaporate.

He dialed the number on the yellow note attached to the file. As he'd anticipated, the senator answered the private number on the second ring with his trademark, "Brannally."

"Good evening, Senator. Are you enjoying that bottle of Courvoisier your wife gave you for your anniversary?"

"Who the fuck is this, and how do you know what I'm drinking?"

"Let's say I'm a concerned citizen who knows a lot about your private habits. I've made it my business." Davis swirled the amber liquid from his own glass. Was it ironic they liked the same drink, though different brands? "I have a proposition for you that you need to listen to."

"A proposition?" Concern, and a touch of caution, crept into the senator's voice. At least he didn't immediately end the call.

"There's a bill coming to the House next week that your party is planning on quashing. I need you to make sure it goes through."

"And why would I do that?"

"Because if you don't, I'll ensure the press receives a medical report verifying that you are the biological father of one Colin Fitzgerald, currently known as Troy McPherson."

"No one will care."

"I beg to differ. I think there will be at least three people who will find it very interesting. Your wife, for instance. Hasn't her family money funded your campaigns all these years? I believe she has a prenuptial agreement revoking all access to her contacts and money should it be proven you have committed adultery. Then there's Colin himself whom you've lied to about who you really are."

"He'll understand why I had to maintain the ruse."

Would he? "And how do you think Troy will feel when I point out to him that the timing of your visit to Ireland and his *father*'s death was more than coincidental."

He counted the beats before Brannally answered, suspicion rife in his voice. "What are you getting at?"

"You know that he blames himself for his father's death. You even encourage it. Yet he wasn't the one who arranged for Paddy's murder, was he?"

"You have no proof."

Cooper could have laughed at the confidence the good Senator had. "Yes. I do have proof. And if you don't cooperate with me, if that bill fails to pass, then I'll ensure that Troy accidentally meets my contact and learns of your part in his stepfather's death. And how you let him think he was responsible."

"It won't matter to him. He wanted Fitzgerald dead too, otherwise he wouldn't have ratted him out to the RUC."

"We both know the RUC weren't planning on killing Paddy. They wanted to turn him. To use him as a mole. But you couldn't have that, could you, Senator? Because Paddy knew who Colin's real father was, didn't he?" The senator's silence confirmed Cooper's guess. "He contacted you after Mary's death. I'm guessing you saw it as blackmail."

"He wanted money to get out of Ireland. Said if I didn't give it to him, he'd go to the press and sell them the story about Mary and her son."

"So you took care of the matter. With Paddy Fitzgerald out of the way, you spirited young Colin back to the States. You even came up with a fake relative of his mother's who granted you guardianship of young Colin. Then you kept him away from any nosy reporters while telling yourself it was in his best interest."

"It *was* in his best interest. If he'd stayed in Northern Ireland, they would have recruited and trained him as a goddamned terrorist. He'll forgive me."

"Perhaps. But I doubt Evan Fitzgerald will be so forgiving that you killed his brother, will he? Especially when I reveal that the men who killed Padraig weren't RUC but your own men. Did you know that Evan's still in the terrorist business? Oh, not for the IRA anymore. No, now he's for hire by whatever group can afford him. And he's very, very good at his profession."

The silence grew heavy. "I'll see what I can do to make sure the bill passes," Brannally finally said. "But I want your assurance that information never gets out."

"Oh, you have it. As long as the funding in that bill continues, you have no cause for worry. I will be watching you, Senator. And if you fail to convince your fellow party members, I will make this report public."

Davis hung up softly and leaned back in his chair, a smile quirking his lips. Sometimes he loved his job.

TWENTY-TWO

THE CUCKOO in the clock by the front window whirred and popped out his door. Sandy put down her Kindle and counted each melodic chirp. Ten o'clock. Shouldn't they have heard something by now?

Rosie and Chad's wife, Lauren, had shown up at the safe house two hours before with bags filled with take-out Chinese, declaring it a girls' night out. But as the meet time approached, the happy chatter had gradually grown silent. Sandy eyed Lauren, who sat curled up in a chair by the fireplace, reading a paperback on hostage negotiation, and Rosie, at the far end of the couch, amused herself by playing solitaire on her iPad.

"Is there any danger to them?" Sandy finally let herself ask. "I mean, they're just waiting for him to show up and then they grab him, right?"

Lauren bookmarked her page and closed the paperback. "It's always hard to know what's going on. If they're lucky, Rowlands walks right into their trap and it's an easy collar."

"What if he doesn't? What if he realizes they're there?" Jazz asked from where she stood staring out the window.

"Then we find another way to catch him." Rosie shrugged. "They may have already caught him and now they're hung up talking to the cops and filling out paperwork. It's rarely as exciting or dangerous as they show on TV."

"And not one of them can find the time to send us a text message?" Jazz flopped on her belly on the floor and played with Xander. "I don't know how you stand it. I'm worried and I'm not even dating any of them the way you two are."

"Three," Lauren corrected. "You forgot Sandy is dating Troy."

"Nope." Jazz shook her head. "Sandy broke up with Troy this morning."

Three sets of eyes narrowed on Sandy. "I didn't break up with him. Not really."

"Uh-uh." Why wouldn't Jazz let it go? "From what I hear, Troy asked you to move in with him and you pulled your usual *see you later, I'm out of here* routine."

"Sheesh. I was late for work and had to leave instead of discussing it to death, that's all."

"That's a fucking excuse and you know it. You ran, didn't you? Just like you always run." Jazz folded her arms and glared. "He didn't ask you to give up your job or your name or anything. Just asked you to move in with him. But oh no, you go getting your panties in a twist and immediately assume he's going to tie you down or control you like Glen did when he wouldn't do that."

"I did not."

"Not everyone's Glen, you know. Troy's a nice guy and he loves you, yet you kicked him to the curb like he's a piece of trash."

"You don't know what you're talking about. Anyway, you should talk. We wouldn't be in this mess if you hadn't dated Mitch." She clapped a hand over her mouth as soon as she realized what she'd said.

The color drained from Jazz's face. "If you care to remember, you were leaving with Mitch before Troy interrupted you. So you can go climb back onto your high horse and go fuck yourself."

Jazz dashed out of the room, her footsteps echoing down the hallway as she ran up the stairs. The operative assigned to guard Jazz followed her after shooting Sandy a look of annoyance.

"She's right." Sandy stood, intending to follow Jazz. She'd been sick with guilt when she'd read Andy's report outlining how Mitch had abused Jazz. "I was leaving with him that night. It could have been me instead of her."

"Let Holly calm her down a bit before you go up." Rosie patted the cushion beside her. "In the meantime, sit down. I think we should talk."

Shoot. "If this is a talk about how I shouldn't have gotten involved with Troy in the first place, Sam's already read me the riot act, okay?"

"I'm not judging you. Heaven knows, I'm not one to talk when it comes to making a commitment. I literally ran away from Sam. All the way to New York."

"And I ran from Chad," Lauren added.

"But that was different. I mean, I only heard bits and pieces of the story, but you weren't sure Sam was over his old girlfriend, right? And Lauren, you didn't leave Chad willingly, that was Thalia's doing, right?"

"Either way, we shouldn't have left the way we did." Lauren moved from the chair to the other end of the couch. "So is Jazz right? Is Glen a ghost-of-boyfriends-past that's haunting you and stopping you from getting serious with Troy?"

"Or is Troy just a casual affair?" Rosie asked. "Because that's totally okay as long as he knew that all along."

"See, that's it exactly." Sandy grabbed at Rosie's question like a lifeline. "He changed the rules on me. I made it very clear that I wasn't looking to settle down any time soon and all of a sudden he's saying he loves me and he wants me to move in with him."

"Moving in with him doesn't mean giving up your life or giving up your identity. It means learning more about each other. Finding out the things that may bother you that you wouldn't know not living with him. Things you need to find out before you say 'I do'."

"No. It doesn't work that way. Once I move in with him, my mom will be all, 'Oh, Sandy, you should be getting that ring on your finger instead of giving the milk away for free.' And that'll be followed by, 'you're not getting any younger, you know. You shouldn't wait too long to give me grandbabies.' And if there's ever an argument between me and Troy, she and Gram will take Troy's side and tell me it's my responsibility to keep the peace. To keep my man happy. Don't you see? It's a slippery slope if I move in with him. First he expects me to give up my own place, then he'll ask me to marry him and change my name. My identity."

Which name would she have to take? McPherson? Or Fitzgerald?

Rosie tilted her head as she considered Sandy. "Do you think I've given up anything by moving in with Sam? Am I any different than I was before?"

"No?"

"Of course I'm not. I'm the same person I was before. And Troy's not that much different than Sam. He may be quieter about things, but in reality they're a lot alike." Rosie tucked one leg under the other and faced Sandy. "Do you care for Troy? Do you think you could get to the point where you could love him?"

"Yeah. I do." She did love him. She hated the idea that he might get hurt, or might move back to England where she couldn't see him every day, but... "I just—"

Rosie's phone rang. "Hang on."

Sandy's stomach did flips when the expression on Rosie's face turned bland. She'd seen that same look on Sam's face when he'd heard that Chad had been shot. "What's happened?"

Rosie held up her hand and shook her head. "Where are they? Thanks, Jake." She ended the call and hurried to the bottom of the stairs and called for Holly. The agent appeared, a mascara-smudged Jazz trailing her. "A friend of mine from dispatch called. There's been a situation. We need to get to St. Jerome's. Can you stay here with Jazz?"

St. Jerome's *Hospital*? Oh shit.

Lauren paled and grasped Rosie's arm. "Who? How bad?"

"I don't know." Rosie glanced sideways at Sandy. "All Jake said was that there were several ambulances at the scene."

No one spoke as Rosie drove at a breakneck pace through the Bethesda streets. The look on Troy's face as she'd stepped into the elevator that morning burned in her memory. The story of how he'd betrayed his father, something he'd not even told his best friend, should have told her how much he trusted her. He'd told her he loved her without asking her to say it back to him. Yet she'd thrown that trust, his confession of love, back in his face by walking out.

She clutched the armrest as Rosie ran a yellow light and careened around a corner onto the 495 on-ramp. Lauren turned on the radio and fiddled with the switches until she found an all-news channel.

About ten minutes in, the announcer reported a "breaking news story"' about a shoot-out in Bethesda. "According to the Maryland Police, there were two fatalities. We'll have more on the story as we get the details."

Rosie put her foot to the floor and weaved through traffic in moves worthy of a NASCAR driver.

Two fatalities.

Oh God! What if Troy died thinking she didn't care about him? Thinking that the one person he'd finally trusted didn't give a damn. What had she done? What if she never saw him again?

ROSIE LET them off at the emergency entrance and they raced inside while she parked the car. Chad and Scott rose from a bank of chairs in the darkened waiting room, the television the only light source, washing any color from their faces.

While Lauren slowed and sank into Chad's embrace, muttering, "Thank God," Sandy rushed past them looking for any sign of Troy. Scott caught her. "Troy's been shot but it's not life threatening. He's in surgery, but he's going to be okay. Don't worry."

Her knees weak, she clung to his arm. "How bad is it?"

He pressed her into one of the chairs and took her hands in his, squeezing lightly. "He took a bullet to his thigh, but he's going to come out okay. I promise."

There was a major blood vessel there, wasn't there? Unable to get her head around the concept that she'd almost lost Troy, might still lose him, Sandy clutched Scott's hands like a lifeline.

"What about Sam?" Lauren asked. "Rosie's coming in once she parks the car. I think she's pretty freaked."

Almost as much as Lauren had been, Sandy reckoned.

"Sam's fine," Chad assured them, "but he's still at Sandy's dealing with the police and the media. He'll be by as soon as he can get free."

"Who was killed then? Rowlands?"

"Yeah, him and a shooter we haven't identified yet. Andy's waiting for us up in the surgical waiting room on the fifth floor," Scott said quietly. "You want to go up there and wait?"

Sandy nodded. Scott wrapped his arm around her waist as they walked down the hall toward the elevators, while Lauren and Chad followed them. A police officer leafed through a magazine while Andy paced, his hair sticking up in every direction.

Sandy's stomach heaved at the dark stain on his jeans. But whether it was Troy's blood or one of the other men's, she didn't want to know.

"Hey, Andy, any news?" Scott asked.

"A nurse came out a few minutes ago and said they were almost done with Troy." He looked at Sandy with concern. "How you doing, Sandy?"

Why was everyone so concerned about her when it was Troy lying on an operating room table? She opened her mouth to answer but found she couldn't so she shook her head and let Scott lead her to one of the chairs.

"What happened anyway? Who shot Troy?"

"The op itself went fine." Andy ran his hand through his hair. "Rowlands walked right up to the door, not expecting anyone other than Jazz to be waiting for him. We cuffed him and called the cops who arrested him."

Scott picked up the tale. "We were following the cop taking Rowlands out of the apartment when a guy stepped out of the stairwell and started shooting. Rowlands went down and we returned fire. Before we killed him the shooter's last shot went wild and hit Troy in the thigh. Then he—Troy—insisted he was fine but he passed out and conked his head, so they're checking him out for a concussion too. But he's gonna be fine. Honest."

SHE SAT THERE, images of Troy hurt, pale and bleeding, flooding her mind. Chad and Lauren sat across from her, holding hands. Andy continued to wear a hole in the tiles. When the elevator doors opened and Sam walked out, Rosie looked up from the thumbnail she was worrying and leapt to her feet. "Sam!"

Sam caught her as she flung herself at him, lifting her off the ground so he could kiss her.

"It's all right, Rosebud. I just had to make sure the police got everything squared away. Didn't mean for you to get worried." She should be happy for Rosie that Sam was safe. But with Troy in surgery, she found it hard to squelch the jealousy surging through her.

Still holding Rosie off the ground, Sam glanced over at Chad. "Any news?"

Chad shook his head. "Not yet."

He let Rosie down but kept his arm around her. "Hey, Sandy, how you doin'?"

"Worried," Sandy admitted.

"He'll be fine, honey. He was bleeding like a stuck pig but the paramedics got to him real quick."

Rosie swatted him in the chest. "*Stupido*, she didn't need to hear that last bit."

The group got quiet again as they waited. Each time the door to the operating rooms opened everyone would look up hopefully. When the orderly or nurse walked past without sparing them a glance, everyone slumped back in their seats. As the silence grew heavier, Sandy picked at a seam on her purse, wishing she could go back to this morning, that she'd had the courage to tell Troy she loved him too.

It seemed forever before the double doors opened and a woman in scrubs appeared. She took one look at the group and headed straight for them. "McPherson?"

Sam rose with a nod, no trace of his trademark smile on his face. "Yes, ma'am."

"I'm Dr. Rosslyn—I operated on Mr. McPherson. He's stable. Luckily for him there was no artery or bone damage. We won't know about nerve damage until he's fully out of the anesthesia but if all goes well, we'll probably be able to release him tomorrow."

"Tomorrow?" Sandy squeaked. "How can you release him so quickly if he's been in surgery for so many hours."

All heads turned to her. "Sandy," Scott said, his tone gentle, "Troy's been in surgery less than an hour."

Less than an hour? That couldn't be right. But she glanced at Rosie who nodded in agreement. "I could have sworn... It felt like..." forever.

"He's being moved to recovery now." Dr. Rosslyn's gaze swept the group but lingered longest on her. "You can visit him, but only two at a time and only for five minutes each."

All gazes swiveled to her as Sam said, "Sandy, do you want to see Troy first?"

Sandy nodded. "Yeah, I do." Her knees shook when she stood. Even though she knew he was all right, she didn't know if he'd want to see her. "Scott? Would you come with me?"

His smile put her at ease as he stood. "Of course I will."

The trip down the hallway to the recovery area was only a couple dozen steps, but it stretched before her as if it were miles.

The doctor stopped in front of a blue printed curtain halfway down the room. "He'll still be groggy but he's awake." She pulled the curtain aside then left them alone.

Scott pushed Sandy toward the bed. "Go on, talk to him."

Her breath catching in her throat, Sandy walked closer. Troy's eyes were closed, his dark lashes accentuating the pallor of his skin, his leg was encased in a huge bandage. She stood at the side of the bed, wanting to take his hand but afraid to disturb the IV leads. "Hey," she said softly.

His eyes fluttered open and turned in her direction, his pupils large and unfocussed. "Sandy?"

She smoothed the hair off his forehead. "You sure gave us a scare."

"Why are you here?" He blinked and frowned. "Wait. Scott. How's Scott?"

Scott stood on the opposite side of the bed. "I'm right here. You're the only one who was stupid enough to get shot."

Why are you here? What did he mean? Did he not want to see her? She took a deep breath. "Do you want me to leave? Should I send Chad or someone else in?"

Troy gave his head a small shake and lifted the hand on the other side, the one without the needles. "Want you here. Always."

She choked back her sob and reached across to touch his hand. "Oh, God, Troy, I've been so worried about you. When I heard there'd been shots fired—" I'd thought maybe I'd lost you. That I'd never get to tell you I love you too.

"Don't be afraid of me."

Of him? Because of what he'd told her about killing Garcia, or his father? "I'm not afraid of you. I'll never be afraid of you. *For* you, yeah, totally, but never *of* you."

"Yes, you are." His words were mumbled and slurred. She cast a worried glance at Scott who shook his head and mouthed *"it's the drugs"*. His eyes drooped until they closed and his voice dropped to a husky whisper. "Love you."

"I love you too, Troy." She lifted his fingers to her lips then pressed her cheek against them. "God, I love you so much it scares me."

She waited for a reaction, a response, something, but his eyes didn't open, and his lips didn't curl into a grin.

"He's asleep, honey," Scott whispered. "Come on, let's let him rest. The nurse over there is giving us the evil eye and tapping her watch."

As he guided her back to the waiting room, Sandy strained to look back until she couldn't see Troy anymore. As she trudged down the corridor back toward the cramped waiting area, she couldn't help wondering, "Do you think he heard me?"

"I don't know. I guess we'll find out when he wakes up."

TWENTY-THREE

THE TELEVISION in the next cubicle blared the inane chatter of one of the morning talk shows and the crackled voice over the intercom squawked altogether too loud. After a hospital worker delivered a breakfast tray, Troy lifted the cover hopefully and cursed under his breath to find a clump of oatmeal, suspiciously pale scrambled eggs and two rashers of limp bacon.

An hour later a nurse who looked like she'd barely graduated high school, let alone nursing school, poked her head around the curtain and frowned at the remains of his breakfast. "You didn't eat anything, Mr. McPherson. Are you not feeling well?"

He gestured to the tray. "Anyone would get grumpy eating that slop. There's no way in frickin' hell those were real eggs, the coffee was little better than dishwater, and every damned thing was colder than a witch's tit in the arctic in January. I can't sleep with the noise around here and my fucking leg hurts like a son of a bitch."

"Oooh, somebody's grumpy, I see." Did they give perky lessons in nursing school? Because someone really needed to tell those instructors that perky could bug the shit out of a patient stuck in a hospital bed.

"I haven't had any visitors, have I? A blonde a couple inches taller than you?" he asked, unable to hide the hope in his voice.

"Not yet but visiting hours aren't for three hours and you should be released by then."

"I could have sworn..." *I'd heard her voice.* Strange, he was certain someone had touched his forehead while he'd been sleeping. Probably a nurse.

"Let's see how you're doing, shall we?" Cold air hit his dick and his balls when she flipped aside the covers, baring the big-ass bandage on his thigh. Okay, so he was in a corner unit and the curtain between him and the bed beside him was drawn but the nurse didn't need that type of peep show. Not to mention the fucking hospital was cold and his balls had shriveled to the size of grapes.

He grabbed the covers and scrunched them over his groin then hissed in a breath when she ripped the tape from his skin, tearing a handful of hair along with the adhesive. No matter how he tried not to look, he couldn't stop his eyes from dropping. Oh shit. It was a fucking good thing he was lying down or she'd guess what a wimp he'd morphed into. Even so, sweat gathered in his armpits and the back of his knees and his muscles reduced to gelatin at the sight of the line of little black stitches holding his skin together.

"There's no blood, if that's what you're afraid of."

"I don't mind blood." When it's someone else's.

"Mmm." She wasn't buying it. "It looks good." She placed a much smaller, fresh bandage over the wound with chirpy efficiency. "Have you arranged for someone to pick you up today?"

"That would be me." The curtain rippled as Scott stuck his head into the cubicle. He grinned at Troy's hand clutching the bedding over his groin.

"Excellent." The nurse straightened the covers and turned to Scott as if Troy had ceased to exist. "The doctor's already been to see him and the discharge papers are all set. I'll run down to the nurses' station and get the prescription and instructions for care of the wound, shall I?"

Scott stepped aside as the nurse pushed the curtains open and left. He raised an eyebrow as he caught Troy staring past him. "If you're looking for a certain blonde, she's not here."

"I was checking out the nurse. She's got a great ass."

"Liar," Scott said without any heat.

Troy thumped his head into the pillow. "Yeah. I am." He scrubbed his hands over his face. "I fucked up with Sandy. I moved too fast and scared her away."

"You didn't blow it. She loves you too." Scott set a bag on the bed and pulled out a folded pair of underwear along with track pants and socks. "Here, put these on and let's get you home."

"Thanks." He went through the motions of getting dressed. As much as he hated wearing sweatpants in public, they were a hell of a lot easier to pull over the bandage than his jeans would have been. He grabbed the crutches they'd given him earlier and stood. He nearly fell back on his ass as his vision greyed and his head swam at being vertical so quickly. "Let's get out of here."

Ignoring the nurse's startled expression, he stumped toward the bank of elevators. Nurse Perky chased after him, calling his name but he kept walking. Bugger the paperwork. He had to get out of here. Sandy hadn't phoned him or come with Scott. That confirmed his fears. Despite Scott's assurances, he'd lost her.

On the drive home Troy stared out the window at the trees coated in the latest snowfall. Despite the sun glittering off the white blanket, the place was drab and dreary. Bugger this. So she didn't want to hear that he loved her. Screw it. Who needed her? Put her behind you and get on with your life.

Fuck, that thought sucked. He decided to focus on something not Sandy-related. "What happened with Rowlands? He die?"

"Yup. You know how Chad said one of his clients was connected with the mob? Well, apparently he'd given Rowlands a deadline to get his money back. They're trying to track down who the shooter was and how he's connected to the case, but they figure he was behind it." Scott eased the car into the left lane as they approached the condo. "In the meantime the D.A.'s finally putting Mrs. Rowlands into protective custody while they grill her for any information they can get about how he'd been laundering money for the mob."

"How is Jazz, by the way?"

"Shaken, but she'll get through it."

He stayed quiet until Scott pulled into the underground garage. Okay, it had to be said. He took a deep breath. "I owe you an apology, don't I? It got pretty intense back there and you didn't fold when I thought you would have. I misjudged you. And I'm sorry."

Scott shoved the car into park. "Yeah, you did. But Chad's a good boss and I'm working active cases again, so..."

"Yeah." So...

Ignoring the throbbing in his leg that had started during the ride over, he followed Scott to the garage elevator. Thankfully Scott wasn't any more talkative than him. There was no way in hell he could have concentrated on a conversation the closer he got to his unit. The yards between the elevator and his door were far too short and covered far too quickly. At least in the hospital, he wouldn't have to look at his bed and know Sandy had been there once. He wouldn't have to smell her perfume or her shampoo on his pillow. Once the smell of her faded, the paint on the walls would be a permanent reminder. Oh, sure, he could paint over it, but he'd now always see his apartment with her lying on his bed, surrounded by his things.

Scott unlocked the door, pushed it open, then stepped aside. "Welcome home."

He stayed in the hall, unwilling to be assailed by the knowledge of what he'd once had and lost. "It's not a home. Not without her here."

"Get your ass inside before you start feeling too sorry for yourself." When he didn't move, Scott grabbed his arm and shoved him inside. The door closed behind him, keys jingled on the other side of the door, locking him in.

Troy stumbled to a halt when he saw Sandy standing in the middle of the living room. For a brief moment—one glorious, beautiful moment—he was giddy with relief, beyond happy to see her. Then he remembered the day before and his happiness shattered. She might as well have taken an ice pick and split his chest open. "What are you doing here?"

She flinched and lowered her eyes, her smile disappearing in a flash. "I was worried about you."

"Not worried enough to meet me at the hospital." He shrugged out of his coat, trying to ignore the pain in his chest.

"I didn't figure we could talk there. Not the way we need to."

"Talk? The time to talk was yesterday, but you ran away like a scared rabbit." He stumped into the bedroom, exhausted far more than he wanted to show. "It's obvious you don't want to be with me and I don't need your pity so I don't know what else there is to say."

Sandy followed him, placed herself directly in front of him. "I do want to be here, and I'm not here because I pity you. I'm sorry. I shouldn't have run out yesterday."

He closed his eyes at her statement. It was all well and good for her to apologize but what would happen next time he said he loved her? Because he wanted to say it to her. Over and over again.

"I was a wimp and a coward and I'm so sorry if I hurt you," she continued. "But you scared me."

"I told you I loved you. I've never said that to a woman before." Hell, he'd not had anyone to say it to since his mother had died. "You threw it back in my face, and now you stand here...and...and... expect me to forget it happened?"

"I love you too. I know I should have said it back to you but I've said it to someone before and it didn't work out well."

God, what he would have given yesterday to have heard those words. Why did it feel different hearing them now? He wanted to believe her but he couldn't set aside her reaction the day before. "I know you don't want to be tied down but I need those ties. I haven't had them in so long and I liked them. I liked knowing you were here, waiting for me at the end of a trip. Knowing I'd wake up in the morning and you'd be right there beside me. I've never asked a woman to move in with me before. I've never trusted anyone enough before."

"I know," she whispered. "I'm so sorry."

"How do I know you'll be there tomorrow? Or the next day? Or the next month? Because I don't think I could stand losing you again." He lifted his hand and let it hover a half-inch away from her cheek but couldn't bring himself to actually close the space between his fingers and her skin. After flexing his fingers, he let his hand drop. "You don't have to marry me, though I'd be there in a heartbeat if you wanted. I'm not asking you to have kids if you don't want to. Just be with me. Stay with me. Let me love you.

"But if you don't want to be with me for the rest of my life, then leave now. Rip the bandage off fast." It would hurt like hell, but maybe, one day, he'd get over it. Though he imagined that day would be long in the future.

From deep inside her purse, Sandy's phone rang. Instead of digging into her purse, she just stared at him, her beautiful plump lips parted, her eyes soft and glistening. The ringing stopped and immediately started again.

The moment broken, he stepped back and gestured at her ringing purse. "Answer the damned thing, will you?"

With a sigh she retrieved her phone and grimaced. "Hey, Mom."

He turned away, unable to look at her anymore. Leaving her in the bedroom to hold her conversation in private, he wandered into the living room. But distance couldn't mute the clear tones of her voice. "I told you, I'm fine."

The shooting had probably made the news and Mrs. Hallquist was calling to check on Sandy. He'd never had anyone call to check on him before he'd joined Hauberk.

"Are you going to be home this weekend?" Her voice got louder, as if she'd followed him. "I'm thinking of flying up to see you."

His chin dropped to his chest. So she was leaving.

"I want you to meet my fiancé."

Her fiancé? Troy whirled to face her. Ignoring the holy-fucking-crap-that-hurt pain that bloomed in his thigh, he grabbed Sandy's shoulders. "You want to marry me?"

"Yeah." She nodded, letting the phone drop to the couch, her mother still talking. "Yeah. I do."

He picked up the phone and put it to his own ear. "She'll call you later with all the details, Mrs. Hallquist."

He clicked off the phone and tossed it back on the cushions. Cushions that hadn't been there yesterday. Cushions that yesterday had been on the couch at her place. The very same couch that was now right here in his living room. "Where did this come from?"

He glanced around and realized the room now contained a lot of furniture and knickknacks that yesterday had been in her apartment. She'd moved in.

"That's why I couldn't meet you at the hospital this morning. Andy and Sam and Rosie and Chad and oh, everyone, helped me move my stuff over here." She cradled his jaw in her palm. "I love you, Troy. I don't care whether we live here in D.C. or in London or in a room at the Rouge. I want you in my life forever too."

The anvil parked on his chest shifted but it didn't drop completely. "You're not going to change your mind about this?"

She slowly shook her head. "No. I'm not."

Her tone was sure and steady, her face clear of any type of guile. "Do you realize how long forever is?"

He closed his eyes when she reached up on tiptoes and brushed her lips across his. "I do—and it won't be long enough."

His crutches fell to the floor with a clatter, or maybe it was that damned anvil that had been squeezing all the air from his lungs. He wrapped his arms around her waist and pulled her flush against him. "It's about time you figured that out, Miss Hallquist."

"Don't you mean, the soon-to-be Mrs. McPherson?" Her voice raised in question on his last name.

"Soon-to-be Mrs. McPherson is a bit of a mouthful, don't you think?"

She leaned back and cocked her head to consider him, a devilish glint in her eye that had him bracing. "Are you saying you want a quickie wedding?"

"I'll take you any way I can get you. If you want a big wedding,

I'll help you arrange the biggest damned wedding in history. If you want to run away to Vegas, I can make the reservations right now."

"First things first. You're listing. Let's get you to bed, Mr. McPherson." She nestled her shoulder under his and boosted him as he limped back to the bedroom.

"I'm not sure my leg's up to much in the way of gymnastics at the moment, sunshine." Not that it stopped him from pulling her into the bed with him.

The grin she shot him both filled his chest with love and his groin with expectation. "Figures you'd wimp out on me because of one little bullet wound." Her smile faded. She rested her head against his chest. "I was so scared I'd lost you."

He buried his face into her hair, loving how she smelled of flowers and sunshine even in the middle of winter. "You'll never lose me, Sandy. I'm yours. Forever."

DEDICATION

There are so many people who helped me out in writing this book, from the police sniper I met at the Writers' Police Academy in North Carolina who shared his thoughts on guns with those red laser siting systems, to my friend Tabatha S who kept me writing on those days when I wanted to pack it all in.

And to my husband for pitching in and sliding dinner under my nose when I'm on deadline. And even when I'm not. Love ya, babe.

ABOUT THE AUTHOR

Leah lives in Ontario Canada with her husband, their dog Seamus who behaves like a cat, and cat Turtle who thinks he's a dog. She loves escaping the ever-multiplying dust bunnies by opening up her laptop to write about sexy heroes and the women who challenge them.

Find out more about Leah on her website or sign up for her mailing list to get news about her upcoming releases and sales of her titles.

Follow Leah here:
leahbraemel.com
leah@leahbraemel.com

ALSO BY LEAH BRAEMEL

Contemporary Romances

Feeding the Flames

Unashamed

All I Need for Christmas

HAUBERK PROTECTION SERIES

First Night

Private Property

Personal Protection

Deliberate Deceptions

Perfect Proposal

Hidden Heat